THERE BE DRAGONS HERE

S.L. ROWLAND

ALSO BY S.L. ROWLAND

Tales of Aedrea

Cursed Cocktails

Sword & Thistle

The Halfling's Harvest

There Be Dragons Here

Pangea Online

Pangea Online: Death and Axes

Pangea Online 2: Magic and Mayhem

Pangea Online 3: Vials and Tribulations

Sentenced to Troll 1-6

Path to Villainy: An NPC Kobold's Tale

Collected Editions

Pangea Online: The Complete Trilogy

Sentenced to Troll Compendium: Books 1-3

Sentenced to Troll Compendium 2: Books 4-6

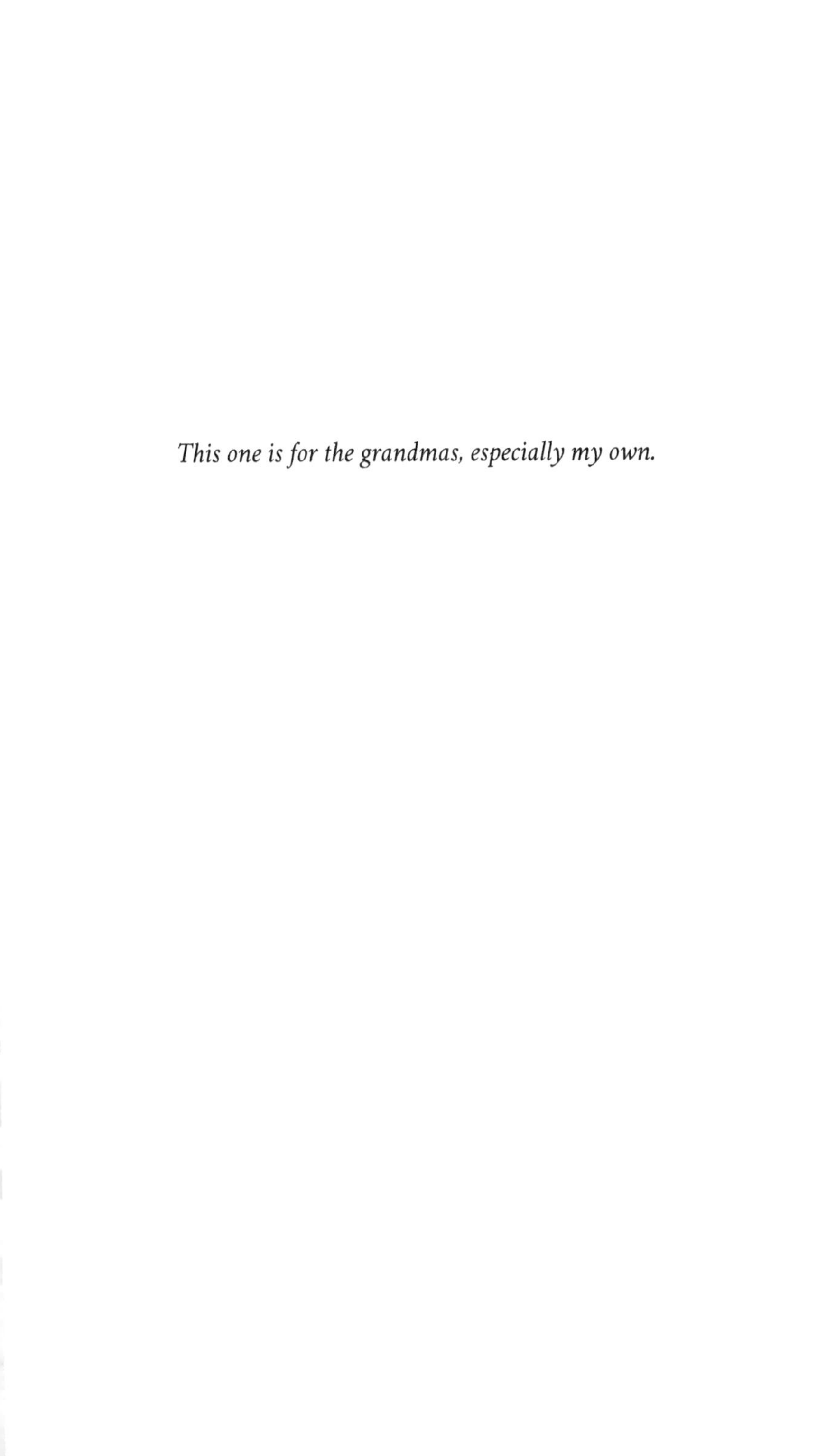

This one is for the grandmas, especially my own.

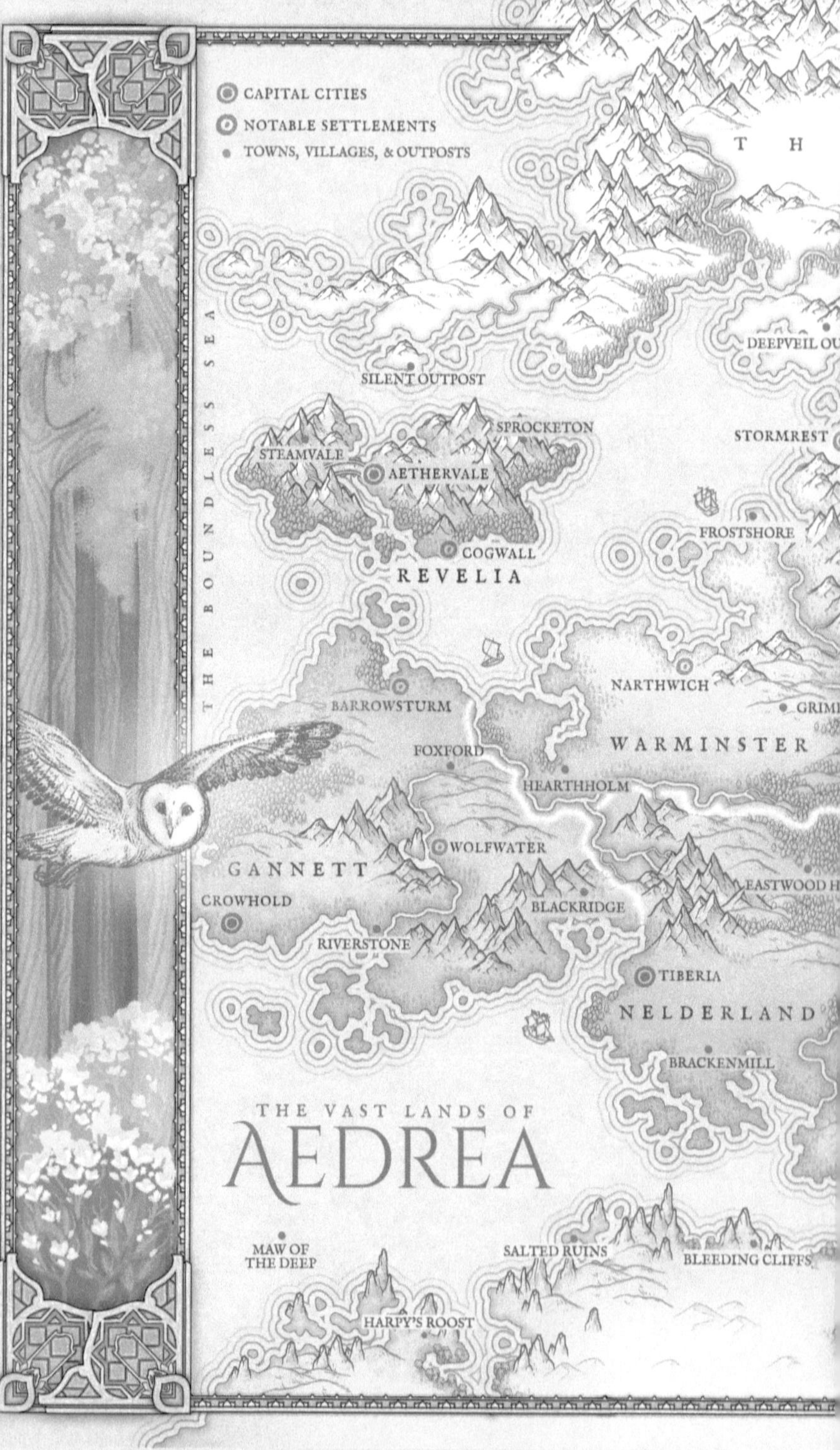

CAPITAL CITIES
NOTABLE SETTLEMENTS
TOWNS, VILLAGES, & OUTPOSTS
THE BOUNDLESS SEA
T H
DEEPVEIL OU
SILENT OUTPOST
SPROCKETON
STORMREST
STEAMVALE
AETHERVALE
FROSTSHORE
COGWALL
REVELIA
NARTHWICH
BARROWSTURM
GRIMP
WARMINSTER
FOXFORD
HEARTHHOLM
WOLFWATER
GANNETT
EASTWOOD H
CROWHOLD
BLACKRIDGE
RIVERSTONE
TIBERIA
NELDERLAND
BRACKENMILL
THE VAST LANDS OF
AEDREA
MAW OF
THE DEEP
SALTED RUINS
BLEEDING CLIFFS
HARPY'S ROOST

FROZEN NORTH
NORTHPASS
STONEWATCH
HOLLOWTON
MOUNT TOR
CASCUS
DURENDREG
NOCTURNE'S REST
DUSKWATCH
ASHRIDGE
SANGUIN
STONEFIST HOLD
DRAKE CANYON
BLACKTHORNE REFUGE
REACH
HAMMERPOINT
TOR'S ANVIL
ROCKDALE
ADARNA'S REST
FEYBROOK
ILVERPEAK
HELLS' CRAG
COPPERHILL
WHITEHAVEN
BOULDER RUN
DARM
BEARMOUTH
REDSTONE WAYPOINT
SHIVERDAWN
OAKHOLLOW
HILLSIDE
SILVERBOUGH
FERNHILL
WHITBLOSSUM
APPLEWOOD
NIA
WILLOWBROOK
HONEYDALE
TYNE
VUSORA
GREENBRIAR MARSH
MOSSY HOLLOW
EASTBORNE
ICRAMEL
ERMMIR
MOONPETAL GLADE
WHISPERING VALE
ACKENED ISLE
TO THE WILDS
BLIGHTWOOD
WASTELANDS

PROLOGUE

The bowstring rested against Hilda's fingertips, her hawklike gaze following the three other members of her party as they navigated the narrow ridge in her direction. A glint of silver caught her eye as something descended from overhead.

There was a twang as the arrow released, followed by a crunch and hiss as the barbed carapace of the cave spider thudded against the ground. The arrow protruded from between the creature's many eyes.

A soft glow ignited Frey's features as he looked from the spider to the sprawling cavern above. The dwarf's black beard fell to his chest in an intricate braid adorned with stone beads. The head of his enchanted axe had a tinge of green pulsing through the metal, a signal that goblins were near, though they had yet to see any.

He pulled the arrow free and kicked the corpse over the edge. There was a long silence before it hit the bottom.

This deep inside the mountain, the luminescent moss upon the cavern walls provided enough light to travel without torches, but there were shadows everywhere. Each one an opportunity to be attacked unaware, or to lose oneself to the heart of the mountain. The air was damp and ancient with a pervading earthiness that never relented—the same air breathed by their ancestors for millennia. Glowing water dripped from stalactites, and as the three dwarves approached the corridor where Hilda had scouted ahead, the moss shrouded them in ghastly hues.

"Nice shot." Frey handed Hilda the arrow. The faint minty-pine scent of the frostbloom oil he used to tame his beard lingered as he passed.

By seniority, Brok should have been the leader of their party, but Frey had never been one for tradition. He had a bravado that led him into every battle like a hellhound starving for flesh. His brashness was annoying at times, but Hilda couldn't imagine him any other way.

She scanned the cavern as Frey entered, looking for the glowing reflection of goblin eyes. She saw nothing, but that was little comfort. There were tunnels and crevices throughout the cavern, and the creatures were like spiders, always watching and waiting for the opportune time to attack.

Brok passed next, a warhammer tossed over his shoulder as he whistled, oblivious to the perilous depths beneath the ridge. He was the eldest of the party and had completed more quests than the others combined. He'd been adventuring for almost a century, crushing skulls and claiming rewards before the others had fuzz on their chins. His beard was unkempt and streaked with gray, with a mustache that fanned outward like spindly wings. Bushels of hair sprouted from his ears and eyebrows. He was powerful, with arms that rippled with corded muscle. "Old dwarf strength," he called it. For all his strength, he had the reflexes of a tortoise, which was fine. Every anvil needed a hammer.

Snorri peeked over the ledge before latching her shield across her back and entering the corridor. She was one of the few remaining shielddaughters of Mount Tor. Hilda had read stories of the fearless dwarven maidens as a child, enamored by their bravery as they fought with shield and sword alongside the great heroes of the past. It was part of the reason she'd chosen the life of an adventurer.

For nearly a decade now, Hilda had been a member of Stone & Splendor. She was the youngest member by nearly thirty years, so it had been a surprise when they took her on. But the truth was that as a ranger, there was no shortage of parties in need of her tracking, trapping, and navigation skills, especially for those who kept to strictly dwarven company. Shielddaughters might be a rarity these days, but dwarven rangers were downright scarce.

Hilda lingered a moment, scanning the ridge to ensure they weren't being trailed. Satisfied, she lowered her bow and marked a symbol on the wall with chalk for their return. She refused to become a lost soul of the mountain. With a final glance, she hurried to join the others in the passage.

Thick, golden braids fell across the circular shield

strapped to Snorri's back. Ahead of her, Frey and Brok crept down the corridor with all the stealth of an ogre in a crystalarium. They were the muscle, pure and simple. The type to smash first and ask questions later. She'd learned early on that they were more suited to smash-and-grab quests than covert operations. If something needed stealth, Hilda preferred to go alone.

According to their intel, this mountain range had once been home to a band of dwarven mercenaries during the Age of Empires. Supposedly, there were still treasures hidden within its depths four thousand years later. So far, they'd cleared three caves, and all they had to show for it were a few trinkets. It hadn't been a total waste, though. Hilda had collected a fang from a grayfang spinner to add to her collection of monster teeth.

Up ahead, Frey said something Hilda couldn't hear. Brok shook his head, wearing a look of annoyance. Frey tapped his axe against the elder's breastplate.

Despite their age difference, those two bickered like brothers.

While Hilda waited for them to continue moving, she trailed her fingers across the lichen along the cavern wall. The green tendrils wriggled beneath her touch. Whiskers of the Mountain, her mother had called them. Most dwarves cared more for stone and gems than what grew from the mountain, but Hilda had always been drawn to the life that could thrive in such treacherous terrain. Mountains were more than rock and ruin. There were clues and knowledge everywhere if one knew where to look.

There was a grunt up ahead, and Brok's warhammer fell to the ground with a thud.

"Oh, yer gonna pay for that." Brok pushed Frey against the passage wall, and the two tussled, cursing and shoving one another.

"By the gods, will you two quit it?" Snorri hissed, hitting the dwarves with the flat of her sword.

"I'll rip off yer sorry excuse for a beard—" Frey grabbed Brok by the braid, ignoring Snorri's reprimand.

"Aye," Brok scowled, sinking his fingers into the tuft of black hair on Frey's chin. "Two can play at that, you brittle piece of flint."

Hilda rolled her eyes. Just once, it would be nice to complete a quest without a scuffle breaking out. Sometimes, she wondered if they truly had rocks for brains.

She pulled her fingers to her lips and whistled. In the narrow passage, the shrill noise blared like a siren, echoing through the cavern. The two dwarves released one another, grimacing and plugging their ears.

"Gods, Hilda." Frey had a finger knuckle-deep into his ear. "So much for the art of stealth."

"Stealth?" Hilda's eyes widened, and she tried to swallow her irritation. "You want to talk about stealth? The whole mountain could have heard you two cretins—"

There was a guttural screech from behind just before something slammed into Hilda's back with enough force that she crashed into Snorri. The shielddaughter stumbled forward, and a sharp pain flared in Hilda's shoulder. Grating, raspy growls filled the corridor as wiry, moss-green fingers wrapped around her neck.

"Goblins!" Snorri shouted as she crawled to her feet.

Teeth gnashed in Hilda's ear, and hot, fetid breath assaulted her. She turned, slamming her back into the wall, but the goblin held tight. Pain radiated through her shoulder as the creature squirmed, fabric tearing as its taloned feet clawed against the back of her cloak.

Snorri didn't hesitate, stabbing her sword past Hilda's head. The goblin's grip immediately slackened, and Hilda rolled to the side before Snorri brought her shield down with a crunch.

Brok and Frey rushed by as a mixture of growls and chittering resonated outside the corridor. In the faint glow of the moss, Hilda counted at least a dozen goblins on the ridge. The lanky humanoids were a little over half as tall as most dwarves, all bones and sharp edges from their pointed ears down to their clawed feet, with ravenous yellow eyes, dangerous teeth, and skin that mirrored the gray and green tones of the mountain. They wielded spears and daggers, some crudely made, others clearly looted, snarling and hissing as they thrust them at the dwarven challengers.

Snorri extended a hand and helped pull Hilda to her feet.

"You good?" Snorri asked.

Hilda nodded. She found her bow, and burning pain shot through her shoulder as she reached to pull an arrow from her quiver. With a grimace, she nocked the arrow and let it fly.

Outside the mouth of the corridor, Frey and Brok spread joyful chaos as they pushed the attackers back. Brok's warhammer sent a goblin plummeting into the depths below. Frey's axe blazed an eerie green as he cleaved another in two. Among the yowls and clamor, Brok and Frey's laughter rang out as they pressed their way down the ridge until no goblins remained.

When Frey and Brok returned, there was a familiar

calmness about them. It was hard to explain to someone who hadn't lived this life, but for some, there was peace in living on the brink of death, of knowing that one moment was all that stood between them and the great beyond.

Brok stopped in front of Hilda, the massive warhammer once again tossed over his shoulder. His bushy brows furrowed, like two sheep kissing, as he examined the wound. "They got you good. Are you okay?"

Blood had stained through Hilda's cloak and trailed down her back, warm and sticky. She could smell the metallic tang mixed with another scent she couldn't place.

"I'll be fine." She grimaced, pulling a vial of red liquid from her pouch. "Nothing a potion won't fix."

She downed the sickly-sweet liquid and waited for it to work its magic. She never left without an ample supply of healing potions. Once, she'd slipped while tracking an elk through a mountain pass, and a jagged rock had shredded her muscle to the bone. She'd sat upon the stone, watching with amazement as the wound stitched itself together from the inside out. For an adventurer, healing potions were worth their weight in gold, especially when they were far from the aid of a cleric.

"Have a rest while it heals—" Frey began barking orders, "Brok, Snorri, keep a lookout. Make sure there aren't any more of the little shits lurking about." He gestured toward the openings at each end of the corridor before wiping blood from the blade of his axe. The metal had returned to a calm silver. Maybe that was the last of the goblins. He knelt before Hilda. "Here, let me take a look."

Frey unclasped the fastening on Hilda's cloak, removing it and peeling back her tunic. It was moments like these that showcased why he was their leader. He might be a pain in the ass more times than not, but when things got messy, Frey was always there to take charge and lead them.

"This doesn't look good. It's not deep, but it's not healing." He met Hilda's gaze. "What'd he stick you with?"

She frowned. "I couldn't exactly see."

Frey rummaged around the goblin's corpse until he found the weapon. It was made from a silver metal, almost white, with burgundy runes on the blade that appeared liquid in the dim light. There was a black stone set in the pommel, and a dark red ribbon crisscrossed the grip. Hilda couldn't explain it, but the dagger gave her a sense of unease.

"How in the hells did a goblin get hold of this?" Frey frowned as he held the dagger up to the glowing moss. "This is an elvish blade."

"Elvish?" Hilda's eyes widened. They were a long way from elven lands. Maybe they were finally near the rumored treasure.

Frey took a potion from his pouch and poured it directly on Hilda's wound. She hissed at the stinging sensation.

"Dammit, Frey." Hilda shoved him away. "Let me heal in peace."

"Hilda." He gave her a knowing look. "Have you ever known a potion to burn when you applied it to a wound?"

She froze. In ten years of adventuring, she'd needed the aid of a potion more times than she could count. Every time, they offered sweet relief.

Hilda leaned against the wall and sighed. Brok and

Snorri were no longer watching the exits. They both stood over her with worried expressions.

"What's going on?" Snorri asked, concern radiating from her deep brown eyes..

"We need to get Hilda to a cleric." Frey held up the dagger for them to see. "She's been stabbed with a cursed blade."

1. THOSE WHO REMAIN

142 Years Later

Drums thundered through the Hall of Embers. The steady, solemn beats echoed off the polished walls of the mountain, reverberating through Hilda's chest as she stood over the corpse of Frey Ashborn.

The dwarf's body rested on a stone dais. His beard, once black as obsidian, was now the gray of spent coals. It had been oiled, braided, and adorned with fire opal beads that shimmered like cinders in the firelight. He looked peaceful wearing the old adventuring garb from years long past, his hands resting on the enchanted axe laid across his chest. Hilda smiled at that. Frey had never been one for tradition; of course, he would forego the ceremonial armor.

Her friend had been a hellion, with a playful smirk permanently etched into his features. Flames danced in the surrounding braziers, casting shadows that made him seem almost alive. When the light hit just right, she could see hints of that roguish grin beneath his mustache.

She caught a familiar scent she hadn't smelled in ages —the sweet mixture of mint and pine that followed Frey like a protective aura. He'd paid a fortune for the small vials of frostbloom oil, their price reflective of the scarcity of frost laurel leaves that only grew on the highest peaks in Mount Tor.

Frey swore it brought him good luck and would douse his beard with the oil before every quest. Whenever pressed on whether it actually worked, he simply responded with, "I'm still alive, aren't I?"

Hilda placed a hand on Frey's chest, her wrinkles and sunspots reminders of how much time they'd shared together. For over seventy years, they'd adventured across the realm, collecting bounties and making memories. It had been eighty years since she had retired to start a family, but it still felt as if no time had passed at all. With Frey's death, Hilda was the last surviving member of Stone & Splendor. It wouldn't be long before the memories of their triumphs and failures were confined to the pages of her journals and the guild archives.

Leaning down, the wisps of Hilda's beard touched Frey's as she whispered, "So long, old friend."

She moved aside so that the others could pay their respects. Frey had been a dwarf of the people, burning like a lamplight in every tavern they visited. He'd sung vulgar songs and captivated entire rooms with salacious stories and crude jokes. Even after all this time, hundreds had made the trek to his ancestral home to send him off. *Those who remained.*

Hilda recognized some dwarves, elves, and gnomes

from their glory days. No humans, though. Compared to the lifespans of the others, they were the ephemeral race.

She frowned as her shoulder complained—a dull, burning ache telling her it was time to rest for a moment. The trip from Stonefist Hold to Ashridge had been a journey, and it had taken its toll. She leaned against a towering pillar and massaged her shoulder.

Across from her, a twin column gleamed in the torchlight, specks of white sparkling within the dark gray stone. The Ashborn Clan were some of the greatest stoneworkers in Mount Tor, and the Hall of Embers was no exception.

The pain ebbed, but it never fully receded. It had been over a hundred years since she'd been stabbed with the cursed blade, and there were days when the discomfort felt like it had been yesterday. Some wounds even clerics couldn't heal.

While Hilda rested, she searched the hall for her eldest son, Flint. She'd been surprised when he'd volunteered to take weeks away from the mines to join her on this trip. The lad was just like his father, all work and no play, so it was no surprise he'd been talking with the Ashborn stonemasons last she'd seen him. Part of her suspected that had been his intention all along.

The drums fell silent before Hilda spotted Flint, and the pyres surrounding the dais erupted. The recessed stone around the edge of the hall filled with fire, bathing the walls in orange light as a wave of heat passed through the chamber. A dwarf wearing a red robe stepped behind Frey's body. A fire mage. He looked ancient, leaning on an obsidian staff for support. His beard was long and wispy, trailing down to the black cord tied about his waist.

When he spoke, his deep voice contradicted his venerable appearance, carrying across the hall. "We are gathered in the Hall of Embers to honor the passing of Frey Ashborn. As is tradition of the Ashborn Clan, his body will be commended to Elohr upon the Forge of the Fallen. From stone to ash, as it was, shall it ever be."

A small chorus of "from stone to ash" echoed around the hall. While the majority of dwarven clans prayed to Pidros, the god of mining, some, like the Ashborn, paid tribute to the god of fire. Upon death, their bodies would be cremated.

The mage continued, "Frey might have been rowdy and raucous, but he was a good dwarf. Known by many as the Rogue Ember, he forsook his claim as head of the Ashborn Clan to travel the realm. While his flame may have drifted from the hearth, his light never dimmed. He brought glory to himself, and our clan, by forging his own destiny. For that, we honor him."

Drums thundered once again, this time in rapid succession, as flames jumped from the braziers and arced through the air before engulfing Frey's body. There were gasps among the crowd from those who had never witnessed a dwarven cremation. The fire burned intensely, powered by the mage's magic, concealing all evidence of the body within. Only a few moments passed before the flames burned out, leaving a pile of ash and the glowing red head of Frey's axe.

Following the cremation, the procession moved to the great hall to feast and celebrate Frey's life. Wine and ale flowed freely, and tables were topped with platters of savory meats, roasted vegetables, pies, breads, and a litany of desserts.

While Hilda searched for Flint, she spotted an old friend leaning against one of the massive tables, a cup of wine in her hand. Tiegan's face lit with recognition. The elf had been approaching two hundred years when Hilda had first met her, and a century later, she looked as youthful as ever. Her golden hair was braided into elaborate butterflies on each side of her head, and she wore a shimmering gown that fit her body like a glove.

"Hilda Rockfall." Tiegan grinned as she took in the dwarf's appearance. "It's been an age since I last saw you. How have you been?"

"Not as well as you." Hilda looked the elf up and down. "I don't think I've ever seen you in anything other than leathers."

"Only the best for our dear friend Frey." She nodded toward a table. "Shall we sit? I hear this feast is to die for."

"You haven't changed one bit." Hilda shook her head, but she couldn't hide the smile. It was a joke Frey would have appreciated. With a room full of former adventurers, this was sure to be an interesting night.

Hilda fixed a plate for herself and Flint before joining Tiegan. As she sat down, there was a commotion as three mages entered the great hall. There was a human in blue robes, an elf wearing red robes, and an elderly dwarf in brown robes. The dwarf was old, but the human looked to have one foot in the grave. He hunched against his staff, taking shuffling steps while the elf held his free arm for support. She could have been fifty or five hundred for all Hilda knew.

"Who is that?" asked Hilda.

Tiegan smirked as she looked upon the trio. "You don't recognize the founding members of Fire, Wind, and Earth?"

Hilda's eyes widened as she recalled the trio of mages who had toured Aedrea around the same time she had. "No. That can't be Erlodius Cloudwalker. How is he still alive?"

Tiegan shrugged. "You never know with those magical types. There have been a few human mages to live past two hundred, and some say the elvish triumvirate are thousands of years old." She poured two glasses of wine and handed one to Hilda. "To Frey—" Tiegan raised her glass. "And the ties that bind us."

"The many ties." Hilda raised her own glass. "To Frey, I'm going to miss the old bastard." She sipped the wine, its flavor so rich that she closed her eyes and savored the vibrant notes of blackberry and plum that transitioned to a smooth, oaky finish. "This is a far cry from the swill we used to drink."

Tiegan waggled her brows. "I still partake in the swill from time to time."

"That's right." Hilda took a bite of roasted mutton, relishing the bold, musky flavor. "I heard you were still adventuring."

"From time to time." Tiegan grinned. "I'm more of a consultant these days. Someone has to make sure these young idiots don't get themselves killed."

"We were young idiots once." Hilda gave her a knowing look.

"My point exactly." The elf took a long swig of wine. "I spend a lot of time in various guild halls providing demonstrations and ensuring that the youngbloods set out with proper equipment. You know how they are—willing to spend a fortune on weapons and armor while forgetting to buy rope and chalk." She rolled her eyes. "I try to remind them that preparation is half the battle. Occasionally, I'll tag along if the job is particularly interesting. What about you? Last I heard, you'd formed yourself a small clan."

"We're getting there." Hilda smiled. "Six children, five spouses, and twenty-two grandchildren at last count." As much as she'd loved adventuring, she'd found an equal amount of gratification in building a family. Most days, her home was filled with laughter and the pattering of stubby young feet. "Speaking of which, here's one now."

Flint strolled over. He was a stout dwarf with broad shoulders and thick arms built in the mines. His beard was the same earthy brown as his father's, and his eyes were like golden wheat fields. He kissed his mother on the cheek. "Here you are."

"Here I am?" Hilda raised a brow. "I've been searching everywhere for you. Where did you get off to?"

Flint blushed. "I, uh, was talking with Gormel. He has this new Runetech smelting kit he wanted to show me." His eyes brightened with excitement. "It's portable, powered by runes that heat the crucible, and it allows his team to test ore quality on-site. If I can convince Pa to order one, he's going to love it."

"You're just like him." Hilda slid over and patted the bench. "There will be plenty of time to talk with Gormel before we leave. Now, have a seat. I made you a plate." She gestured to Tiegan. "This is an old friend, Tiegan Velfern.

One of the best archers I've ever witnessed. Tiegan, this is my eldest son Flint."

"Pleasure." Flint nodded. "An archer, eh? That's a skill I wish I'd mastered."

Tiegan tilted her glass in Hilda's direction. "You could always ask your mother for tips."

Flint laughed. When no one else joined it, his brow scrunched. "You're serious?"

"I'm a fantastic shot, but your mother is the only dwarf to ever hustle me out of hard-earned coin."

Flint frowned, looking between the elf and his mother. "Really?"

"Truly." Tiegan nodded. "I was furious, believe me. And once, I made the mistake of challenging her to a game of Shot-for-Shot." Upon Flint's blank expression, she continued. "It's a drunken shoot-off archers would play when we were especially bored. For every bullseye, your opponent had to take a shot of whiskey. We were ten deep, and she still hadn't missed. I don't recall losing, but I do remember waking up in my own filth the next morning."

Hilda smirked. "You were always cocky. Even for an elf."

"Yeah, yeah. I learned my lesson that night." Tiegan downed the rest of her wine and stood. "Anyone need a refill?"

Hilda drained her glass. "If we're reminiscing on the old days in front of my son, best to bring the bottle."

As the wine flowed, more of their old acquaintances joined the table, sharing stories of Frey and their younger days. Hilda's head buzzed, not just from the alcohol but from the companionship. It wasn't often that she had the opportunity to relive her past with people who truly understood. She'd married into a family of hard-working miners. They were good, honorable people, but they could never truly understand what her life had been like before.

They talked into the wee hours before finally retiring for the night.

"So, it's really true?" Flint had an eyebrow cocked as they made their way toward the inn. He'd sat in near silence for most of the evening, undoubtedly seeing his mother in a new light. "You were an honest-to-gods adventurer?"

Hilda stopped, placing a hand on her son's shoulder. "You think your mum's been telling you fables the last eighty years?"

"Honestly? Yes." He shook his head, as if still making sense of it all. "I just thought you were a better storyteller than Pa. It's hard imagining you raising a weapon against anything." Flint grinned. "Unless someone was trying to steal a bite of your honey crumble."

"And you'll do well to remember it." Hilda pulled him in close. "If you've learned anything here today, Flint, know that people are always more than what they seem. Even the old codgers roaming these halls were all young once."

"I know, Mum." Flint squeezed her, his muscles hard as rock from manual labor. "I never would have pictured you as the cracked stone of the family. Aunt Dorna, maybe, but not you."

Cracked stone. Hilda chuckled. He wasn't far off. She'd been Hilda Flintbreaker before she married into the Rockfall lineage. She was the first adventurer in her family in seven generations, and there hadn't been another since. And bless her husband's heart, but the Rockfalls were about as stubborn as stone when it came to tradition. With a family motto like "Our Worth Lies Beneath," it was no surprise that mining was a family business.

Hilda patted Flint on the back as they entered the inn. "Get some rest, son. We've got a long journey ahead of us tomorrow."

2. HOMEWARD BOUND

Two war goats, Bartemus the Third and Morsel, pulled the wagon up the mountain. They moved slow and steady, occasionally bleating their opinion of how the journey was going. Bartemus's dense black fur gave his orange eyes the appearance of burning coals. Morsel was a grayish brown, and when viewed from a distance, her coloring could almost blend into the mountainside. Each of them was the size of a horse but twice as sturdy, having originally been bred by dwarves during the Age of Strife for traveling along rocky terrain.

Hilda sat next to Flint as the wagon bumped along. Her shoulder ached terribly. It always did after a night of drinking, which was part of the reason she'd given up the habit long ago.

She reached into the back, grabbing for a small metal box about the size of her head. She opened the lid, and cool air wafted from within. Inside, there was a glove and a blue stone etched with a white rune. A thin layer of frost coated the polished rock—a coldstone, etched with a gnomish rune that kept it constantly chilled.

Hilda put on the glove and held the coldstone to her burning shoulder.

After the incident with the cursed dagger, she'd discovered that ice was the only thing that brought relief when the wound flared. No potion or cleric's blessing could alleviate the discomfort, but ice provided temporary reprieve. She'd paid a small fortune for the item, but it had been invaluable over the years.

"Shoulder bothering you again?" Flint gave her a concerned look.

"It's always worse after a night of drinking." She sighed as the burning sensation slowly ebbed.

Flint arched his brow. "Maybe you shouldn't drink, then?"

"Wise words, my son." She grinned. "I'll keep it in mind for the future."

"I'm just saying. I learned the first time that if I hammered my finger, it's going to hurt." He shrugged. "I don't know why you'd willingly punish yourself."

Hilda laughed. "I take it as a consequence, not as a punishment. Who knows how many opportunities I'll have to reminisce with old friends? None of us are getting any younger, and a day of dull aches is a small price to pay."

"I still can't believe you were a famous adventurer." Flint flicked the reins, and the goats sped up. "Does Pa know?"

"Does your father know?" She cackled. "Son, how do you think we met?"

Flint wore a confused expression. "I thought you met in the mines?"

"We did." Hilda smiled fondly at the memory. "Your father's team found a nest of cave spiders, and someone cracked an egg thinking it was a rock. By the time my party and I arrived, the little bastards were everywhere. After we cleared the cave, your pa offered to buy me a drink. We spent the whole night drinking and talking, and then we stumbled up to an overlook where he liked to watch the stars. After seventy years of adventure, it was nice to talk to someone who enjoyed the simple things. One thing led to another, and then a year later, we welcomed you into the world."

"Ma!" Flint's cheeks blazed red as he stared at the road ahead. "I don't need to know all the hedonistic details."

"Oh, son." She grinned. "Don't be such a prude. You can't possibly think you were formed from the earth like the first dwarves."

Flint groaned, burying his head in his hand.

The journey home to Stonefist Hold was filled with long days and bumpy rides. Hilda and Flint spent their evenings in small inns and taverns, and every night, she'd share stories with whoever would listen. Hilda had no shortage of tales from her decades traveling the realm. She'd taken quests from the boundless sea to the edge of the wilds and everywhere in between.

For the first time since Flint was a child, he peppered his mother with questions about her adventures. She was happy to share. With each of her six children, the cycle had been the same. They loved her stories when they were young, but as they grew older, they began to question how their mother could have possibly done all those brave, stupid, and adventurous things. This was the woman who baked pies and patched their old clothing, after all.

She couldn't blame them. Not truly. In her prime, Hilda had been a force of nature, and many of the tales were far-fetched, like something they'd read in a storybook. In time, the children quit asking, their thoughts consumed by their own lives and sprouting ambitions.

Once the children were adults, Hilda's adventures were confined to the pages of her journals and the small moments that triggered fond memories. Then came the grandchildren. Twenty-two of them so far. Hilda spoiled them rotten with hard candies and pastries, and once again, she had a chance to share the stories of her youth. Even now, some of the older grandkids questioned the truth of the stories. Eventually, there would be great-grandchildren, and the wheel of time would turn again.

This evening, Hilda and Flint booked two rooms at the Broken Horn Tavern in Dunhollow, a small logging town two days from home. A large skull with a broken horn was mounted over the front of the building. She recognized it as a crag bison. She'd always wanted a tooth for her collection, but the creatures had been hunted to extinction millennia ago and were in short supply. Occasionally, their bones were unearthed during an excavation.

After settling in, Hilda and Flint reconvened downstairs for dinner, where a pot of rabbit stew simmered in the hearth, its savory aroma enveloping the room. They both had a bowl of stew and slices of herbed bread. A handful of guests were scattered about the tables, and a surly-looking bard lurked in the corner, strumming on a lute while he drank from a large tankard.

Hilda sat across the table from Flint. Her son's brow knitted tightly as he moved chunks of carrots with his spoon. Hilda didn't need a mother's intuition to know that something was off.

"Everything okay, son?" she asked.

His golden eyes met her gaze. "I'm glad I took this trip with you."

"Is that what has you so dour?"

Flint narrowed his eyes. "I'm not dour. I just..." He dropped the spoon, and it clanked against the bowl. "I can tell how much you've enjoyed talking about your past. It means a lot to you, and I wish I'd listened more. I don't know why I ever stopped believing your stories were true. It won't happen again."

"Don't worry about it." She squeezed his hand. "There's a time when every child stops seeing their parent as a hero. You're a good son and a good dwarf. There's nothing for you to be ashamed of."

"You know, there was one story that always stuck with me." Flint smiled. "The one where you and your party were helping with pruning season, and you were attacked by ogres. Frey, Brok, and Snorri had all been knocked unconscious, and you were down to your final four arrows, yet you managed to defend them all by yourself until help arrived."

Hilda recalled that day fondly. She had been fierce and relentless back then.

His smile twisted into a frown. "I told my friends that

you were a hero, and they laughed in my face. I think that's when I stopped listening."

"That's how it goes sometimes. The Steps might technically be a part of Stonefist Hold, but make no mistake, our little borough is a mining town set within a city. That's not a bad thing, but it's a different way of life. Some of our citizens live their entire lives without ever leaving its borders." Hilda held Flint's gaze until he nodded. "Now, eat up. Your stew is getting cold."

3. HOME IS WHERE THE HEARTH IS

When Stonefist Hold came into view, it was easy to discern how the city had earned its name. From a distance, the mountain looked like a closed fist punching toward the heavens. It boasted the tallest summit in the southern range, extraordinary in the fact that the rocky zenith was a flat mesa nearly twenty miles wide.

The white stone stood out against the surrounding forests like the moon on a cloudless night. Its appearance was so unique that several legends surrounded its formation. Some said that the mountain's peak had been cleaved off by an angry god. Others believed that it was the fist that had pushed the first dwarves from the earth.

Flint smiled as he looked upon the mountain. "No matter how many times I leave, coming back to this never gets old."

"It's one of the most beautiful sites in the realm." Hilda patted her son on the leg. "One of the Eight Great Natural Wonders of Aedrea."

"Really?" Flint wore a surprised expression. "I knew it was famous, but I didn't know that. What are the others?"

"Let's see. There are the Bleeding Cliffs located on the northern tip of the wastelands. They're named for the vibrant red water that pours over the white cliffs." She put up a finger for each one she counted off. "Then there's Wolfwater Lake, named after the rock formation in the center that looks like a howling wolf. The Maw of the Deep, a constant whirlpool that has been the doom of many sailors. There's Moonpetal Glade in Ermmir, with its white-leaved trees that glow in the moonlight. Blackridge, known for the solid black mountains. The wilds, of course. And then there's the Silent Outpost, an ice-and-snow-covered island in the north where sound doesn't travel."

"You've been to all of them?"

"Most of them. I've seen the Bleeding Cliffs from a distance. I thought we'd sailed upon a massacre when I first saw it. Moonpetal Glade was one of the most magical scenes I've ever witnessed. Never got to the Maw of the Deep or the Silent Outpost, and I don't ever plan to. They say those who are close enough to see the Maw are already doomed. And I don't know anyone who'd willingly travel to the Silent Outpost." Hilda grimaced at the thought. "For whatever reason, sound doesn't travel on the island, and the lack of noise has driven many to madness, leaving the outpost abandoned for ages."

Flint grinned at his mother.

"What?" She raised a brow.

"You've led a fascinating life." He gazed toward the mountainous fist of their homeland. "Will you tell me again about the time you saved Frey from a mimic?"

Hilda smiled as she settled in, comforted by the fact that her son, for the first time in a long time, was excited to listen.

Bartemus and Morsel's hooves clacked against the stone street as Hilda and Flint made their way up the Fist. The sounds of the mountain welcomed them, from the distant clink of pickaxes as they passed the mines to the roaring furnaces and the metallic grind of gears and chains that carried imports and exports up and down massive shafts to the city above. The dry scent of stone dust and the tang of metal wafted from open tunnels as they passed.

Centuries of dwarven craftsmanship had shaped the mountain into what it was today, but it was ever evolving. Numerous tunnels and shafts had been carved into the rock, and wide streets curved around the mountain at a low incline. While much of the city was atop the Fist, the mountain's roots ran deep. There was a vast network of industry in the undercity that thrived below the surface.

The sun had dipped beyond the mountains by the time they reached the summit, where the open gates of Stone-fist Hold—two towering stone pickaxes—welcomed Hilda and Flint into the city proper. In all her years of living in the city, she had never once seen the gates closed, likely due to the defensive nature of having a city built on top of a flat mountain.

Flint nodded to the guards as they entered, and the guards tapped a gauntleted fist to their chests in acknowledgment.

Beyond the gates, there were large sections of trellises,

towers, and green walls that made up Stonegrove, growing everything from carrots and potatoes to lettuce and strawberries. Chickens and goats roamed freely throughout the streets, and a pervading scent of musk lingered in the air. Hilda pulled her cloak tighter to hold back the bite of the evening chill. This high up, even the summer nights could be brisk.

Despite appearing flat from a distance, the top of Stonefist Hold was actually composed of three tiers— Stonegrove, Hearthstead, and Ironheart—each one slightly elevated above the last. Stonegrove ran the perimeter of the city, where it was used for growing produce and raising some of the livestock that fed the populace. With no room for the city to expand outwards, the government was forced to innovate, leading to large sections of vertical gardens that could produce significantly more yield than traditional farming while using less water and land space.

Further down Main Street, they entered Hearthstead. The streetlamps had been lit for the evening, casting the city in a warm glow. Hearthstead was the largest tier by far, and home to the city's general population and businesses. If they traveled far enough, they would eventually reach Ironheart, the city's center and home to the nobility, mages, and the governor's palace.

The musk of the outer ring gave way to aromas of baked bread and the yeasty scent of the many alehouses and taverns in the market district. Laughter and boisterous voices carried into the streets from many of the workers relaxing after a hard day's work. They passed through the Armory, where the clang of metal on metal had faded with the daylight, and into the Miner's District, commonly known as the Steps because of the wide staircase in the center of the borough that descended into the mountain.

"I'll drop you off first, and then I'll take the goats to the stables." Flint tugged on the reins, and the goats veered onto a side street before coming to a stop. "See you tomorrow, Mum."

Hilda patted him on the leg. "Give the little ones a hug from Grammy."

"You know I will." He squeezed his mother's hand. "Tell Pa I'll see him in the morning."

Hilda stowed away the coldstone as the wagon came to a stop. She flexed her neck from side to side, and with a grimace, she grabbed her bag from the back.

Their home was similar to the others on the street. It was a square stone building, two stories tall, with slate shingles shaped like dragon scales. A chimney protruded from the center of the building where a wisp of smoke trailed into the night air. On the ground floor, a welcoming glow came through the smoked glass windows, and above the door, the Rockfall Clan crest was carved into the stone exterior—a mountain with an eight-pointed starburst at the bottom. In blocky letters beneath the crest, the clan motto: Our Worth Lies Beneath.

Hilda's gaze drifted from the crest to the door, where a small sign read "home is where the hearth is." For the past eighty years, that had served as her personal motto.

Home sweet home.

She opened the door to find her husband sitting in the chair by the hearth, his head buried in a book as the fire crackled beside him. Boric Rockfall looked up, and his gray mustache twitched from the smile beneath. When his dark eyes looked upon her, Hilda's insides melted. He had his beard braided neatly, oiled, and adorned with jeweled clasps. Though his face was etched with wrinkles and his hair had turned from russet brown to ashen gray, he was every bit as handsome as the day they'd met.

Hilda dropped her bag on the floor. "Hey, Papa."

"Hey, Mama." Boric set the book aside and stood. For two hundred years old, he was as striking as ever. His forearms were thick with muscle, and Hilda loved the way his belly rumbled beneath his barrel of a chest when he laughed. After a moment of admiration, he stalked over with purpose, enveloping his wife in a bear hug. "Oh, how I've missed you."

Frey and the others had often asked how she knew it was time to give up the adventuring life. When Hilda looked into Boric's deep brown eyes, she wondered how she couldn't. Every day with him was proof that she'd made the right choice.

"Where's everyone?" she asked, looking around the empty room.

"They left about an hour or so ago." He kissed Hilda on the forehead. "I've done my best to fill your absence, but the little ones are vicious. They told me I don't tell stories as well as Grammy, and my pies are too runny."

"That's because you're impatient." Hilda chuckled as she pressed a finger to his chest. "Maybe one of these days, you'll listen when I say you need to let it cool first."

"I know, I know, but some habits die hard. I didn't get strong by waiting for food to come to me." Boric let go and picked the bag up off the floor. "Tell me all about your trip."

She took a deep breath and began the story.

Hilda sat in a chair by the fire, eyes closed as Boric massaged her shoulders. With each firm stroke, the tension released and eased the ache within. She told him of the funeral and her time reminiscing with old friends.

"It's hard to believe he's gone." Hilda swallowed hard. During the funeral, she'd been content to celebrate Frey's life, to smile and laugh over the memories they'd shared together. Now, though, the weight of his passing had finally settled in her chest.

He was gone. Truly gone. And while he'd lived a full life, that didn't make his absence any easier.

Boric's fingers had stopped massaging and rested on Hilda's shoulders. "I know he was like a brother to you. If there's anything you need from me, just ask."

Hilda took his hand into her own, feeling the warmth that radiated beneath the rough calluses. "Thanks, Papa." She kissed his fingers. "It was nice spending time with Flint, though." She chuckled. "Can you believe it took a funeral for him to believe his mother was an honest-to-gods adventurer?"

"Well, he was always a little thick in the head." Boric resumed massaging.

Hilda didn't have to see his face to know her husband was smiling. "I wonder where he got that from."

"Must run in the family," he said, humor in his voice. "No matter what the kids may think, the little ones still believe you could move mountains."

She turned, meeting his gaze. "For now."

"Be that as it may, you'll always be a legend to me."

Boric moved around the chair until he was facing his wife. "I have a surprise for you."

Hilda arched her brow suspiciously. "Do you, now?"

"Close your eyes."

She did as was told, listening to Boric's heavy footsteps, followed by a rattling drawer, a moment of silence, and his return.

"Alright, open your eyes."

Hilda opened them. Boric stood in front of her, offering a square of moist honey-colored cake. He'd even managed to layer the cream filling between two pieces of sponge, and topped it all with delectable, golden-brown crumbles drizzled with thin lines of honey.

"You made this?" Her jaw hung open.

Boric grinned. "It took a few tries, but I think I finally made a serviceable honey crumble."

Hilda stood, setting the plate aside and embracing her husband. She rested her head on his chest and closed her eyes, listening to the hammer beating within. "Eighty-two years and you still find ways to surprise me."

"What can I say?" Boric stroked her cheek with his thumb. "I learned from the best."

Hilda smiled contentedly. It was good to be home.

4. FAMILY MATTERS

"Grammy!" Children swarmed into the house like a pack of gremlins, their small feet thumping against the aged wood.

Tonight was Flint and Darrin's evening to bring their families over for dinner. With six children, five spouses, and twenty-two grandchildren, Hilda and Boric had decided long ago that it was easiest for everyone to have a rotating schedule for family meals.

Darrin was always running behind, so it was no surprise that Flint and company were the first to arrive.

Flint stood in the doorway next to his wife, Maela, and eldest daughter, Frida. He wore an amused expression as his four youngest—Zarra, Brom, Killy, and Elrik—flocked to their grandmother. Each of the boys had Flint's dark brown hair, and Zarra had inherited the strawberry blonde of their mother. And then there was Frida, whose hair was the same fiery red that Hilda's had been before turning gray. She crossed her arms, holding back a laugh as her younger siblings nearly toppled their grandmother.

"Easy now." Hilda wrapped her arms around the little rascals as they peppered her with so many questions that she couldn't decipher them all. "One at a time."

Frida waited until they turned their attention to Boric before approaching her grandmother. She had her hair in twin braids and wore a leather tunic, along with a thin gray cloak and fingerless gloves, perfect for gripping the string of the bow she carried. Of all the grandchildren, she'd always been the most interested in Hilda's stories, so much so that she had joined the archery club at her school.

She wrapped her arms around her grandmother and kissed her on the cheek. "Missed you, Gram."

"I missed you too, kiddo." Hilda released the embrace, patting Frida on the shoulders and sizing her up. "I swear you grow a foot every time I see you."

No sooner had the door closed before another knock came. Darrin and his husband, Orik, entered, along with their three adopted children, Bori, Kori, and Tilda. Tilda was enamored with Frida and had taken to carrying a small bow everywhere she went.

"You look ready for an adventure." Hilda kissed the top of Tilda's head and welcomed everyone inside.

"Good to see you, Hilda." Orik embraced his mother-in-law, his curly blonde beard soft against her cheek. "How's that shoulder of yours holding up after such a long trip?"

Hilda grimaced. "Better now, but you know how it goes."

He rapped his leg with his knuckles, and a hollow thunk rang out. "Never truly goes away, does it?"

If anyone could understand her experience, it was

Orik. He hadn't been stabbed by a cursed blade, but he'd been the unfortunate victim of a basilisk bite while surveying a cave outside the city. The clerics hadn't been able to save the leg, and he often experienced phantom pains where it had once been. Fortunately, he'd been fitted with a gnomish prosthetic that allowed him to live a relatively normal life.

While the grandchildren played, Hilda worked in the kitchen with the adults preparing the meal. Chatter, laughter, and sibling arguments bounced off the stone walls.

Flint joined his mother's side, nudging her with his elbow. "Want to make a run for it? It was a lot quieter on the road."

"Not a chance in hells." She looked over the chaos around her. "This is the sound of family."

"Dad," Flint's youngest son, Elrik, came running into the kitchen. He tugged on his father's pant leg. "Zarra pulled my mustache again."

Flint closed his eyes, pinching the bridge of his nose. He took a deep breath before locating his daughter, who stood by the hearth wearing a mischievous grin. "Zarra, what did we tell you about pulling on your brother's mustache?"

The young girl placed her hands on her hips. "I'd hardly call that thing a mustache."

"It's thicker than yours!" Elrik shouted, and it was all Hilda could do to contain her laughter.

"Children, please." Maela let out an exasperated sigh. "In Pidros's name, could we go five minutes without bickering?" She narrowed her eyes at Flint. "They get this from you, you know."

"Me?" Flint's mouth dropped open. "What did I do?"

Maela rolled her eyes. "All the stories you tell them about the trouble you made and the pranks you played on your siblings."

Flint held up his hands. "I would never."

"You most certainly would." Darrin wrapped an arm around his brother. They were of similar height and build, both with dark brown hair, but Darrin's beard was streaked with copper. "Ma can attest, you put the rest of us through one hell or another." He pointed a finger at Elrik and then Zarra. "If you want to know what kind of a menace your father was, listen up, little ones." Darrin playfully tugged on Flint's beard. "Even though he was older, my beard sprouted several years before your father's did. Dear Flint would never admit it, but he was jealous of my luscious bristles. One night, while I was sleeping, he tied my beard to a brick and placed it on the side of my bed. I've always tossed and turned in my sleep, so you can imagine the pain when I was suddenly yanked from a peaceful dream and pulled to the floor by the hair on my chin."

Elrik and Zarra both cackled.

"Please don't give them any ideas," Maela pleaded.

This continued for the next couple of hours as they prepared dinner, Hilda delegating like a chef as she put her husband and children to work.

Boric frowned as Darrin licked his finger and stuffed it in his brother's ear. "If those two aren't wrestling by the time dinner is served, I'll eat my boot."

As much as their offspring liked to pretend they were adults, they behaved like children themselves when they were around one another.

Hilda looked up from the carrots she was chopping. "What was it you always told me, dear? Boys will be boys."

Boric shook his head. "They never truly grow up, do they?"

Hilda was fine with that. She hadn't had a large family growing up. Being the only child, her parents showered her with love, but she never experienced that familial camaraderie that so many of her friends and classmates had with their siblings. It wasn't until she joined Stone & Splendor that she felt that type of bond with others. Frey and Snorri had been like a brother and sister, and though Brok was much older, their bond had been just as unbreakable. She was happy to have found that type of loving chaos once again in her own home. As much as they bickered, her children would do anything for one another.

***

"Did Flint tell you about Gormel's new toy?" Hilda asked Boric. She wore a playful smile as they sat at the table for a dinner of stuffed chickens, roasted vegetables, thinly sliced potatoes covered in herbs and cheese, and several loaves of bread. For dessert, cakes were already cooling on the counter.

"Tell me?" Boric scoffed, followed by a grin. "He wouldn't shut up about it."

"Flint does love his contraptions," Darrin said with a mouth full of potatoes. Specks of cheese had fallen into his copper-streaked beard. "What is it this time?"

Hilda tuned Flint out while he went into detail about the gnomish smelting kit again. While her son rambled, she turned to her granddaughters. "So, Tilda. Your father tells me you've been training with your bow."

"I have." The young dwarf's face beamed with excitement. "Frida's been helping me after school, too. My teacher says I'm the best shot in the class."

"Is that so?" Hilda winked at Frida. She found it admirable that the girl had taken her younger cousin under her wing. It warmed her heart to know they'd both inherited their grandmother's love for archery.

"Yes, ma'am." Frida nodded seriously. "We both want to hunt monsters and go on all kinds of adventures, just like you did."

"Keep at it and you just might."

"We already have a name for our party." Tilda grinned.

Hilda set her fork aside and leaned forward, whispering, "And what is it?"

The two girls exchanged glances and then answered at the same time. "Braids and Quivers."

"A beautiful name, and very fitting for two talented archers. I love it, dears."

After dinner, Hilda gathered the grandchildren around the hearth while the adults set to clearing the table and washing the dishes. She sat before them all, a long, pointed tooth the size of her forearm resting on her lap.

"Does anyone know what creature this came from?" Hilda held up the tooth.

"A dragon!" shouted Bori.

"Nope. Guess again."

"A troll?" Kori looked uncertain.

"Nope. Any other guesses?"

"A behemoth," said Brom, and the other children gasped at the mention of the monster.

"If this belonged to a behemoth, I doubt I would be here telling you this story." Hilda leaned forward, tilting the tooth so that they could see the hole in the tip. She rotated it, showing that the inside of the tooth was hollowed out like a funnel. "I'll give you one more guess."

"It's a spider fang," Frida said proudly.

"Are you certain?" Hilda raised a brow.

"Absolutely." Frida nodded. "It's not technically a tooth; it's a chelicera, and the reason they're hollow is so that the spider can inject venom into its prey."

"Someone's been paying attention in school." Hilda smiled, handing the fang to Frida. "She's right. This tooth belonged to a grayfang spinner, a cave spider that can grow bigger than a war goat."

At that, the younger children groaned and made sounds of disgust.

"Who wants to hear the story of how I came to possess this fang?"

The disgust quickly transitioned into shouts of approval.

"I was young, half the age your parents are now, when my party and I ventured into the mountains in search of long-lost treasure. We'd come upon a tip that there was treasure hidden in the Iron Mountains."

"Wait!" Flint yelled from the kitchen, where he had his brother in a headlock. "I want to hear this one." He abandoned the scuffle and a moment later, Flint was sitting cross-legged on the floor between his children. "Carry on."

Hilda laughed. "Now, where was I? Stone & Splendor had been on a quest a few weeks prior, hunting down kobolds that were raiding farms and stealing chickens. We were on our way back to the guild hall when we stopped at an inn to rest. While we were eating, we overheard a man who was sitting at a nearby table talking in a hushed voice about a letter he'd discovered when clearing out his late father's desk. Apparently, his ancestors had been mercenaries during the Age of Empires and had stashed some of their treasure in the mountains. They'd died during a skirmish, and no one had ever tracked down the treasure. I didn't think much of it, but Frey was certain it was worth looking into. So, he bought the man drinks all night long, and eventually, we got the full story. Once we had a location—"

She paused as a knock came from the door.

"I'll get it." Boric waved a dismissive hand as he walked over. He opened the door, followed by the murmur of conversation.

"When we had a location…" Hilda's words trailed off when she saw who Boric was talking to. A dwarf wearing the Ashborn crest stood just outside, holding a small wooden crate.

Boric turned around, gesturing for Hilda to join him with a nod.

"Give me a moment, children," Hilda said, followed by the protest of her grandchildren as she warily approached the door. "Everything okay?" she asked her husband.

Boric stepped aside. "There's a package for you from Frey."

"From Frey?" Hilda frowned as she looked to the messenger for confirmation.

"Sorry to disturb your evening, Mrs. Rockfall." The dwarf bowed slightly. His black pants were covered in dust from traveling. "A note was discovered while organizing Frey's desk sometime after the funeral. He'd updated his last wishes. You'd already left, so I was sent to track you down."

"Updated his last wishes?" Hilda's brow scrunched further. "What do you mean?"

"It's all explained in the letter inside." The messenger held the crate out.

Hilda took it. There was a clunky rattle from within, but whatever it was wasn't very heavy. "Thank you."

"You all take care." The messenger bowed again and left.

Hilda stared at the box in her hands, wondering what could possibly be inside.

"Do you mind if I open this in private?" she asked Boric.

He rubbed her back. "Whatever you need, Mama. I'll distract the little ones until you return."

Hilda took the stairs to her private study and shut the door behind her. Floor-to-ceiling shelves lined the room, each one filled with books, journals, and trinkets from seven decades of adventuring. Behind her large wooden desk, there was an assortment of teeth and feathers displayed alongside her old bow and handaxe.

Her chest tightened as she placed the crate on her desk, and minutes passed as she stared at the box. The messenger had said there was a letter inside. Whatever it contained were the last words Frey had written her. Opening this box would be the last memory she ever shared with him.

She contemplated leaving the crate on the desk and waiting for the children to leave, but her curiosity won out. She took a dagger from a nearby drawer and pried the lid open. Inside, there was a stone vessel carved from obsidian. It had two thin handles and silver latches that held the top securely in place. The Ashborn crest was etched into the stone and set within was a reddish metal that gleamed in the candlelight. Beneath it, there was an envelope.

Hilda opened the envelope and with a shaky hand, she removed the letter, opening it gently.

Dearest Hilda,

If you're reading this, I'm either dead or a servant has been pilfering through my desk and sent my last wishes ahead of time. If this is the latter, well, that's a bit embarrassing, but not nearly as much as the time I tore the seat of my pants while climbing that ledge in search of griffin eggs. It was truly a full moon that evening.

If, in fact, I have perished and left the mortal realm, then I have one last request for my oldest and dearest friend. As you know, it is Ashborn tradition to have our ashes scattered among the mountains so that we may once again return to the earth from whence we came.

Traditionally, the scattering is done by the immediate family. But you know how I am for tradition. On my best days, I'll honor it halfway. I've always dreamed of soaring with dragons, and I don't have to be dead to know that none of my children have the mettle for this kind of adventure. I don't mean this as a slight to them, but as a testament to you. You've always seen things through, oftentimes when logic or reason would say it unwise. I've included a map marked with the location of my final resting place.

I know it's a big task, but what do you say? Will you take one more adventure with your old friend?

-Frey Ashborn

Tears brimmed in Hilda's eyes as she folded the letter and tucked it away. She removed the urn, placing it carefully on her desk. At the bottom of the crate, she found an old, folded piece of canvas, yellowed with age.

She opened the canvas, revealing a map on the other side. The map was faded, almost unreadable in the creases, but she recognized the topography as the northern mountain ranges of Mount Tor. Far to the left was Northpass, and to the right, Stonewatch. There was an entire mountain range between the two cities that was empty wilderness. The Forgotten Peaks. Those lands had been settled in the past, but the ruins had been abandoned for over two millennia. Nowadays, only fools traveled to those parts, searching for treasures that didn't exist.

In the center of the map, Frey had marked his final resting place in those perilous mountains. Beneath the X, a message was scribbled in long-faded ink. Hilda had to squint to make out four words that sent a chill down her spine.

There be dragons here.

5. ONE LAST RIDE

"Bastard." A smile tugged at the corner of her mouth as she folded the parchment and placed it in her pocket. "You always had to have the last laugh, didn't you." She patted the urn. "Alright, old friend. One last ride into danger."

She mentally prepared herself for the objections that were about to arise. In her younger days, she would've been called a fool for attempting to traverse the Forgotten Peaks. At her current age, they'd call her mad.

At least the entire family wasn't here to offer their protests.

The normally chaotic household went silent as Hilda descended the stairs, every eye focused on her. Even the youngest of the grandchildren could sense that something was happening.

Boric waited for her at the bottom of the stairs. "What is it?" he asked, hands held together and concern coating his voice.

Hilda wordlessly handed him the folded parchment.

As her husband read the letter, his expression shifted from amusement to curiosity and settled on something between unease and discontent.

He met Hilda's gaze. "Where does he want you to go?"

She handed Boric the map, and his brow creased with deep furrows. He closed his eyes, and a moment passed before he finally opened them, releasing a long sigh. His face had softened, but there was worry buried within the depths of his eyes.

He swallowed hard. "Don't suppose I could talk you out of this, could I?"

Hilda shook her head. This was the last wish of someone she'd considered a brother. How could she not honor his request?

There may be dragons in the mountains, but she was a ranger. A damn good one, too. She'd spent a lifetime honing her skills in dangerous situations, and they hadn't faded just because she moved a little slower. Besides, what was one more quest in the grand scheme of things? Was this not the perfect storybook ending—a chance to take a final quest on her terms?

"Does anybody want to tell the rest of us what the hells is going on?" asked Flint. His gaze narrowed as it pinged from Hilda to Boric.

Boric gestured to his wife.

She looked over her adoring family. Seeing the concern on their faces, part of her wanted to abandon the idea entirely. Why should she make them worry because of a dead man's last wish? As soon as the thought came, she banished it. This was what friends did for one another. If traveling into the Forgotten Peaks would allow her oldest friend to rest in peace, then that's what she'd do. Frey would have already been on the road if the roles were reversed.

"I'm going on an adventure." She chose her words carefully. The last thing she wanted was to make them worry. "I received a note from Frey containing his last wishes. He wants me to scatter his ashes among the mountains."

"That's not so bad." Darrin chimed in. "But why does Pa look so forlorn about the prospect?"

"Yeah." Flint nodded. "Where exactly does Frey want you to scatter them?"

Hilda smiled. Most of the time, her boys were the hammer, stubborn and unyielding, but there were times when they were the pick, too sharp for their own good. "The Forgotten Peaks."

At this, the house erupted in a mangled mess of complaints and disapproval that contained the words "too dangerous," "too old," and "death wish" more than once.

"Enough!" Boric's voice boomed off the walls, leaving a void of silence in its wake. "I might not agree with it, but this is your mother's decision. She has survived more close encounters and dangerous situations than the lot of us combined. If she believes she can handle the journey, then we will respect her decision."

"This isn't a trip to Ashridge." Darrin shook his head in disapproval. "I'm sorry, Ma, but this isn't one of your stories either. There's a reason those lands are not settled. We all know what happened at Deepwarden. The entire region was forced to abandon their homes and move south because of dragons. Dragons that are likely still there. What if one carries you off and we never see you again? You can't possibly be considering doing this."

Hilda forced down her smile at the mental image of being carried away by a dragon. That would be a different kind of storybook ending.

Flint met his mother's gaze, and she could see the turmoil raging within his golden eyes. Two weeks ago, he would have undoubtedly agreed with his brother. Flint took a deep breath and turned to Darrin. "Yes, she can."

"Brother, you've lost what little rocks you had in the noggin of yours if you think—"

"I was at the funeral, Darrin. You should have heard the way they talked about her there." Flint pointed to his mother. "You might not believe the stories anymore, but they're true. Our mother is one of the bravest and most adventurous souls to ever walk the realm. And while I wish she wouldn't go, I support her if she does."

"It's happened." Darrin ran his fingers through his hair. "They've all lost their minds. Orik, back me up here."

"Sorry, hon." Orik patted his husband on the back. "But I'm siding with your mother on this one."

"Traitor," Darrin muttered under his breath.

"Maybe she could hire someone to go with her," Maela offered. "A couple of adventurers could help carry the load."

Darrin groaned. "I don't like it, but that's better than nothing, I suppose."

"I'll go with her." Frida stood and held her bow in the air. "I've been training."

"Me, too," echoed Tilda.

"Absolutely not." Flint and Darrin shouted at the same time.

"Children." Hilda smiled, grateful for how much they cared. "I appreciate your worry, but I'm not some helpless old woman who needs an escort. I'm not even two hundred yet, but by the sound of your protests, you'd think I've already got two feet in the tomb."

"But your shoulder," said Darrin.

"I adventured for sixty years after being stabbed with a cursed blade." She crossed her arms. "I'll travel lightly and camp often. My shoulder will be fine."

"Sometimes, I wish you weren't so stubborn." Darrin sighed. "There's nothing we can say that would change your mind?"

"Son," Boric chuckled. "I think you'd have better luck moving a mountain."

Hilda walked over and squeezed Darrin's hand. "If you're all done complaining, I have a story to finish."

She took her seat by the hearth, finishing the tale while everyone enjoyed a piece of honey crumble. There were no more protests, but the hugs lingered longer than usual when it was time for everyone to leave. She couldn't blame them for worrying. They were right in some regards. She was no spring griffin. Much had changed in the last eighty-two years since she retired, but in her heart, she was still the same woman who thrived on risk and reward. It would be good for her to stretch her muscles one more time.

After the kids left, she made her way back to the study. Boric followed, watching as she pulled her bow and handaxe from the wall, laying them on the desk beside the urn. "If I didn't know any better, I'd offer to go with you."

"Some things need to be done alone."

Boric nodded. "I know."

Hilda wrapped her arms around his barrel chest. "Thank you."

He kissed the top of her head. "What for?"

"For still believing in me after all these years."

"You'll be fine." He chuckled. "I'm more worried for the unlucky dragon that tries to get in your way."

Hilda pressed her forehead to his. "I'll be back before you know it."

6. LET SLEEPING DWARVES LIE

The next morning, Hilda inspected her gear while Boric fetched a war goat from the stables. She'd stayed up late polishing her bow and fitting it with new string. Sharpening the old handaxe brought back fond memories. After wrapping the grip with new fabric, it looked as good as new. With a few adjustments, her old leather tunic still managed to fit, if a bit tighter than it had been before.

As far as quests went, this one was pretty straightforward—find a mountain peak, scatter Frey's ashes, and try not to get eaten by a dragon in the process. But seeing as she hadn't gone on a true adventure in eight decades, her stomach fluttered with nervous excitement.

Hilda had already triple-checked her inventory, but one more time wouldn't hurt. She riffled through the two satchels, locating her bedroll, cookware, waterskin, and assortment of tools and supplies. She'd packed more than she'd likely need, but it was better to be safe than sorry.

Packing for a quest was vastly different from packing for a trip. Once she was in the wilderness, there would be nowhere to resupply, no comfortable inns to visit for a rest and a warm meal. She needed to account for every inconvenience before stepping out the door.

Hilda folded her cloak and placed it at the top of her pack. Of all the items she'd acquired over the years, the elven dreamcloak had been one of the best, serving her time and again, even after her adventuring days were behind her.

The cloak was made from elvish dreamweave, a fabric spun from the wool of Vusoran sheep. It was lightweight, warm in the winter, cool in the summer, waterproof, and shifted color depending on the terrain. Hilda had no idea how it worked and since the sheep were only bred within the borders of Vusora, the fabric was difficult for outsiders to acquire. Dreamweave cloaks were a rarity, even among adventurers, but she'd been given one as a token of thanks after saving an elf while tracking down a rare ingredient in the Blightwood. That was a tale for when the grandchildren were older, if they still wanted to listen.

Hilda snapped the satchels shut just as Boric hitched the goat to a post out front. She still needed to make a few stops before leaving the city, but most of her adventuring gear had held up remarkably well over the years.

Morsel nibbled on a flower potted near the hitching post, bleating when she noticed Hilda. She scratched the goat beneath the chin as Boric draped the satchels over the beast's flanks. A small wagon or cart would have been nice, but there was no telling how the terrain would be a few days north of the city.

"She's ready." Boric cinched a strap and gave the satchel a good pat. "You have everything you need?"

"Mostly. I don't trust these old ropes and potions, so I'll resupply before heading out." Hilda held his gaze. "I'm going to miss you."

"I know." Boric ran a thumb across Hilda's cheek and kissed her, his scruffy beard tickling her skin.

As he pulled her in tight, Hilda felt a tug deep inside that said this was foolish. This was exactly why she'd decided to leave so soon after receiving the letter. Every day she waited was a chance she might reconsider.

She'd had her adventures, a lifetime of them, and then she'd had a second life that was equally fulfilling. She loved baking, cooking, and watching the grandchildren grow like weeds. Why was she risking that comfort for a taste of adventure?

When she looked over the peaks in the distance, their white caps kissing the clouds, she knew the answer. A single label could never encapsulate Hilda Rockfall. She was a grandmother and an adventurer. A homemaker and a ranger. She'd raised hell as well as she'd raised children. All those things were true at once, and they hadn't changed just because she was older.

She gave her husband a final kiss. "I'll see you in a month or so. Sooner if the winds blow in my favor."

"You got this, Mama." Boric patted her shoulders and gave them a firm squeeze. "I'll be waiting to hear all about it."

Hilda climbed into the saddle and set out across the city.

A bell chimed as Hilda pushed open the heavy wooden door into the Adventurer's Guild. The sleeping dwarf behind the desk stirred at the sound, a mumbled acknowledgment escaping from beneath the gray beard. He sat leaning back in his chair, feet propped on the desk as powerful snores roared like the bellows of a mountain furnace. This early in the day, most of the adventurers were likely asleep, either weary from travel or hungover from a night of revelry. If it had been an especially good quest, then probably both.

Hilda couldn't remember the last time she'd set foot inside. A decade at least. In the years after she'd retired, she came down every so often to catch the latest gossip and connect with old friends. As time passed and her family grew, she visited less and less.

The foyer hadn't changed much. The walls were a mixture of stone and exposed beams. There was a griffin head mounted on one wall, the head of a direwolf on another. Dented shields and broken weapons adorned the wall behind the sleeping dwarf, where two doors led into the guild hall and areas that were off-limits to non-members.

Hilda perused the notice board that was peppered with available quests. There were low-ranked quests like finding missing pets, locating stolen items, or special deliveries. Some required particular skillsets, like tracking down ingredients for alchemists or escort missions through dangerous terrain.

Her gaze drifted around the room until she was facing the door she'd entered through. Its center was marred with gashes from the night she and Frey had drunkenly decided to use it as target practice for throwing knives.

The guildmaster had given them hell for that one, forcing them to polish the boots of every guild member staying in the hall that night. Brok and Snorri were livid at being forced to help because they'd watched it happen.

Hilda smiled at the memory. All these years and the door still hadn't been replaced.

Behind her, a door groaned as someone entered the foyer from the guild hall. Hilda turned to see a much younger dwarf set a scroll and a stack of journals on the desk. He had rounded shoulders and wore a blue linen tunic that stretched around his midsection. Judging by the length of his beard, the lad couldn't be much older than fifty.

He frowned at the sleeping dwarf, and his eyes widened slightly as he noticed Hilda. "Sorry about him, ma'am. Some of these old farts can barely keep their eyes open at times." He chuckled. "Can I help you with anything? If you have a quest, you can leave it with me, and I'll pin it to the notice board."

Old farts. Hilda fought the urge to roll her eyes. *The lad is barely a pup.*

"Ma'am?" The young dwarf raised his voice as he asked again. "Anything I can help you with?"

Hilda forced a smile. "I need to buy some rope and potions."

"Sorry, ma'am, but we only sell supplies to guild members." He pointed toward the door. "There's a general store a few blocks down Stone Street."

Hilda pinched the bridge of her nose, swallowing her irritation. "Son, I carved my name into these walls when you were nothing more than a whisper of a dream in your father's loins. Call me 'ma'am' one more time and I'll see to it that you're cleaning the latrines instead of growing soft and pudgy behind that desk. Do we understand one another?"

She wasn't sure she held that kind of sway with the current guildmaster, but her tone had gotten the point across well enough.

The young dwarf gulped. "Yes, ma—er. Sorry." He nodded. "I mean, uh, y-yes. We understand one another."

He looked like a deer in the lamplight as he tried to inconspicuously tap the elder dwarf's foot in a desperate attempt to wake the sleeping bear. The elder only snored louder until a firm nudge sent the dwarf's feet tumbling from the desk, jerking him awake. He sprung from the chair like a pit viper, hand drawing a dagger with practiced precision as he thrust the blade toward the young dwarf's throat.

"Who wants to feel the sting?" the elder asked, his eyes wild.

The young pup stumbled backward, tripping over a chair and tumbling to the floor.

Hilda laughed, and awareness returned to the older dwarf's eyes.

"Seven hells, Grover." He lowered the weapon. "What did I tell you about startling someone awake?"

"Durhum," Hilda barked with laughter. "I didn't recognize you with the gray beard. Dreaming about the old days?"

"Hilda Rockfall." Durhum looked from Grover to Hilda and shook his head. "What in Pidros's shiny arse are you doing here?"

She raised her eyebrows suggestively. "Well, old friend, I'm in need of supplies."

After giving Grover a stern lesson on how to respect one's elders, Durhum escorted Hilda to the supply room.

"He called me 'ma'am,'" Hilda scoffed. "Can you believe it?"

"Oh, I believe it. With each new batch of trainees, they either have their heads in the clouds or so far up their own arses that they can see the daylight through their teeth." He stopped outside the door to the supply room. "You want to tell me what it is that you need supplies for?"

She told Durhum of Frey's death and his last wishes.

"The Forgotten Peaks?" Durhum sighed. "Hells, Hilda, are you so keen to join him?"

"I was a ranger for seventy years. I think I can handle a trek through the mountains. Besides, Frey would do the same for me if the roles were reversed."

"Frey was a smug bastard, but I always liked him." Durhum opened a cabinet filled with potions, tonics, and elixirs in a variety of colors. "It's honorable, what you're doing. I don't agree with it, but I do understand it." He paused, his hand resting on the red vial of a healing potion. "I mean no offense, but don't you think we should leave the adventures to the young bloods?"

Hilda gave him a wink. "Why should they have all the fun?"

"I can see in your eyes that I'd have better luck taming the wind than changing your mind." He placed several potions on the table and then began measuring the rope. "You and Frey had that much in common. Both of you were as stubborn as a direhog once your minds were made up." He cut the rope, winding it from his hand to elbow until it was a compact circle. "Promise me you'll be careful. Once you're out there, you're on your own. Not even the glory chasers travel through those parts nowadays."

Hilda packed the potions and tossed the rope over her shoulder. "Don't worry about me. I've had enough glory to last me a lifetime."

7. END OF THE ROAD

After gathering supplies, Hilda sat upon Morsel's back as they traveled northward through winding roads. It was a beautiful afternoon, the sun sparkling against distant peaks as the harsh sounds of the city faded, replaced by the trill of insects, birds cawing overhead, and wind rustling through the tree branches. The city had its advantages, but she'd be lying if she said she didn't miss traveling on the open road.

Morsel turned her massive head and bleated, refusing to quiet until Hilda scratched her behind the ears. Although the goat was most commonly used for pulling wagons, she was a gentle soul and always seemed to enjoy the opportunities to carry a rider.

"Easy, girl." Hilda ruffled the goat's soft brown fur. "You don't want to be doing that once we're in dragon country. Bartemus would never forgive me if I let you get carried off because you were being needy."

Morsel huffed in response. Apparently, some pleasures were worth dying for.

In ages past, war goats had been the predominant mount of most northern dwarves. Their large spiral horns, sturdy bodies, and steady feet were perfect for mountainous regions. Many times, citizens had defended their lands by using the goats to ram their adversaries off narrow passes. Nowadays, war goats had become a rarity throughout the kingdom, and almost non-existent in the wider realm, though Hilda had heard tales that the Northern Guard still used them on occasion when traveling into the wilderness to fight behemoths. In dangerous terrain, there wasn't a creature she trusted more to remain calm and steady in a tense situation.

Hilda made good progress over the first few days. Towns gave way to villages and settlements, and each inn grew smaller than the last. Compared to the populous trade route that stretched from Durendreg to Drake Canyon, the northern route was practically desolate. She encountered the occasional adventurer or trader, but not much else. Each night, she made a point to enjoy the hearty meals and company while it was available. Soon, she'd be eating rations, and Morsel would be her only companion.

By the third day, Hilda's cursed wound had begun to ache, dull and steady. After a dinner of roasted mutton, she retired to her room to rest, laying in bed with the coldstone pressed against her shoulder until the discomfort ebbed.

On the fifth day, there were no more villages, only miles between the ramshackle steads of sheepherders and farmers. People in these parts were of the old blood, generations of dwarves who had bent but not broken when an entire region was forced to relocate in the aftermath of dragon attacks.

As the sun faded, the road seemed to deteriorate before her eyes. Vegetation crept in from the surrounding countryside, narrowing the path. Owls hooted and wolves howled into the night with the chorus of crickets and other wildlife. It reminded her of adventures long ago, traveling through ruins and the far reaches of the realm.

Hilda began to scour the countryside in search of a place to camp for the night when she came upon a dilapidated stone building hidden behind a thicket not far from the road. It was two stories tall and maybe three rooms wide. Vines had laid claim to half of the structure, blanketing it with green ivy. Many of the stone tiles on the roof were cracked or missing, the windows were caked with grime, and the wooden slats on the porch were splintered and warped. A faded sign hung askew just above the porch, the words "Inn'd of the Road" barely readable.

She would have assumed it abandoned if not for the faint glow from beyond one of the murky windows.

End of the road, indeed. Hilda tied Morsel to a pillar and climbed the rickety steps. Something stirred beneath the porch, and a cat hissed before darting into the woods.

Hilda knocked on the door, and she heard footsteps a moment later.

The door squeaked, swinging inward. An elderly female dwarf stood inside, holding a pipe that trailed smoke from the end. Her tattered tunic had seen better days, and she wore pants patched at the knees. Despite the state of her clothing, the woman's silver beard was perfectly woven into a fishtail braid. There wasn't a stray hair in sight, but her mustache was stained a golden brown from years of smoking.

She frowned at Hilda beneath a pair of bushy eyebrows. "Can I help ya?" she asked with a raspy voice.

Hilda looked past the dwarf, but she couldn't see much in the dim candlelight. "Is this an inn?"

A cat meowed from inside as it stepped into view and nuzzled against the elderly dwarf's legs.

"Once upon a time." The woman scoffed. "Just me and the cats nowadays."

"Sorry to bother you." Hilda bowed and took a step back.

"Yer already here, ain't ya?" The woman opened the door further, and the smell of earthy vegetables wafted outside. A few more cats moved in the shadows. "It ain't much, but dinner's almost ready. Still gots a bed upstairs, but if I'm honest with ya, ya might prefer the floor."

"I appreciate the honesty." Hilda grinned at the woman's candor. "Is there anywhere to stable my goat?"

The woman shook her head. "Barn doors haven't worked in ages. You can tie her up, though. Ain't no need to worry about someone taking the beast. Yer the first person I've seen in weeks."

After unpacking Morsel and tethering the goat in the barn, Hilda came inside. A single candle flickered at the center of a thick, wooden table, and a low fire burned in the hearth, where a half-dozen cats basked in its warmth. A kettle of stew simmered quietly, steam wafting up the chimney.

"That smells delicious," Hilda said as she placed her satchel on the bench.

"Root stew." The woman puffed on her pipe, and the

end pulsed orange. "Turnips, carrots, taters. No meat. Still garden but I don't hunt like I used to."

If Hilda had to guess, the woman was nearing three hundred. Wrinkles lined her eyes and forehead like a map of the world.

"Have a seat." The woman gestured to the table before pulling a bowl from the shelf. "What's yer name, dearie?"

"Hilda. Hilda Rockfall." She sighed as she sat down, her muscles happy with relief.

"I knew a Rockfall once." The woman ladled soup from the kettle. "Decent fellow."

"Most are, in my experience. What's your name?"

"Gwynera." She set the bowl in front of Hilda. "Best to eat while it's hot."

Hilda scooped a spoonful of stew, blowing on it before taking a bite. The vegetables were so tender that they practically melted in her mouth. Creamy potatoes complemented the sweetness of the carrots and the bitterness of the turnips. There was a hint of pepper and other spices that brought it all together.

She slurped a spoonful of broth, savoring the earthy flavor. "This is wonderful."

Gwynera smiled for the first time. "My pa taught me how to make the best of what we had."

"How long has the inn been around?" Hilda continued devouring the stew.

"Generations. Once upon a time, it was the last stop this side of the mountain between Stonefist Hold and Grayhall. Now, it's just a memory. I 'spect the inn will die with me."

Hilda wasn't sure how to respond to that. There was no sadness in Gwynera's tone, only cold finality. Hilda thought of her own family and how they were likely already worried about her. She wondered if the woman had ever had a family of her own, or how long she'd been living with just her and the cats.

"Don't feel sorry for me." Gwynera chuckled, waving her pipe in a dismissive gesture. "I chose this life. I have siblings a few towns over. They visit from time to time, but I like the peace and quiet. Tell me, what brings a lady like yerself out this far?"

"I don't know if I'd call myself a lady." Hilda laughed. "I'm heading north to keep a promise to an old friend."

"Who needs enemies when you have friends like that?" Gwynera took a long draw of her pipe. "Nothing good up that way, I can assure you."

"Still, a promise is a promise."

A cat jumped on the bench, sniffing at Hilda's bowl.

"Sorry about that." Gwynera looked amused as the cat placed its forepaws on the table for a better sniff. "They run the roost."

After dinner, Gwynera showed Hilda to a room. True to her words, the bed was in even worse shape than the building's exterior. After testing the lumpy mattress, Hilda elected to sleep on her bedroll.

She was lying on the floor, listening to the chirp of crickets outside, when she heard music coming through the floorboard.

Quietly, she snuck down the hallway, pausing at the top of the stairs to listen. In the dim glow of the fire, Gwynera sat in an old rocking chair, strumming a lute for the cats sitting at her feet. At least one of the instrument's strings was broken, but there was still beauty in the sound.

Gwynera cleared her throat. Then, she sang, the raspy words and solemn, mournful tones seeping into the ancient wood.

"The goats are gone, the ale sits still,
Where wind now haunts the windowsill.
My mother's quilt, left on the chair,
Her spirit lingers in the air.
We built our hearths with love and care,
Now only ghosts are settled there.

Smoke in the trees, fire in the night,
We lost our boots, we left our lives.
No time for axes, no time for gold,
Just memories and hands to hold.

Some say we'll return one day when it's cold,
When dragon bones are cracked and old.
Til that hour, we wander and roam,
And sing the loss of our mountain home."

A pang tugged at Hilda's heart for the families who lost everything because of dragons. And once again, she wondered if she was making a mistake.

8. INTO THE UNKNOWN

With the inn behind her, Hilda breathed in the fresh air of open wilderness. It was a crisp morning, and fog settled in the valley like a blanket. Animals chittered from the trees, and leaves rustled beneath pillowy clouds speckling the calm blue sky. She passed a herd of deer drinking from a stream, oblivious to Hilda and Morsel as they trekked along the faded path. The buck raised its head, dew-covered antlers sparkling in the sun. It gave Hilda and Morsel a passing glance before returning its attention to the crystal-clear water.

Morsel's long brown fur rippled in the breeze. Hilda leaned forward, scratching the goat behind the ears. "Just you and me, old girl. Once more into the unknown."

Morsel bleated in response.

In their rearview, Stonefist Hold was just another towering mountain, its colossal white fist pointing toward the heavens. Ahead, hundreds of miles of wilderness stood between Hilda and the Forgotten Peaks.

Durhum was right. No one had traveled these routes

in a long time. The old roads were little more than animal trails at this point, with the occasional vestige of ancient civilization lurking beneath overgrowth, and moss-covered stones that served as a reminder of what had been.

If she ever wanted to turn back, now was the time.

Gwynera's song replayed in Hilda's mind, those mournful tones sending chills down her spine. *Some say we'll return one day when it's cold, when dragon bones are cracked and old.* How many years had it been since the residents were forced to abandon their homes, and still no one had resettled these lands? The land had become untamed, unforgiving, and uncaring of Hilda's or anyone else's place in the world.

Dragons might be hundreds of miles away, but their presence cast a long shadow.

A branch cracked some ways behind her, sending a flock of birds cawing as they fluttered from nearby trees. Hilda turned but saw nothing. Probably some animal passing through the underbrush.

Around midday, she stopped by a stream to rest, and if she was lucky, catch a fish. She had enough stonebread packed in her satchels to last a month, so there was no worry of going hungry. The dwarven bread was great for traveling since it didn't spoil, but flavorful, it was not.

Morsel drank from the gurgling water and then grazed in the tall grass while Hilda took out the last of the honey crumble Boric had made.

Frey's urn sat beside Hilda, the dark, polished stone gleaming in the daylight.

"I'd offer you a bite—" She held out the cake to the urn. "—but I wouldn't want to soil your ashes."

Morsel looked up from the grass she was chewing and bleated.

"No one asked your opinion."

The goat bleated again.

Hilda took a bite of the cake, savoring its sweet deliciousness. She wondered what her husband was up to now. Probably down in the mines, listening to their children complain about what a foolish endeavor this was. That was fine. She didn't need them to understand her choice, only to respect it.

With cake in her belly, Hilda set her sights on more nourishing sustenance. Using her dagger, she dug in the soft soil beside the stream until she found a worm. She wrapped it around the hook and extended her rod over the stream, dipping the line in the flowing water.

Fishing had always been one of her favorite ways to pass the time while on the road. It was rare that an activity could be both integral to survival and the pinnacle of relaxation. Unlike hunting, which required a great deal of effort and cunning, not to mention it could be quite messy, fishing was simple. It required technique, sure, but the mind could wander. Hilda did some of her best thinking with a rod in her hand.

She sat on the bank, enjoying the sun's warmth kissing her cheeks and the gentle breeze tousling her beard. A flash of white caught her eye as a griffin broached the far tree line, its prey clenched between its talons. Nowhere else could she see something like that. She smiled, relishing in the tranquility of nature with its myriad of sounds, scents, and textures— the splash of water as it flowed downstream, the fresh scent of wildflowers, the cool earth beneath her fingers.

Sometimes, she wondered why her people were so obsessed with stone and jewels when the real treasure was all around them. If dwarves were born from the earth, she liked to imagine it was the soft loam of the forest floor, not the inflexible heart of a mountain.

The rod dipped as something nibbled on the line. Hilda leaned forward. Beneath the clear water, a silver fish darted about, pecking at the worm. Like a game of cat and mouse, Hilda waited patiently for the fish to bite. When she felt a solid pull, she jerked. When the tension increased and she was certain the hook was set, she pulled her line from the water. A silver fish the size of her hand flailed from the end.

It wasn't the biggest fish she'd ever caught, but it'd make a decent lunch.

Hilda gathered sticks from the surrounding area and quickly had a small fire going. She cleaned the fish quickly, content that her skills with a blade had not dulled with time. Soon, it crackled over the open flame.

She watched as its skin slowly darkened, fat glistening from the flaky meat beneath. Her mouth watered at the smell.

A shrill cry cut through the moment of peace like an axe swing. Hilda turned to see a figure running in her direction, hands waving as they shouted for help. Behind them, a black bear pursued, followed by two young cubs in the distance.

"Idiot." Hilda reached for the bow hanging from Morsel's pack but instead grabbed her cooking pot and took off in the direction of the bumbling person. "Damned fool! You never run from a bear, especially a black bear."

As Hilda grew closer, she noticed a mop of red hair concealing the woman's face as she looked over her shoulder at the pursuing bear. The woman's dwarven legs moved swiftly through the tall grass. The animal was gaining on the woman, but she had the sense to toss her pack aside.

"Help!" the dwarf shouted. "Gram, help!"

Hilda nearly froze in her tracks when she realized it was Frida. What was her granddaughter doing this far from the city? She pushed the thought aside and took action.

"Behind me!" Hilda ordered, stepping in front of her grandchild and raising her arms high above her head in an attempt to appear as formidable as possible.

She roared with all the power her lungs could muster, and the mama bear halted. Hilda roared again, this time banging the butt of her axe against the pot. Thunderous gongs rang out across the valley.

The bear grunted a challenge. Hilda continued to bang her pot until the bear took a step back. Mama Bear nuzzled one of her cubs in the side, and with a final look over her shoulder, led the trio back toward the woods.

Hilda turned around, eyes wide as she took in Frida's appearance. "What in the seven hells are you doing here, Frida?"

9. A PROPER ADVENTURE

Hilda walked in silence, Frida following her. She wasn't sure if she should be furious or impressed that her granddaughter had managed to track her for six days without being spotted.

Once the bears disappeared into the woods, they'd retrieved Frida's pack, along with the other items she'd tossed aside during her escape, and were now making their way toward Morsel and the camp. The girl's pack rivaled Hilda's, complete with rations, waterskin, bedroll, knife, plenty of arrows for her bow, and an assortment of gear.

She'd packed well. No one could argue that the girl hadn't paid attention at school. Well, aside from the incident with the bear.

By the time they made it back to the stream, the fish was nothing more than blackened char. Hilda offered it to Morsel, and the goat ate it happily.

"Sit." She pointed at the grass, and Frida sheepishly obeyed.

Hilda took a deep breath. There was a lot to unpack here, but first and foremost, she needed to dispense some knowledge.

"Never run from a black bear." She met her grand-daughter's gaze. "Ever. They are fast and they are danger-ous, but if you stand your ground and make as much noise as you can, they will usually avoid conflict." Hilda looked over her shoulder in the direction the bears had fled. "You came upon a mother, and she was protecting her cubs. That made her more aggressive than usual, but even so, you do not run. Do you understand?"

"Yes, Grandmother."

Grandmother. Hilda swallowed her amusement. They only called her that when they were in trouble.

She massaged her eyes and focused on Frida, cutting straight to the point. "Why did you follow me?"

Frida bit her lip, as if choosing her words carefully. "I wanted to come with you on an adventure. You've always told us about how great they are, and I knew if I asked, everyone would say no."

"You're damned right." There was more bite than Hilda had intended, and Frida recoiled from her grandmother's words. She softened her tone but remained firm. "This isn't playtime, Frida. These are dangerous lands. Where I'm going is even more so. Out here, if you get hurt, there are no clerics to save you." Hilda stared off into the distant mountains. While she hoped things would go smoothly, nothing was guaranteed.

"I know that, Gram." The girl stared at her grand-mother defiantly. "I might be young, but I'm not a child. You weren't much older than me when you became an apprentice. I've wanted to be an adventurer since the first time I heard one of your stories. I've been training for this."

Hilda crossed her arms. She wanted to tell Frida that that was childish thinking, that she herself had apprenticed for ten years as a ranger before she ever joined an adventuring party in her own right, but she couldn't do that to the girl. She couldn't kill her dreams. As far back as Hilda could remember, Frida had been enamored with the life of an adventurer, more so than any of her other grandchildren. Not just the action and heroic bits, but all of it, from rainy nights playing games in taverns to campfire stories under the stars. The girl carried her bow everywhere and had joined numerous clubs to help develop her skills. Flint assumed she would grow out of it in time, but Frida had held steady. This was more than just a childhood phase.

"Does anyone know you followed me?" Hilda asked.

The girl smiled timidly. "I left a note."

"Of course you did." Hilda chuckled. Not that she would have done anything differently. It was always easier to ask for forgiveness than permission.

With the time it would take to escort Frida home and return, she could be halfway to the Forgotten Peaks. Danger awaited where she was heading, there was no denying that, but she'd navigated far worse situations with less capable companions. Frida was right, she wasn't a child, as evidenced by the fact she'd made it this far.

"Tell me..." Hilda sat on the ground next to Frida. "How'd you manage to follow me?"

The girl's timid smile spread into a full grin. "First, I had to outsmart Pa and Ma, so I packed my bag the night before you left. I knew they would ask questions. They always ask so many questions." Frida rolled her eyes. "So, I told them we were practicing the best way to store our gear at school. I woke up early and waited in the alley across from your place until you left. Then, I kept my distance while you made your stops. After that, I slept in barns, so I'd wake early, and did my best to follow Morsel's tracks when you were out of sight. I wanted to wait a couple more days before I revealed myself so you had no choice but to let me come but…" She frowned at that. "I know you're not supposed to run from black bears, but I panicked. Everything happened so fast."

"It happens to the best of us." Hilda squeezed Frida's shoulder. "There was one time, back when I was still an apprentice, when goblins raided our camp during the night. Everything was pure chaos. I grabbed my bow and ran out into the fiery carnage, only to realize I didn't bring any arrows."

"You forgot your arrows?" Frida's mouth was agape.

"I did." Hilda grimaced at the memory. "It was the first and last time that happened. We all make mistakes. What's important is that you learn from them."

"I want to learn, Gram." A fire burned in the girl's eyes. "This is all I've ever wanted to do. I'm only four years younger than you were when you became an apprentice."

"Really?" Hilda raised her brows, wondering where the years had gone. "Are you really seventeen already?"

"I will be in a month." Frida wore a mischievous smile.

"Oh, child." Hilda laughed. "What am I going to do with you?"

Frida clasped her hands together and batted her eyelashes. "Let me come with you?"

Hilda watched the girl for a long moment. The

yearning in Frida's voice tugged at her heart. There were times, long ago, when Hilda had dreamt of one day taking her children on a quest through the mountains. Eventually, she realized that all of them had taken to her husband's interests. They were more concerned with mining, industry, and craftsmanship than the wonders of the world. This was an opportunity to make memories that would last Frida the rest of her days, no matter what course her life took. She nodded. "Your parents are going to kill me. I hope you know that."

"Thank you! Thank you! Thank you!" Frida wrapped her arms around her grandmother and squeezed. Her grip was strong, further evidence that she was on the verge of adulthood, as much as Hilda would have loved to believe otherwise.

She pried herself from Frida's grasp, looking her granddaughter in the eye. "I meant it when I said this isn't playtime. I'm glad for your company, but if I haven't reiterated this enough, our path ahead is perilous. That means you will do as I say when I say it. From here on out, you are not my granddaughter. You are my apprentice. You have an opportunity that few your age have—to learn through real-world experience. Do not squander it."

Frida squealed with delight and thrust her hands in the air. "This is the best day ever!"

Hilda shook her head and pulled a piece of stonebread from her satchel. "Eat up, youngblood. We still have a ways to go before nightfall."

They trekked for most of the day, until the tip of Stonefist Hold was barely visible over the peaks in the distance. Hilda quizzed Frida on her training, stopping occasionally to point out edible plants or the tracks of various wild animals. While Frida had a great deal of theoretical knowledge, putting it into practice could mean the difference between survival and starvation.

The sun hovered above distant mountains when they finally stopped to make camp in a clearing beneath a large oak. Lush grass spread across the glade.

"Do you know how to start a fire?" Hilda asked as she tied Morsel to a tree.

"Yes, ma'am." Frida opened her pack. "I have flint and steel. Pa got me a Seer's Lens for my birthday last year, but it only works if it's sunny. And I know how to start a fire with sticks, though I'm not as good at that."

"That's about three more methods than I knew at your age." Hilda pointed to a copse of nearby trees. "Gather some tinder, and I'll prepare a firepit."

While Frida went out in search of wood, Hilda dug a small pit and lined the circle with stones. This was her first night camping beneath the stars, and judging by the breeze whistling through the trees, it was sure to be chilly. Hilda's elvish dreamcloak would regulate her temperature, but she didn't want her granddaughter catching a cold. Besides, it was good for the girl to practice making a fire in windy conditions.

Frida returned a few minutes later with an armful of sticks and twigs in various sizes, and Hilda watched as the girl put her training to use. She placed a bundle of tinder in the center, and then topped it with small sticks and twigs in a cone for kindling. Next, she surrounded the kindling with larger sticks for fuel, stacking them in a tent formation. Not too many to where it would blaze like a beacon, but enough to burn low for hours.

She looked to her grandmother for approval. "How's that?"

"You did well. The wind's not so bad that we need a lean-to formation, so this should suffice."

Once the fire was going, they both set up their bedrolls. Hilda pulled out the coldstone. Cooling the cursed wound was part of her nightly routine for the foreseeable future. At least until they returned home.

Frida propped herself on her elbows, watching her grandmother. "Does it hurt?"

"Not like it used to." Hilda set the stone aside and massaged her shoulder. "It's a different kind of pain now. Dull. Aching. Like there's a knot that you can never truly work out. Sometimes it burns, but those days are few and far between. Usually when I overdo it." She kept the fact that a month-long trip through the wilderness at her age was likely the epitome of overdoing it. "All the more reason why you should always remain vigilant when you're on the road. It only takes a moment for your life to change forever."

"Gram, look!" Frida sat up, pointing toward the valley.

Hilda reached for her dagger out of instinct, her muscles tensing. She scanned the area for threats, but all she saw was a pulsing yellow light. Her gaze settled on the glow, and her body relaxed. The light moved through the darkness like a streetlamp on a foggy night, hazy and ethereal. A moment later, there was another flicker, this time in a golden hue. Soon, a dozen twinkles of light pulsed across the valley like fireflies in shades of yellow, gold, and orange.

"What are they?" Frida whispered, as if the mere act of talking might make it all disappear.

"Will-o-wisps." Hilda said, remembering the last time she'd seen the creatures. "No one really knows what they are since they don't have bodies. Nowadays, you only ever see them deep within forests or in the wilderness. Depending on who you ask, they're either a good omen or evil spirits trying to lead you to your doom."

"What do you believe?"

Hilda recalled traveling through Feybrook with her old party. They'd come across hundreds of wisps glowing in the center of the lake, their reflections shimmering like stars even though it was an overcast night. They'd camped by the shore, sharing bottles of elvish wine they'd purchased in town as they talked and watched the wisps long into the night. Snorri had believed that they were the souls of those who'd chosen to stay connected with the earth instead of parting to the great beyond.

"I think people like to find meaning in anything they can." She turned to Frida. "But we're adventurers. We forge our own luck. Now, get some rest. We've got a long day ahead of us tomorrow."

Frida gave a salute and then laid down, pulling her bedroll to her chin.

Soon, the wisps disappeared into the trees, and Frida's gentle snores rumbled like the purr of a cat. Hilda watched her granddaughter sleep. Strands of red hair hung across Frida's face. While sleeping, she still looked like the girl that Hilda had bounced on her lap and tucked into bed at night, not the young woman she was becoming. As concerning as it was to bring Frida on such a daunting journey, there was a part of Hilda that was excited to share the experience with her family.

She patted the urn resting beside her bedroll. "Between the three of us, this might be a proper adventure."

10. CLASHING STEEL

"These are two of the most common mushrooms you'll find throughout Mount Tor—Gargoyle's Beard and Stonecap." Hilda held up two remarkably similar mushrooms. "One of these will feed and nourish you. The other will make you so sick, you'll wish you were dead. Tell me, young adventurer, which one is safe?"

"I know this." Frida frowned as she examined the two fungi, her brow scrunched in frustration.

Both mushrooms had a dark gray convex cap with a slate-blue underbelly. While they looked almost identical at first glance, the one in Hilda's left hand had gills in the undercap, while the other had wrinkled folds. It also had white speckles along the stem.

Frida pointed at the one with white speckles and folds. "This one is Gargoyle's Beard. It's named that because the folds underneath the cap look like beards do in sculptures." She pointed at the other. "And this one is the Stonecap."

"Correct. And which one is poisonous?" asked Hilda.

Frida scratched her head. "Gargoyle's Beard?" There was a hint of uncertainty in her answer.

Hilda arched her brow. "You sure about that?"

The girl paused, then nodded. "Yes, ma'am."

"Let's find out." Hilda offered her the Stonecap mushroom.

"Seriously?" The girl's eyes widened. "What if I'm wrong?"

Hilda fought away the grin that tugged the edges of her mouth. "Are you wrong?" She could see the war waging in Frida's eyes as the girl contemplated if her grandmother would truly let her eat a poisonous mushroom.

Frida groaned and closed her eyes. When she opened them, she grabbed the Stonecap mushroom without hesitation and stuffed it in her mouth.

"Attagirl." Hilda tossed the poisonous mushroom to the ground. "There's a saying that should help you remember the difference in the future. It goes, 'A stoney cap is fit to eat; beware the beard that looms beneath.'"

Frida laughed. "Where'd you learn that?"

"Snorri always had trouble remembering things, so she had all kinds of sayings to help her." Hilda smiled at the memory. "You hear them enough and they stick with you."

Frida removed her pack and pulled out a small journal.

"What are you doing with that?" asked Hilda.

"It's like you always say…" The girl opened the notebook and scribbled. "What gets written gets remembered."

"It's good advice. I'm grateful that my mentor shared it with me." Hilda had filled countless journals over the years, many of them during travels just like this one. There was something about writing things down that kept the knowledge in her mind. Snorri had her sayings, Brok remembered through repetition and sheer force of will, and Hilda had her journals. And then there was Frey. He was the type to leap from a cliff with the hope he'd find water or sprout wings on the way down.

Hilda had spent nine years as an apprentice to Elgrid Brighthearth, but when she thought back on her adventuring days, it was almost always Frey, Brok, and Snorri that came to mind. This little nugget was all Elgrid, though. She'd helped to forge Hilda into someone capable of adventuring the realm, but it had been the members of Stone & Splendor who had sharpened her edges and honed her into something formidable.

"All this talk of mushrooms has my stomach rumbling." Hilda patted her belly. "What do you say we break for lunch?"

Morsel bleated her support of the idea.

They stopped by a fallen tree to eat. The trail they'd been following was at a steady incline, providing a picturesque view of the valley behind them. Hilda unpacked her rations while Morsel wandered through the nearby underbrush, eating the leaves of whatever happened to be in front of her.

The midday sun warmed Hilda's neck as she portioned out stonebread, jerky, and cheese for herself and Frida. Hilda took a bite of the hard bread and paused, tilting her head at a clinking sound in the distance.

"What's that?" Frida asked with a mouth full of food.

Hilda held a finger to her lips and set her plate aside. She'd recognize the unforgettable clang of clashing steel anywhere. This far from civilization, it was cause for concern. She removed her bow and quiver from Morsel's saddle and cautiously approached the direction of the noise. Frida followed close behind with her own bow in hand.

Steel continued to chime as they ascended, the metallic ring echoing off the mountain. Whoever was fighting, they weren't holding back.

Hilda swallowed hard. Durhum had said no one traveled these parts, but he was clearly mistaken. Who would be bold enough to venture through desolate wilderness, and more importantly, why? It was unlikely that there was anyone out here fulfilling the final wish of an old friend.

She crept toward the ridge, the sounds of battle growing louder with each step. Pausing near the top, Hilda could hear the labored breathing and strained grunts on the other side before each new flurry of clinks.

A large tree at the crest of the trail provided cover as Hilda approached. She peeked around the trunk. There was a steep decline to where two umbral elves were fighting in a clearing below. Both wore light tunics and wielded elvish blades, sharpened on only one side. The elves were tall and lithe, and sweat glistened against their ashen skin as they slashed their weapons. One of the elves was much older, his hair and beard a silvery gray that matched Hilda's. He wore his hair pulled up into a knot, a few stray strands framing his angular face. His opponent was much younger. He had a thin layer of scruff on his cheeks, and his shortish brown hair bounced about his pointed ears with every movement.

The two elves circled one another, feet moving with cat-like grace. Whoever they were, they were well-trained. Each swing and parry was like a dance as they drifted like water, neither one gaining the upper hand.

Off to their right, two horses grazed in the grass not far from packs of gear and camping supplies. A small fire burned nearby beneath a steaming pot of stew. Were they traveling together? Or had one come upon the other?

Metal shrieked, followed by a curse as the younger elf was disarmed. His blade twirled through the air before sticking point-down in the ground. The ribbon on the end of the hilt fluttered in the breeze like a banner.

The elder raised his blade, pointing it at the younger's throat. Hilda wasn't sure if she should intervene or stay hidden. She could disarm the elf easily enough with a well-placed arrow, but she wasn't a spry eighty-year-old anymore. She had to think of what would come after. Even with the high ground, there was no sense in putting Frida at risk when she had no knowledge of what the elves were fighting over.

The elder stepped forward until the tip of his sword pressed against his opponent's neck.

And then he laughed. He lowered his weapon and patted the younger elf on the shoulder. "Well played, son. You almost had me for a minute there."

Hilda lowered her weapon, and some of the tension released from her shoulders. They were a father and son sparring. The elves might not be out for blood, but that still didn't mean they weren't dangerous.

The younger elf retrieved his sword. "One of these days, I'll best you. You can count on it."

"But not this day." The elder laughed again.

"Should we go say hello?" Frida whispered.

"Not yet." Hilda shook her head. She needed to assess the situation before risking a confrontation. They were a long way from the Cascus border, and even though the umbral elves had a strong alliance with the dwarves of Mount Tor, Hilda knew better than to place her faith in a person solely on the reputation of their kingdom. As she watched, the son cleaned the dirt from his sword and sheathed his blade while the father filled bowls with stew from the pot.

"That looks delicious." Frida wiped drool from her chin. "Much better than stonebread."

Morsel must have agreed, because she chose that moment to join them. The giant war goat pressed a wet nose to Hilda's ear and then licked her cheek.

"What are you doing, girl?" Hilda whispered, pushing the goat's massive head away. "Get back. You're going to give us away."

Morsel nuzzled into Hilda's shoulder and let out a bleat so loud that birds scattered from the branches above. Both elves stood, the red of their eyes fixed on the trail above them.

"Who's there?" the son called.

"Stay here," Hilda whispered as she stepped out from behind the tree, a hand raised in greeting. "Hi there. I heard a ruckus up this way and came to investigate. I was told no one travels these parts anymore."

"It certainly seems that way." The father blew on his bowl of soup while he continuously stirred it with a spoon. His sword and bow rested on the tree behind him, but he made no move to grab either. "We haven't seen another soul in at least a week. Which begs the question, what brings you to these parts?"

"Keeping a promise to an old friend."

"Some friend." The father chuckled. "Name's Drazhan. This is my son, Korran."

"Hilda." She nodded toward the weapons. "I caught the end of your duel. You're quite the swordsmen." She met Korran's gaze. "Both of you."

"Perks of having the great Drazhan Myrr as your instructor."

Hilda frowned as she tried to recall where she'd heard the name before.

"I know that look." Drazhan smirked. "People know the name but can never place the face. I was First Sword to the Bulwark of Cascus for many years. Youngest to ever hold the title. If you ever saw Tazyrin Duskrider on a stately visit, I was by his side. I joined his guard at sixteen and served for nearly nine decades before stepping aside to start a family of my own." He walked over and clapped Korran on the shoulder. "Now, Korran here is prepared to do the same."

"That's where I know you from." Hilda stopped at the edge of their campsite. "My party and I were rewarded by the bulwark after saving some of your kin in the wilds. That must have been over a hundred years ago."

"No..." Drazhan scrunched his brow as if he were trying to place her. "What was the name of your party?"

"Stone & Splendor."

"By the gods! We've both gone a little gray about the muzzle, but I do recognize you." Drazhan looked to his son and then pointed to Hilda. "We're in rare company, son. If I'm not mistaken, this is Hilda Flintbreaker. Some of the old guard still tell stories of your prowess with a bow. She's the dwarf who single-handedly saved Ylith Vorn from a lycanthe."

Korran's brows shot up. "Really?"

"That was a long time ago." She smiled. "It's Hilda Rockfall now."

"Congratulations, then." Drazhan bowed slightly.

"Thank you. Pardon my intrusiveness, but you two are a long way from Sanguin." First sword or not, umbral elves weren't exactly known for traveling the realm. Spotting one outside of elvish lands was like finding a chrysalis in the wild. Not unheard of, but always memorable when it happened. Much like the elder elves in the south, the umbral elves tended to keep to themselves.

Korran smiled. "I'll return to the capital soon enough. I wanted to see Stonefist Hold before I take my vows. Not sure how many opportunities I'll have to see the wonders of Aedrea until my oath is fulfilled. Father suggested we travel north for a few days while we're here and see if we could spot a dragon."

"Did you?" Hilda asked.

"Saw a blue one from a distance about four days north." His eyes widened slightly. "That was close enough for me. We're on our way back now."

Only four days from dragons. If the map was true, then that was only the outskirts of where Frey had requested his ashes be scattered. She'd imagined there would be dragons near the end of her journey, but if they had to travel through dragonlands for an extended period of time, that changed everything.

"We were just about to have dinner." Drazhan gestured toward the pot still simmering over the fire. "Rabbit stew. You're welcome to join us if you'd like."

"I thought you'd never ask," Frida called from atop the trail. She poked her head around the tree, along with Morsel.

Drazhan narrowed his eyes at the young dwarf, then gave Hilda a questioning look.

Hilda rubbed her brow and sighed. "That's my granddaughter, Frida."

Drazhan grinned. "Of all the men, monsters, and madness in this world, there exists nothing as fearless as a child."

"You were sixteen when you joined the bulwark guard?" Frida asked Drazhan through a mouthful of stew, inhaling it like she hadn't been fed in a week. "That's the same age I am now, and I had to trick Gram into letting me come along."

"Better to ask for forgiveness than permission, eh?" Drazhan wore a mischievous grin.

"Don't encourage her." Hilda scoffed, narrowing her eyes at the elf. He seemed to remember her fondly, yet she couldn't place ever meeting him. "I'm sorry to say this, but I can't recall us having ever been introduced."

"That's because we weren't." He set his bowl aside and pulled a kerchief from his pocket, draping it across his face so that only his eyes were visible. The depths of his red irises sparkled like rubies against his dark complexion. "How about now?"

Hilda chuckled. "That's right. The masks." Unlike guards for most royalty, who wore shimmering plate mail, the bulwark guard wore loose-fitting tunics and pants of deep crimson, with golden wraps about their ankles and wrists. Their faces were concealed behind a mask and hood so that only their eyes were exposed. It might not be as intimidating as plate armor, but it allowed them to move quickly and silently, intercepting threats before they came to blows.

"Members of the bulwark guard only remove our hoods in private, never when we're on duty." He set the cloth aside. "It's part of our oath. While we wear the mask, we observe and protect silently."

"You could learn a thing or two." Hilda gave Frida a knowing look.

"It all worked out, didn't it?" Frida slurped the last of her broth, and Korran offered her another helping.

"This time." Hilda blew on her stew and then took a bite. It had the gamey flavor she associated with rabbit, but there was also a sweet earthiness of root vegetables and savory umami from slivers of mushroom. "This is quite good."

"Thank you. We found a heap of wild carrots and mushrooms a couple of days north. They balance out the leanness of the rabbit." Drazhan tilted his bowl in acknowledgment. "If you don't mind me asking, what has you traveling this far north? There's nothing but ruins and wilderness as far as we've seen."

Hilda pointed to Morsel, who was grazing next to the two horses, occasionally bleating her opinion to the equines. The top of Frey's urn peeked above the satchel. "That urn holds the ashes of a dear friend. He asked me to scatter them in the north."

Drazhan pursed his lips. "Anyone I might know?"

"Frey Ashborn."

"Ah." Drazhan grinned.

"What?"

"Ylith called him a lovable asshole."

Hilda burst into laughter. "That about covers it."

"Some folk have thorns to protect the rose within. He must have been a good friend for you to do this for him."

"He was."

Drazhan turned to Frida. "You've got quite the journey ahead of you. Good thing you're in capable hands."

Frida sat up proudly. "I'm here to learn from the best."

"Has she ever told you how she saved Ylith from a pack of lycanthe?" asked Drazhan.

"What's a lycanthe?" asked Frida.

At the mention of the word, Korran perked up.

Drazhan pressed his palms together as he asked Hilda, "Would you mind sharing the story of how you saved Ylith? I've heard her account, but I've always wondered what it was like from your point of view."

Hilda had shared many stories with her grandchildren, but this was not one of them. When you adventure for as long as she did, some stories weren't suitable for such impressionable minds. She had no problems telling them about battles with giant spiders or fighting off harpies at the edge of the wilds, but the Blightwood… She'd only been once, and some of the things she'd witnessed still made her skin crawl.

"You're old enough now, I suppose." She met Frida's gaze. "The elves call them lycanthes. They go by other names across the realm. Fleshhowlers. Moonborne. Wyrwolfs. No matter the name, they are a terror to behold."

"Wyrwolfs are real?" The girl arched her brow skeptically. "I thought they were old fables for when Pa wanted us to behave."

"Live long enough and you'll realize every story has some basis in truth." Hilda took a deep breath and let her mind travel back to that fateful day. "We'd been hired by the Alchemist's Guild in Grimbarrow to acquire an ingredient that only grew within the Blightwood. Bloodsap, they called it. A key ingredient used in potions against the undead. It wasn't a particularly rare ingredient, but it was quite the journey, and for all of their boasting, the number of adventurers willing to traverse a cursed forest are few and far between. The payday was good enough due to rumors of a necromancer in the Arenian Forest, so Stone & Splendor set out in search of gold and glory…"

A long time ago…

Hilda knelt, examining the footprint pressed into the soft soil of the Blightwood Forest. The print was large and humanoid aside from the gouges from large claws at the end of each toe. The edges of the print hadn't yet crumbled, and the mud was still glossy and damp, a shade darker than the surrounding soil.

She waved Frey over. "Keep an eye out. These tracks are fresh."

He nodded, his face unreadable. "Any idea what made this?"

"My guess is something we'd rather not meet." Hilda had done her research beforehand, but it was hard to tell where rumors ended and truth began with places like this.

Everything from bloodfiends to wyrwolves and gaunt trolls were said to haunt these lands.

There was a heaviness to the air here, an almost electric feel that Hilda had experienced before storms at sea, and the earthy must of decay rivaled even the dampest caves.

"I don't like the look of this." Brok glanced skyward as rain pattered against the black canopy overhead. "I say we wait until daylight."

Frey patted the older dwarf on the shoulder, teeth flashing as he grinned. "You can't see the glow of the sap in the daylight."

Brok shook his head. "We could at least wait until the storm passes."

"Scared of a little rain, old man?" Frey laughed.

Brok grabbed him by the tunic. "Call me old again, you sorry sack of—"

"Will you knock it off?" Snorri shoved her shield between the two dwarves before they could escalate any further. "It's every damn time with you two."

Hilda rolled her eyes. It didn't matter if they were in the bowels of hell, Frey would find a way to antagonize Brok.

Lightning flashed, igniting the gnarled trees of the forest, followed by a thunderous clap. Rain poured from the heavens, and Hilda pulled up her hood.

"Great." Brok held his hands up in resignation. "Just great."

"Come on." Hilda gestured ahead. "We'll go this way."

She held her bow at the ready as she scoured the darkness, searching for the faint glow of bloodsap. According to her research, the crimson coloring was caused by an infection in the roots. The sap itself had a dull glow, but the roots were said to be so intense that if the soil was dry enough, it looked like the earth was burning beneath the tree.

Not that that would be an issue with the current downpour.

Another flash of lightning, and dozens of eyes flickered within the darkness. Hilda's grip tightened around her bow, her pulse thrumming within her chest as thunder rumbled, followed by an eerie howl that set the hair on the back of her neck on end. She stroked the waxed bowstring with her thumb for comfort.

Two more howls echoed, closer than the first.

"I don't like the sound of that." Snorri pulled her sword from its scabbard.

"Sounds close." Brok looked to Frey.

Frey hesitated. "Maybe you're right." His black beard glistened with rain. "We can make camp tonight and—"

A loud scream tore through the night.

Hilda met Frey's gaze. "Was that a woman?" They'd been in the forest for two days and had yet to see a trace of another living soul.

"Godsdammit." For all of his faults, Frey was not the type of person to abandon someone in trouble. "Follow me."

He took off in the direction of the scream, his heavy footsteps splashing in the mud. Hilda and Snorri followed, and after cursing, Brok trudged along behind them, massive warhammer tossed over his shoulder.

The old dwarf wiped rain from his brow. "I knew this was a bad idea."

Mud sloshed beneath their boots as the rain intensified, thick drops pelting through the trees. Puddles and streams sprung up around them, making it difficult to gain traction.

Lightning crashed again, and thunder reverberated through Hilda's chest as a tree burst into flames. A large branch snapped, and embers drifted like burning snow as it cast the forest in an orange glow. All around them, eyes reflected in the depths of the night.

"There!" Frey pointed with his axe, where the silhouette of a mighty beast stood over a woman.

She had her back pressed to the tree, the glow of bloodsap framing her silver hair as she swung a sword wildly. She grimaced, and Hilda noticed the elf's leg was bent at an odd angle.

Without hesitating, Hilda nocked and loosed an arrow, hitting the creature in the shoulder.

It unleashed a savage howl, turning in Hilda's direction with eyes that burned like molten metal.

The creature was over seven feet tall, built like a giant with the head of a wolf. Thick black fur, soaked with rain, covered its body. Its hands were long and spindly, tipped with blood-soaked talons. The monster snarled, revealing a mouth of dangerous incisors and canines. It sniffed and then howled again.

Two howls answered as more wyrwolves stepped into the light of the burning tree.

"By the gods…" Frey's voice trailed off. This was the first time Hilda had ever seen the dwarf speechless.

"Help!" the elf screamed. She tried to use her good leg to push herself up against the tree, but it kept slipping in the mud.

The wolf turned back to its prey, but Hilda loosed another arrow, hitting the beast in the opposite shoulder.

"On me!" Frey called as he ran into battle.

Brok and Snorri followed without hesitation. And then everything went to shit.

The two new wyrwolves snarled, their eyes glowing like raging fire as they charged. The wolf looming over the elf turned, hitting Frey with enough force that he hit a nearby tree. He crumpled against the trunk and fell to the ground, out cold.

The second wolf lunged at Snorri, who barely had time to raise her shield before claws shrieked against the metal.

Hilda steadied herself as she aimed, pinning the first wolf's hand to the tree before it could hurt the elf. She loosed another arrow, hitting the second wolf in the neck. It thrashed wildly, knocking Snorri to the ground. Brok swung his warhammer at the third, but for all his strength, the wyrwolf was twice as fast, knocking the dwarf to the ground and then stomping his plate mail until Brok was buried in mud.

The wolf lowered itself, mouth salivating as it sniffed Brok's neck. Hilda shot it in the eye, and it collapsed upon the unconscious dwarf.

Snorri swung as she lay on her back, backhanding the wolf. It yelped as rainwater misted from the impact.

The first wolf pried its paw free and abandoned the elf, focusing its ire on Hilda. It charged, and she did the same. A few feet away, she dropped to the ground, bow raised as she slipped through the slick mud toward the towering monster.

She slid through its legs, releasing an arrow as the wolf

bent down to grab her. The arrow pierced the creature's jaw from below, pinning the wyrwolf's muzzle to a large limb. Its body fell limp, dangling from the tree.

Behind Hilda, Snorri was pinned to the ground, her shield the only thing keeping the wolf from rearranging her face.

Hilda spun in the mud, crimson braids whipping as she found a kneeling stance and released her final arrow, toppling the beast.

Present day.

"It was a slow trek home after that," Hilda paused, sipping on the fireweed tea Korran had made. She loved the minty citrus flavor, but it was difficult to find outside of Sanguin. "Ylith had a broken leg, Brok had broken ribs, and Frey had a concussion. I made Ylith a splint, and Snorri and I carried her on a litter for three days until we could hail a wagon. Ylith never did tell us what she was looking for in the Blightwood, but she gave me this cloak as a thank-you for saving her life."

"Part of me always imagined Ylith had embellished the tale." Drazhan stared at Hilda with a look of wonder. "If anything, she didn't do it justice."

"Three lycanthe." Korran whistled, then smirked at his father. "I doubt even the legendary Drazhan Myrr could manage a feat like that."

"I'd probably suffer the same fate as Ylith." Drazhan laughed. "There's a reason people stay clear of the Blightwood."

"I had the right tool for the job." Hilda patted the bow

resting beside her. "Sometimes, that's all you can hope for."

"That's the truth of it." Drazhan poured water on the fire, dousing the embers. "I'm glad to have officially made your acquaintance, but I'm afraid we must get a move on. If you ever find yourself in Sanguin, don't be a stranger."

Hilda shook his hand. "Thank you for your hospitality." She turned to Korran. "And good luck on your endeavors with the guard."

Frida tilted her bowl, draining the last bit of broth. "Thanks for the stew."

"You're welcome." Drazhan patted the girl on the shoulder. "Keep an eye out for your gram."

Hilda bit her lip as a thought struck her. "Say, could I ask a favor of you by chance?"

"If it's within my power."

"Could you deliver a letter for me on your way back?" Flint and Maela were probably worried sick about Frida's disappearance. A letter might not completely assuage their fear, but at least they'd know she was with Hilda.

Drazhan shrugged. "I don't see why not."

"Thank you." Hilda pulled a journal from her pack and handed it to Frida. "Well, youngblood, you have some explaining to do."

12. NESTS

Thick clouds hung low over the mountains the next day, blocking the sun as Hilda and Frida hiked to higher elevation. The breeze whispered through the trees, cool upon their cheeks.

They stopped to rest among the stone ruins of what had once likely been someone's home. The roof had long deteriorated, but the thick, moss-covered walls still held the vestige of another time. Nature had claimed it as her own, vines and bushes growing through the openings where windows had once stood, nests and burrows scattered among the brush. A spider made its home in a corner, its silver web speckled with dead bugs and dried leaves.

While Frida ate, Hilda pulled out the map. Despite living within close proximity, she wasn't familiar with these lands. In all her years with Stone & Splendor, they never traveled within a week's journey of the Forgotten Peaks. The main roads connecting Durendreg, Drake Canyon, and the umbral elves' homeland of Cascus all ran south of Stonefist Hold. Those traveling north to North-pass or Stonewatch took wide detours around the kingdom.

Judging by the map, they were a few days south of the ruins of Deepwarden. The city had been built nestled within the valley between two mountain ranges. Once upon a time, it had been known as the Gateway to the North. Now, it was nothing more than a footnote in Mount Tor's storied history. Another city returned to the earth.

"Is this what we're eating for the next month?" Frida tapped the hardened bread against her tooth. "Maybe I should have stayed with the elves."

Hilda laughed as she looked up from the map. "Did you pack anything better?"

"No." Frida groaned. "It's only been a week and I'm already tired of stonebread. Did you really eat this for weeks on end when you were adventuring?"

"If you want to be an adventurer, you better get used to it." Hilda took a bite of the flavorless bread. "Unless you hunt, fish, or forage, good meals are hard to come by on the road. Lucky for my party, I was pretty good at all three."

Frida looked around as if a food source might suddenly reveal itself. "All of those sound better than this."

Hilda gestured at the terrain. "Be my guest."

"Where do I start?"

"I thought you've been training for this." Hilda chuck-led. "You tell me." One thing she was committed to was ensuring that this trip was a learning experience for Frida, which meant not spoon-feeding her. Hilda had let her granddaughter take the lead since leaving Drazhan and

Korran. The girl had navigated well, and Hilda only offered guidance when necessary. They'd passed by several streams that would have been opportune for fishing, but she was waiting for the girl to make the decision.

"Look!" Frida pointed at the branches of a nearby tree. "It's a nest. There might be eggs inside."

"Might be." Hilda winked. "Only one way to find out."

Frida immediately started to haul herself up the lowest branch, her legs kicking as they tried to gain traction against the trunk.

"Be careful," called Hilda.

She'd never been an overprotective parent with her own children, so it made no sense to start now. Bumps and bruises were a part of life, even more so for an adventurer. Besides, a potion could remedy just about anything short of a cursed blade, dismemberment, or dragon attack.

"Dammit," Frida muttered once she'd climbed to the nest. "It's empty."

"Most nests are. Many species only use a nest for a season, usually in spring, though there are some that nest in the summer. You want to make sure you've actually seen a bird nesting before going through all that effort."

Frida crossed her arms. "You could have told me that before I climbed up here."

"Could have, but where's the fun in that? Now, you'll remember." Hilda laughed. "Come on down, and I'll give you some actionable advice."

"Oh my goodness," the girl squealed. "Gram, there's a griffin!"

"Get down now!" Hilda immediately went for her bow and rushed toward the tree.

"Don't worry, Gram. It's far off, but I can see it on the cliffside. You should come look." Frida looked down at her grandmother. "If you can climb up here. I don't think you can see from down there."

If I can I climb up. Hilda didn't know whether she should be amused or irritated at her granddaughter's uncertainty.

"I'm old, not dead." Hilda set her bow aside and pulled the spyglass from her pack, tucking it in her belt.

Her back complained as she reached overhead, wrapping her hands around the lowest branch. She pressed her boot against the trunk and heaved, sweat beading on her forehead as she pulled herself onto the limb and rested on her stomach. A few heavy breaths later, she was in the tree, navigating limbs to join Frida.

"Been a while since I climbed a tree." Hilda wiped sweat from her forehead with the back of her hand. "Now, where's this griffin at?"

"Up there." Frida pointed. "If you look into that crevice, you'll see its head poking out."

Hilda squinted. She could make out the body of what looked like a griffin—a white, cat-like creature with wings —but it was too far away to know for sure.

"My eyesight isn't what it used to be." Hilda took out her spyglass and adjusted the lens. "Used to be I could shoot an apple off someone's head at two hundred yards. I could probably still do it. Doubt I could see the apple, though."

She twisted the lens and the view shifted until she could have been standing twenty feet away. The griffin had built a nest within a crevice in the mountainside. Bones, eggshell, and white plumage littered the area.

In the center of the nest, a mother griffin stood over her fledgling. The mother had a brilliant white head of an eagle, with eyes as blue as the sky. Her body was strong and muscular like a giant cat, all silver and sleek, with paws the size of Morsel's head. Gorgeous white wings tipped with silver tucked at her side. Beneath her, the wiry young griffin toddled about, stumbling as it playfully attacked its mother's massive paws.

Hilda passed the spyglass to Frida. "Take a look."

It took a moment for the girl to locate the nest, but there was no mistaking when she did. "It's a baby." Her mouth hung open in awe. After a few minutes of watching, she passed the spyglass back to her grandmother. "It's adorable."

"It's adorable now." Hilda watched as the mother clicked her beak before preening the fledgling. The young animal thrashed about in an attempt to escape being cleaned. "Griffins are interesting creatures. One of the few that mate for life, and they only lay one or two eggs per cycle, usually waiting several years before mating again. That makes them fierce protectors of those they do have. If you thought that mama bear was dangerous, she's nothing compared to a mother griffin. We're going to have to find an alternate route."

As far as beasts of prey went, griffins never attacked dwarves unless provoked. They were proud, regal creatures. The ancient kings of Warminster were said to have taken them as mounts. Even so, if one felt threatened, particularly around a hatchling, that wouldn't end well for anyone.

"No one is going to believe that I saw a griffin." She

took the spyglass for another look. "Can I try to find a feather?"

Hilda frowned. "Did you listen to anything I just said?"

"Just one feather. I promise I'll be careful."

"Don't you think I'd like to have a feather? Believe me, I would, but I also prefer to remain alive. That goes doubly for you." Hilda had acquired an impressive collection of teeth, feathers, and claws from her many adventures, but she'd yet to claim a griffin feather. She could have bought one easily enough, but she had rules for adding items to her collection. It only counted if she acquired it herself. It didn't matter if she found it through hunting, questing, or tracking, but she had to have a hand in its procurement.

"Look, there's another one." Frida pointed, and Hilda raised the glass just in time to see the male griffin return to the nest. The male was slightly smaller than the female, with a mane of thick fur around its neck. It held a small deer in its beak, dropping it in front of mother and child.

Hilda passed the spyglass back to Frida, and she held it up, watching as the mother ripped meat and fed it to the fledgling.

"Now I'm even more hungry." Frida sighed. She looked longingly at the family of griffins. "You think they'll share?"

"I'm not willing to find out." Hilda squeezed Frida's forearm. "Come on. Let's get down from here, and once we make camp for the night, we'll see how good your trap-making skills are."

13. STORM CLOUDS

Hilda woke to a burning discomfort in her shoulder the next morning, the price of proving she could, in fact, still climb a tree. The cursed wound radiated heat like she'd been stabbed with a hot iron. She lay on her bedroll, surprised that steam didn't hiss every time she pressed the coldstone to her skin.

A small red bird chirped from a limb in the tree above. It hopped from branch to branch, tilting its head to watch Hilda with an obsidian eye.

"Good morning," Hilda said as she sat up, rolling her shoulders to release the tension. The bird tweeted and then dove from the tree, snatching a bug from around the ash of the campfire before vanishing into the forest.

The early bird does get the worm. Hilda thought with amusement.

She stretched her arms overhead, and her spine cracked audibly. She groaned at the stiffness in her back, then she laughed. *Climbing trees at 182. What were you thinking, old girl?*

She looked around the campsite. Frida had disappeared to check the traps they'd set the night before, and Morsel foraged nearby, eating leaves and flicking her tail. The morning sun gave the goat's brown fur a golden hue.

When Morsel noticed Hilda was awake, the goat walked over and licked the dwarf's forehead.

"I appreciate the concern, but could you not?" Hilda wiped away the thick coating of saliva that was flecked with foliage.

Morsel bleated loudly, licking her again.

"I knew I should have taken Bartemus," Hilda grumbled.

"Bartemus is a little twit." Frida emerged from the bushes. "He once ate my favorite scarf." She held up a rabbit proudly. "My first trap! No more stonebread for breakfast."

Morsel seemed to find this cause for excitement, bleating even louder than she had before.

"Hey, pretty girl." Frida scratched the goat behind the ears. "You wouldn't eat my scarf, would you?"

In answer, Morsel planted a wet kiss on Frida's ear. The young dwarf groaned, pushing Morsel's massive head aside.

Hilda grinned as Frida tilted her head in an attempt to drain slobber from her ear. "One rabbit from three traps. Not bad."

The younger dwarf twisted a finger in her ear. "One of the snares had been triggered, but it was empty. You think something stole our kill?"

"Could be. You're not the only one who's hungry. Could have been a deer passing through or a heavy wind knocked it loose. You never know, that's why it's important to set multiple." Hilda nodded toward the rabbit. "How are your field dressing skills?"

Frida shrugged. "I know the steps, but I haven't had much chance to practice."

"Today's your lucky day, then. Grab your knife."

Hilda stood behind Frida as the girl put her skills to work, offering guidance only when necessary. While not the fastest, Frida was methodical and precise, which would serve her better in the long run.

"Speed will come in time." Hilda placed a hand on Frida's shoulder. "With a little practice, you'll be able to do that in under a minute." She gestured away from the camp. "Bury the organs and I'll get a fire started."

It wasn't long before a rich, savory aroma wafted through the campsite. Frida stared at the rabbit roasting above the fire, a bead of drool gathering on her bottom lip. Grease sizzled as it dripped into the flames, and Frida blinked as if pulled from a trance.

"You're acting like you haven't eaten in weeks." Hilda chuckled.

"What can I say?" Frida shrugged. "I'm a growing girl."

"Don't remind me," Hilda said as she removed the skewer from the fire. The girl was on the verge of adult-hood, and that meant the other grandchildren weren't far behind. Hilda sliced the rabbit in half, and hot steam wafted from the meat.

Frida snatched her portion greedily, sinking her teeth into it like a ravenous wolf. "Hot!" She opened her mouth, and steam poured out like a spent dragon. "Hot, hot!" She panted, eyes wide as tears pooled at the edges, meat blistering her tongue.

Hilda snorted, shaking her head. "Patience is a virtue, you know."

Frida grimaced as she swallowed. "So is fortitude." She took a deep breath, massaging her burning chest. "Whew."

"And wisdom." Hilda winked.

Frida gazed at the rabbit longingly. "Might want to let that cool for a minute."

"Attagirl."

By early afternoon, thick clouds had gathered over the valley. There was a sweetness to the air that always came before a heavy rain.

"Keep an eye out for a cave or shelter." Hilda pointed at the gloom overhead. "We'll want to wait this out if we can."

"They look the same as yesterday." Frida frowned, gazing upward. "How do you know it's going to rain?"

"Stay at this long enough and you'll get a feel for it." Hilda massaged her shoulder. The tingle within was always a precursor to a heavy storm, but she'd been able to track a change in the weather long before she'd acquired her curse. "A ranger's senses are their greatest asset for surviving in the wilderness. It's the reason even a half-assed ranger can have their pick of a dozen parties any time there's dangerous terrain involved. Tell me, what do you notice?"

Frida squinted as she stared at the clouds. "Well, they are a little bit darker, I guess."

"Someone alert the king." Hilda grinned. "We have an oracle in our midst."

"This isn't something they teach in school." Frida scowled. "I'm here to learn, you know."

"Don't light your furnace just yet, youngblood. I'm just ruffling your beard."

Frida put her hands on her hips, and Hilda fought the urge to laugh. Flint had done the same thing when he was a child.

"Close your eyes," Hilda instructed. After a moment, Frida complied. "Now tell me, what do you hear?"

"I hear..." Frida paused, listening to the sounds of the wild. "Wind rustling through the trees. I can hear the stream below. Birds cawing in the distance." She opened her eyes. "And Morsel is a very loud eater."

The goat looked up from the leaves she was munching and bleated.

"That's a good start." Hilda gestured for Frida to close her eyes again. "But more importantly, what do you not hear?"

"Umm..." Frida closed her eyes harder as she concentrated. "I don't know. Everything?"

Hilda laughed. "Do you hear any insects? Any birds in the nearby trees?"

The girl shook her head. "No insects. The birds sound far away."

"When the forest goes quiet, you listen. It may mean that a predator or hunters are nearby, or that the weather is shifting."

Frida opened her notebook and jotted the information down. "Okay, good. What else?"

"Take a deep breath." Hilda laughed when Frida inhaled through her mouth like she was about to go underwater. "No, use your nose."

Frida tried again.

"You smell that earthiness in the air, like wet mud? It's called petrichor. It's kind of sweet and pleasant, and you can usually smell it before a good rain. It means that somewhere nearby, rain has already fallen, and the scent of the earth is traveling on the wind. But—" She held up a finger. "—you'll only smell it if it hasn't rained in a while."

"Really?" Frida sniffed at the air. "Now that I'm looking for it, it is kind of sweet. Like a cave but not so stuffy."

"Exactly. If you notice a sourness to it, kind of like licking metal, that means a thunderstorm is coming."

Frida scribbled furiously in her journal as Hilda continued, explaining various cloud formations and how wind shifts and sudden drops in temperature could all offer insight into how the weather might turn.

"Older folk can sometimes feel a storm brewing in their bones around old injuries." She tapped her shoulder. "Mine likes to sing."

"Sing?" Frida arched her brow.

"Well, it yells mostly." Hilda chuckled. "Telling me not to drink too much, or shoot my bow, and definitely not to climb trees."

Frida paused, looking at Hilda with a concerned expression. "Gram, can I ask you something?"

"What is it, girl?"

"Do you ever regret it?"

"Regret what?"

"Becoming an adventurer." Frida focused on a sprig of grass swaying in the wind. "You've had pain for most of your life, all from a single mistake."

"Oh, child." Hilda wrapped an arm around her granddaughter. "What's there to regret? This life has given me everything I ever wanted—adventure, experience, friendship. It led me to the love of a good dwarf and the best children and grandchildren in all of Aedrea. I wouldn't change a single thing." She placed her hand underneath Frida's chin, lifting until their eyes met. "This life isn't for everyone, and there's no shame in learning that it's not for you. But listen to me when I tell you, everyone has pain, everyone struggles. No matter if it's in the mines or on the open road. That's life. But choosing to be an adventurer means choosing your struggles, choosing adversity. It's not an easy life, but boy, is it rewarding."

Frida turned and embraced her grandmother as thunder rumbled in the distance. "I'm lucky to have you."

"Likewise." Hilda kissed the top of Frida's head. "Let's get a move on. These old bones would prefer to sleep somewhere dry tonight."

14. THE CAVE

Rain poured down in thick sheets, making it nearly impossible to see more than fifty feet in any direction. By the time Hilda located a cave, Morsel was drenched. The goat's long hair clung to her body, showcasing the powerful muscles that were normally hidden beneath the thick coat. She snorted, sending a spray of mist onto the stoney floor.

"Me too, girl," Frida said as she squeezed water from her fiery braids.

Hilda tossed back the hood of her dreamweave cloak. Unlike standard wool cloaks, it wasn't just water-resistant. It kept her dry even in the heaviest of downpours without absorbing water.

Frida eyed the cloak longingly. "One of these days, I'll have one of those for myself."

"I don't doubt it," Hilda said, only half paying attention to her granddaughter as she inspected the cave.

The floor was a mixture of packed earth and slick

rock, littered with loose stone, puddled water, and animal droppings. There were remnants of a long-abandoned campfire, a haphazard circle of stones and ash, along with a bundle of sticks packed neatly in a nearby crevice. Down the dimly lit cavern, water seeped through the veins of the mountain, dripping from the ceiling and shimmering on moss-covered walls that faded into darkness.

Outside, the storm rumbled, rain cascading over the cave's opening like a silver curtain.

"This'll do." Hilda gathered some of the sticks and arranged them in the firepit, adjusting the stones. "Unload Morsel and I'll get us a fire going."

Soon, they sat around a small fire, warming their hands as it crackled merrily. Morsel lay nearby, a puddle beneath the massive beast as she slept with her front legs tucked under her frame like a giant loaf of bread. Her snores roared like a furnace.

"I always loved the sound of rain." Hilda petted the wet goat behind the ears. "There's something calming about it."

"It's peaceful." Frida yawned, stretching her arms overhead. "Perfect weather for a nap."

"We'd be wise to explore the cave first. Make sure nothing is lurking in the dark."

Frida's eyes widened. "Like what?"

Hilda shrugged. "Who knows? Spiders, goblins, rats the size of your head. Frey once woke to a kobold trying to steal his boots because he didn't bother checking."

Frida stood, tossing the damp braid over her shoulder. She checked the knife at her waist and pulled a stick from the fire. "I'll make sure it's safe."

"Easy there, hero. Not with that you're not." Hilda sat up. "You'll be lucky if it lasts you five minutes before burning out. Do you know how to make a torch?"

Frida tossed the stick back in the fire. "It's just a wick soaked in fuel, right?"

"That's right. If you had to improvise, what would you use?"

Frida grinned. "I know this. For the wick, you could use dried moss or a piece of cloth."

"Good. You can also use frayed bark or anything fibrous as long as it's dried out." Hilda opened one of the packs near Morsel. "I always keep some cloth on hand since it lasts longer and really soaks up the fuel. It's also handy if you need to pack a wound or make a tourniquet. If you're in a bind, you can always cut a strip from your clothing. What about fuel?"

"Animal fat." Frida bit her lip. "And pine sap."

"Right. Beeswax works as well, but it's much harder to find in the wild. Leftover cooking grease works wonders, too." Hilda pulled out a few strips of cloth and a jar of whitish-yellow gel. "You never know when you might need to take shelter in a cave or explore some dark ruins, and it pays to have the necessary items. Some adventurers like to keep a few torches prepared in advance, but I've always found that kind of messy. It's not that hard to find a stick. You just want to make sure it's dried out or else it'll smoke like a halfling on holiday." She took one from the tinder pile and handed it to Frida. "Show me what you've got."

The young dwarf took the cloth and dipped it in the gel, sniffing the fabric. "Smells smoky."

"It's grease. Always better to let an item pull double duty if you can. Saves weight in your pack."

Frida wrapped the grease-soaked cloth around the tip of the stick several times and then held it toward the fire.

"Easy." Hilda held up a hand. "You'll want to bind it or else your torch will fall apart as it burns." She cut a length of twine and tied it around the torch head. "If you're going to be exploring for a while, you can soak the head in the fuel source for a bit and it will last longer."

Frida nodded. "Can I light it now?"

"You've got the patience of a cat at bath time." Hilda chuckled. "Go ahead."

Wet moss shimmered in the glow of the torch as they made their way deeper into the cave. Short, pearlescent stalactites descended around cracks in the ceiling, water dripping rhythmically from their smooth tips. Compared to some of the sprawling caverns Hilda had explored, this one was practically cozy. Beetles scuttled beneath rocks and into crevices, rodents retreated, and the occasional bat screeched before flying further into the dark.

"How far do you think this thing goes?" Frida held up the torch to cast the light further.

"There's no telling. I've been in caves for days where we never found the end."

"How did you not get lost?"

Hilda reached into a pouch on her belt and pulled out a piece of chalk. "If you come to a fork, you always, always, always mark your way. Caves are dangerous terrain. One wrong stumble or encounter with a monster and the next thing you know, you've lost your sense of direction. The hearts of mountains are littered with the bones of fools."

"What's that?" Frida squinted at something in the distance, raising her torch higher.

Hilda's eyesight wasn't what it once was, but she could also make out the faint glow of something on the cave walls. "Be careful," she said, hand resting on the haft of the handaxe at her side.

Frida led the way, her own hand on the hilt of her dagger.

"Oh, wow." Frida stopped, letting her hand rest at her side. "Are those slimes?"

Sure enough, thick blobs of pink and purple gelatin clung to the cave walls. Their translucent, viscous bodies seemed to glow in the torchlight. They slowly undulated like pudding being set on a table as twigs, rocks, and other debris floated inside their bodies. Some had animals or plant leaves inside their membranes. Hilda spotted one with a partially digested rat, while another had a frog and some beetles.

"There's so many of them." Frida stepped closer, and a wave passed through the slimes, as if they could sense her presence. "I thought they lived alone."

"You're thinking of oozes. They're much bigger and much more dangerous. Slimes very rarely attack anything larger than they are. Some people keep them as pets."

"Really?" Frida watched with a look of revulsion that slowly shifted to intrigue. "They're pretty in their own way, I guess."

"Beauty is in the eye of the beholder." Hilda chuckled, watching the slimes as they pulsed in unison.

She'd spent time studying them in her youth, and they were truly fascinating creatures. Although each one moved of its own accord, it was like their movements fell in sync when they gathered. She'd even witnessed them merge on occasion.

"Ahh!" Frida screamed as a beetle the size of an apple crawled up her arm. She thrashed wildly, flinging the bug and dropping the torch in the process.

Their light source fell to the ground, hissing as a puddle extinguished the flame and leaving them in total darkness.

"Gram," Frida said, panic coating her voice. She bumped into Hilda and screamed again, the noise echoing down the cavern.

"Easy, child." Hilda clasped the girl's shoulder. "It's just me. Hold still and give me a moment."

Hilda opened a pouch on her belt and dim light spilled out. She removed the cloth covering the enchanted glowstone, and it shone like a beacon, bathing the walls in dull amber light.

"What the— You had that the whole time?" Frida's mouth gaped in awe. "Why in the hells did you have me make a torch?"

Her grandmother scrunched her brow. "I thought you were here to learn?"

Frida's head lolled backward as she groaned.

The glowstone lit the way for Hilda and Frida to explore the rest of the cave. They turned a corner and the cavern ended, splitting into cracks and narrow fissures that expanded deeper into the mountain, much too small for either dwarf to pass. Glowing green eyes reflected from the darkness where creatures chittered and scurried within. Nothing big enough to concern Hilda.

Back at the campfire, she passed out rations.

"Great. More stonebread," Frida said flatly. She held a piece of hardened cheese in one hand and the dry, flavorless bread in the other. "Can't even set traps tonight." She groaned, stacking the cheese on top of the bread and taking a crunchy bite.

"You could set them in the cave." Hilda wore an amusing smile. "Catch a rat if you're lucky. Maybe a beetle. And there's always the slimes."

"Yuck." Frida grimaced. "Who would ever eat a slime?"

"You'd be surprised. Some folk consider them delicacies." Hilda chuckled as she unpacked Frey's urn and placed it beside her bedroll.

"Why do you do that?" Frida asked.

"Do what?" Hilda asked, trying not to laugh at the breadcrumbs on Frida's chin.

"Take out the urn whenever we stop somewhere or make camp for the night?"

Hilda placed her hand on the stone vessel. "This is our last quest together." She swallowed hard, emotion welling in her chest. "If part of Frey is holding on until it's completed, I want him to feel like he's a part of the journey."

The girl's shoulders slumped, and her gaze settled on the floor.

"What's wrong?" Hilda asked.

"I shouldn't have come." Frida met her grandmother's gaze for a moment and then hung her head. "This was supposed to be special for you, a chance for you to say good-bye, and I made it about myself."

"Nonsense," Hilda spoke with a comforting tone. "Frey would have loved you. You're nearly as reckless as he was at times. If he's watching us, he's had some good laughs at both of our expenses so far."

Frida laughed softly, then sniffled as she wiped a tear from her eye. "You think so?"

"I know so." Hilda smiled. "Watching me climb a tree at my age. You, running from a bear and then dropping the torch because of a bug. He'd be howling with laughter."

"What was he like?" Frida moved closer so that Frey's urn was sitting between her and Hilda. "I've heard the stories of your adventures, but what was he like when you weren't in a battle or completing some quest?"

Hilda paused for a moment, looking at the urn as she tried to find the words that encapsulated the dwarf, not as a hero or an adventurer but as a person. "He wasn't always nice, but he was kind."

Frida frowned. "Is there a difference?"

The older dwarf nodded. "I've met plenty of nice people who would stab you in the back. Nothing but gold plating covering a rusted core. Frey was hard around the edges. He was curt, brash, and downright rude at times, but underneath all that bravado, he was good. He never left anyone behind. He'd risk his life to help a friend no matter the odds. He was the type of dwarf you always wanted in the mine with you because come hells or high water, he'd stick with you until the end." She patted the urn. "After all we endured together, this is the least I can do to honor his memory."

Frida placed a hand on top of Hilda's. "I wish I could have met him."

"Me, too, child. Me, too." She met Frida's gaze, imagining what Frey might think of her rambunctious granddaughter. "How about I tell you a story?"

15. MEMORIES WITH A GHOST

Thunk.

Thunk.

Thunk.

Frida grinned with pride at the three arrows lodged in the rotting wood of a fallen tree. Two of them were clustered together in the center of the makeshift target, the third about a hand's width to the right.

Shooting hardwood was a great way to damage arrows, but the moisture from the heavy rain the day before had softened the rotten bark even more, making it perfect for Frida's target practice.

"You're a good shot." Hilda nodded approvingly. "Your stance is relaxed but stable, and you have a consistent anchor point. I always pulled to my cheek, but if drawing to your mouth works for you, then keep at it." She walked over, examining Frida's grip on the weapon. "You're strangling the bow, though." Hilda held up her own bow, flexing her fingers around the grip. "Most people think you want a firm grip to steady your aim, but the opposite is true. Holding too tight will cause the bow to twist slightly when you release. If you relax your hand and use a loose grip, then it will recoil naturally, staying in line with the target. It's the little things that separate a good archer from a great one." Plucking the arrows from the dead tree, she handed them to Frida. "Try again."

Frida walked across the soggy ground and turned to face the target. Her face was set with determination.

"Remember, smooth draw, controlled release. Let your back guide the movement."

The girl took her stance, nocked the arrow, and breathed in as she pulled the string until it was just below the edge of her mouth.

"Attagirl."

Frida grinned.

"Now, focus on the target, not the arrow. And when you release, hold your form for a moment. This will carve the movement into your muscle's memory like stone."

Frida loosed the arrow, and it sank into the center of the target. She repeated the action, the second arrow a thumb's width from the first. Her gaze flitted to her grandmother, but her facade held as she pulled back, shooting again. This final arrow found the empty space between the two.

The stone cracked, and a toothy grin spread across Frida's face.

"Not bad, youngblood. Not bad at all." Hilda waggled her brows. "When I was younger, I carried a cork shield everywhere we traveled. Each morning, I'd hone my skills the same way the others practiced their forms."

"I practice every day at school." Frida beamed as she

pulled the arrows from the trunk. She offered them to her grandmother. "Want to try?"

"Some other time." Hilda massaged her shoulder. The ache from the previous day had subsided, but she didn't want to press her luck. "We should get a move on."

"Are we there yet?" Frida turned to her grandmother, asking for the fifth time.

Hilda let out an exasperated sigh, gesturing toward the mountainous landscape. "Do you see any dragons?"

It had been two days since they'd left the cave. The first day had been a slow trudge through mud and wetness; but with the sun now beaming from clear blue skies, they were making steady progress once again.

"We've been traveling for days." Frida placed her hands on her hips. "I thought this would be more exciting."

"The open wilderness not stimulating enough for you?" Hilda shook her head, though she didn't blame the girl for her impatience. She'd been the same way at Frida's age, hungry for action and willing to prove herself. While this hadn't been the most thrilling journey, there was plenty to enjoy among the sprawling expanse of nature.

Frida tossed her hands in the air. "I mean, it's beautiful out here, but where are the monsters? Where's the adventure?"

"I'm going to let you in on a secret, child. Adventuring is ninety-five percent humdrum and only five percent action. Even the greats like Runa Axebringer and Barik Oathbound had their downtime."

Frida collapsed in the grass dramatically. "My whole life is a lie."

"You have my sympathies." Hilda grinned as she flicked Morsel's reins, leaving her granddaughter lying in the grass. If the whole adventuring thing didn't work out, the girl had a place in the theatre.

"Hey, wait up!" Frida shouted, her gear rattling as she hurried to catch up. "I can't believe you were going to leave me."

"You tracked me for six days, I think you can manage five min—" Hilda gasped as Morsel turned the bend, and she tugged on the reins for the goat to stop.

In the distance, Deepwarden—once known as The Gateway to the North—stretched the width of the valley and into the mountainsides. It was a sprawling metropolis, and nothing like Hilda had expected. The city was weathered, and sections had clearly been damaged, but it wasn't destroyed. Far from it. It looked like a city put to sleep. An emerald ghost town where moss and vines covered dwarven architecture with a green embrace, softening its harsh hewn edges, and trees grew in the rubble where great buildings had once stood.

The dragons had left their mark, but they had spared the city.

Even the perimeter wall still stood, its defensive prowess holding strong centuries later. Watchtowers peaked above the tree lines of the mountainside, ivory statues guarded the entrances to long-abandoned mines, and thousands of terraced homes lined the steep hillsides of the valley. A beautiful, crystal-blue lake gleamed just beyond the southern wall, reflecting the picturesque view of the mountains beyond.

Within the city, massive domed buildings resembled the rolling hills of Tyne, while towering chimneys surged skyward from the forge quarter. In the center, the keep rose above all, ringed by tiered walls, with three of its five pillars still standing tall.

Hilda thought of Hells' Crag, the dwarven city that had been razed to rubble by a single red dragon some five hundred years ago. She'd seen its ruins from a distance and had expected to find the same here.

"What is this place?" Frida wore a confused expression as she joined their side.

"Deepwarden," Hilda said solemnly.

"I thought it was destroyed." The girl's voice took on a reverent tone.

"So did I." But now that she thought about it, all of the stories said it was abandoned, that dragons had forced the citizens to relocate. Her imagination had filled in the details, picturing the worst. "It's beautiful, isn't it?"

"It is." Frida pointed at the mountains. "And beyond that mountain range are the Forgotten Peaks?"

"Someone knows their geography."

Frida shrugged. "Seemed like it might be useful to know. That means we're close, right?"

"It means we're getting closer." Hilda took the map from her cloak and showed it to Frida. "This mountain range here is the Northern Ridge. Once we cross it, we'll be in the dragonlands." She patted the urn packed on Morsel's side. "We're probably a week or so from where Frey wants to be put to rest."

Frida rubbed her hands together excitedly. "What are we waiting for, then?"

By nightfall, they made camp among the ruins of a village a handful of miles from the city. Unlike the structures of Deepwarden that had been constructed by stone mages during the Age of Empires, these were not built to endure for ages. The stone had weathered with time. Mortar crumbled in places, leaving gaps within the walls of roofless homes. Some had collapsed entirely, the piles of rock a monument to what had been.

"Are we going into the city tomorrow?" Frida asked as she placed her bedroll beside one of the walls.

"I think so." Hilda looked toward the city, where the light of the moon cast it in a silver glow. The southern gates were ajar, as if welcoming them to pass through. "If the northern gates are open, it should save us a day of traveling around the perimeter."

Frida gathered sticks for a fire. "And if they're not?"

"We'll cross that bridge when we get to it." She stared at the ghost city, where the towering keep blocked the view of the northern gate, making it impossible to know for sure.

Hilda removed the saddlebags from Morsel while Frida started a fire. The goat wandered off, eating the tall grass and shrubbery that had overtaken the village.

We're getting close, old friend, Hilda thought as she placed the urn next to her bedroll. She sat beside him, her thoughts returning to Deepwarden, unable to shake the eerie feeling that came with seeing a city of that size completely abandoned. The words of Gwynera's song replayed in her mind.

· · ·

"Some say we'll return one day when it's cold,
   When dragon bones are cracked and old.
   Til that hour, we wander and roam,
   And sing the loss of our mountain home."

Two thousand years later, it still sits empty.

"I'll set some traps after we eat," Frida said as she offered Hilda rations of jerky, cheese, and stonebread. When Hilda didn't acknowledge her, Frida tapped the plate against her grandmother's shoulder. "Everything okay, Gram?"

Hilda met her granddaughter's concerned gaze. "Everything's fine. Just lost in my thoughts."

Frida sat in front of her, legs crossed. "Anything you want to talk about?"

Another reminder of how fast the young girl was growing up. To most children, they were the center of the world. Everything revolved around them. Frida was perceptive, though, and that was a valuable quality in a ranger.

Hilda contemplated saying that it was nothing important, but instead, she opened up. "It's unsettling seeing something of that size lying empty. To think of the work it must have taken to create a city so magnificent. From mages and stoneworkers to artisans and engineers, Deepwarden was a beacon of dwarven culture for millennia, and now it's just...empty." She paused, not sure of the right words. "If a city like this can be forgotten—" She glanced at Frey's urn. "What hope do the rest of us have?"

"What was it you always say? 'Don't break your back bracing for storms that never come.'" Frida placed a hand on Hilda's knee, the gesture surprisingly comforting. "You'll be remembered by me, by Pa and Ma, by Uncle Darrin, Uncle Orik, and everyone else in the family. Drazhan remembered you, and now his son will too. Probably hundreds of others do as well. And maybe you're worried about people forgetting Frey, but you haven't, and I won't. You've both left your mark on this world, but even dwarves can't chisel the clouds."

Hilda wiped a tear from her eye, surprised at the sincerity in the words. She leaned forward, resting her hand on top of Frida's. "When did you get so wise?"

Frida shrugged, a smile tugging at the corner of her mouth. "Who knows? Maybe you rubbed off on me."

Soon after, they were both lying on bedrolls, the lullaby of crickets sending Frida to dreamland. Hilda listened to the girl's breathing as her chest rose and fell, still unable to believe such wisdom could come from someone so young. Her granddaughter was right, though. Now wasn't the time to worry about Frey's legacy. She had an opportunity not many received, one she couldn't squander—a chance to make memories with his ghost.

16. A CITY ASLEEP

The gates into Deepwarden stood gaping wide. Thick chains anchored the massive stone slabs to the wall like open arms welcoming them into the ancient city. Vines intertwined with the rusted metal links, crawling across the gates and shrouding the elaborate stonework with green foliage.

Hilda wiped away a layer of dirt and pressed her hand to the stone, feeling the cool surface against her fingertips. After all these years, it was still polished to perfection.

Beside her, Frida stared up at the massive wall surrounding the city. "I've never seen something so big."

The elder dwarf had. She'd seen the gate guardians of Durendreg, where two towering statues raised their hammers over the city's entrance, the white stone visible from miles away. She'd seen the majesty of Vusora, an elven city built among the tallest trees she'd ever witnessed. Even so, these walls were special, taller than any within the kingdom of Mount Tor. A remnant from another age.

She could only imagine what Frida was feeling. This was the first time the girl had been anywhere that rivaled the size of Stonefist Hold. While their city was a testament to dwarven engineering with its illustrious mine shafts and tunnels, its walls paled in comparison to the bulwark before them. The outer wall of Deepwarden was easily three times as tall and twice as thick as any back home. Stonefist Hold might have been a looming presence from atop the mountain, but this was an enduring one.

Morsel's hooves clacked against the street as they entered. Up close, the city was more weathered than Hilda had assumed, but she'd hardly call this ruins. If anything, it looked like a city asleep.

Wildlife had claimed the outer level, where grass sprouted between the stone tiles and trees grew among the rubble of buildings built of lesser materials. Birds fluttered about, while bugs chittered among the overgrown bushes and shrubbery. A horned rabbit crossed the road, nibbling on grass before darting into the underbrush.

The outer district was full of dilapidated buildings and storefronts. Glass windows had been shattered, and ramshackle shelves were barren inside, having been looted long ago by those fleeing or bold enough to traverse these lands in the aftermath. Most of the buildings were unrecognizable, their signs faded or destroyed by the elements, but some had stood the test of time. A shield-shaped slab of metal denoted where an armory must have been, and there was a sign with an engraved mortar and pestle that must have been an apothecary or herbalist.

"It's weird how quiet everything is." Frida peered inside an empty building. "I keep expecting to see someone inside."

"Let's hope we don't," Hilda said, but she recognized it too, that unnatural and unsettling feeling of things not being as they should. Back home, the streets were alive with the sound of vendors, the clatter of wagons, and the distant ring of the blacksmith. Even at night, music and laughter could be heard from the nearby tavern. She placed a hand on Frida's shoulder. "Let's get moving. We still have a ways to go."

They passed through several districts before arriving at the inner wall, where large pieces of rock from a collapsed battlement blocked the entryway. A statue of a dwarf had been crushed under the rubble, leaving it headless and pinned beneath a jagged slab gouged with claw marks. The head lay several feet away, its beard shattered into a hundred tiny pieces.

"Poor guy." Frida turned the head over and then looked up at the blockade. "Should we try to climb it?"

"Best to go around." She patted Morsel on the flank. "Looks precarious, and there's no need to risk her slipping on loose stone."

Or myself, for that matter.

Morsel bleated her opinion on the subject and then started walking.

The deeper into the city they traveled, the more Hilda noticed evidence of dragon attacks. Melted rock here, a crumbled building there, gashes in the stone from where something massive had perched along the battlements. With each new discovery, she attempted to put the pieces together.

This had been a selective attack. A warning.

Dragons were intelligent creatures. Some believed they were the most intelligent beings in all of Aedrea. If the destruction of Hells' Crag was any indication, they could have easily razed this city to the ground, so why had they spared Deepwarden?

"You're doing it again." Frida said, pulling Hilda from her thoughts.

She arched a brow. "Doing what?"

The girl tapped the side of her head. "Disappearing into your thoughts."

Hilda chuckled. "Nothing gets past you, does it?"

Frida stood straighter, smiling. "I'm very perceptive."

"I can't argue with that." Hilda's gaze drifted along the battlements, settling on a claw mark that had cut into the stone. She pointed at the damage, sharing her theory with Frida as they walked. It reminded her of travels with Stone & Splendor and the conversations she had with Snorri while Frey and Brok bickered with one another. When Hilda was finished, she turned to her granddaughter. "Why do you think the dragons spared the city?"

"I don't know." Frida's brow furrowed. "My teacher says dragons prefer to be left alone, that they rarely attack us unless provoked. That's why there are no settlements between Northpass and Stonewatch, right? If the city had expanded too close to the dragon lands, or the mining was disruptive, this might have been the only option they had without destroying the city entirely. Maybe they didn't want a Gateway to the North."

Hilda pondered on that. It made as much sense as any other theory. If no one knew the truth after all these years, it was unlikely she'd discover the answer walking through what remained.

They carried on in silence, aside from Morsel's occasional vocalizations. As the sun dipped toward the horizon, shadows fell across the streets from the buildings and high walls. Following the perimeter of the inner wall was still faster than circling the city from the outside, but it was looking unlikely that they'd make it to the northern gate before nightfall.

"We should probably make camp while there's still daylight." Hilda paused, surveying the area.

They appeared to be in an arts district, judging by the number of statues surrounding the square. Some were carved from marble, the tops dusted with a layer of moss. She spotted a copper statue depicting a dwarven smith that had turned green from oxidation, and a giant iron warhammer that had rusted an orange-brown, its metal rough to the touch. The dome of the glassblower workshop still had fragments of the original colored glass lodged in the frame. It must have been a sight to behold once upon a time.

Frida waved her grandmother over, pointing to an open-air amphitheater that descended into the earth. "Looks magical, doesn't it?"

The tiered seating was overgrown with grass and bushes. Vines stretched above the stage where an awning had once shaded performers. Despite its current state, there was something enchanting about the space, like it might spring to life with fae at any moment. There was beauty in the way nature's curves softened the harsh edges of dwarven architecture.

"It does." Hilda nodded. "Shall we camp here for the

night?"

A small fire crackled in the center of the stage. The sky was clear, with the moon shining brightly overhead.

Morsel frolicked up and down the grandstand, bleating her amusement as she chased fireflies through the tiered seating. Hilda lay against her pack, looking up at the stars through gaps in the vine covering. Frey's urn rested beside her, and she wondered what he might think of them now, camping in a location Stone & Splendor had never traveled during their many years together.

"Nobody is going to believe this," Frida said as she dangled her feet off the edge of the stage. She'd gathered a pile of small stones and was tossing them into an empty planter. Her aim was good, and the vessel rattled every time she got one inside.

"Most people don't believe half the stories I have to tell. I like it better that way."

Frida turned around, crossing her legs. "Why's that?"

"Why should I trouble myself with what someone else thinks? I was there. I know what happened." She held out her hand. "Toss me a rock."

Frida did as instructed.

Hilda caught the stone. "It's nice when people remember your accomplishments. Sometimes, they even take on a life of their own as time passes, but not everything needs to be shared with the world. Sometimes, it's just nice to enjoy things for what they are." She held the stone, gauging the distance between her and the planter.

Then, she closed her eyes and tossed, opening them when the rock rattled inside the empty planter.

Her granddaughter whistled. "I guess so." She crawled across the stage to join her grandmother, and pulled a stone from her pocket, aiming it at the planter. "But it's still nice to be believed if you do share something." Closing her eyes, she let go of the stone. There was a hollow ring as it hit the outside. "We can keep that one between us."

———

"Gram." Frida nudged her in the shoulder. "Gram, wake up."

Hilda wiped the sleep from her eyes. "What is it, child?"

"Listen."

Hilda cocked her head, but she heard nothing. It took her a moment to realize that that was the problem. There were no crickets chirping, no hoots from owls or creatures calling into the night. Absolute silence, save the breeze passing through the vines overhead.

She reached for her bow out of instinct, then she heard it. A distant roar. Guttural. Primitive in a way that stood her hair on end. A second roar answered, further away. This one more dulcet, if that was possible.

"Is that what I think it is?" Frida's eyes were wide.

Before Hilda could answer, she heard the slow thrum of heavy wings beating among the clouds. They flapped rhythmically, growing louder with each passing moment. Frida startled at the sound of a loud crack, like canvas sails snapping in a storm, as a dragon flew higher.

There was an eerie silence as it soared overhead, a gargantuan silhouette outlined in silver. The moonlight disappeared behind the dragon, and Frida's fingers dug into Hilda's arm. Morsel whimpered as the dragon passed by, its wings spread wide.

Hilda swallowed hard. They'd found the dragons.

No one slept particularly well that night. Although the dragon encounter had been brief, its presence lingered long after it disappeared and the distant roars of its fellows faded into nothingness.

Hilda pondered what had caused the dragon to appear as she, Frida, and Morsel made their way toward the northern gate. Were the dragons hunting, or did they perform regular patrols over the area to ensure the dwarves had not returned?

Despite the danger, Frida's spirits had never been higher. The girl led the way, anxious to see what waited beyond the city.

"Do you think we'll see another?" she asked excitedly, gazing out toward the nearby mountains as if a dragon might appear at any moment.

Hilda led Morsel by the reins, the goat's hooves clacking against stone. "I suspect it won't be the last one we see before our trip is finished." While she had a healthy trepidation at the prospect, there was no denying the rush that accompanied witnessing such majestic and terrifying creatures.

"I can't wait!" Frida's body vibrated with enthusiasm. "Have you ever seen one so close before? I thought my heart was going to pop out of my chest."

"A few times." Even for someone as well-traveled as Hilda, dragons were a rare sight. More often than not, they were seen from a distance, passing over forests or high in the mountains. "There was one time when we were traveling north of Drake Canyon. We were pursuing a band of bandits that had been raiding merchant caravans. We'd made camp for the night, and a dragon snatched one of our war goats that had wandered off while grazing. I had to share a ride with Snorri for the rest of that quest." Hilda met her granddaughter's gaze. "Dragons are beautiful and terrifying creatures, but don't let their majesty fool you. Above all else, they are predators."

"Do you think the stories are true?" Frida ignored the warning, her mind preoccupied. "About the dragon riders of old?"

There were legends from the Age of Ancients, long before the history of Aedrea had been recorded, that spoke of men who tamed dragons and rode upon their backs like horses. Hilda assumed it was all made up. If men had tamed dragons, they'd have conquered the continent. She was reminded of an old saying from the Adventurer's Guild. *If you see a dragon's shadow, all you can do is pray.*

Hilda shook her head. "I can't imagine anyone taming a beast that proud."

Frida thought about it for a moment, and then

shrugged, changing the subject. "Who do you think would win in a fight? A dragon or a behemoth?"

"Playing twenty questions, are we?" Hilda laughed.

The girl narrowed her eyes. "What else is there to do?"

"Frey was the same way." Hilda rested her hand on the urn. "A moment of silence was like a blade to his groin."

"Well?" Frida placed her hands on her hips.

Hilda was no stranger to this game. She'd played it herself as a child, rationalizing what would happen if the most powerful creatures, both real and imaginary, encountered one another in the wild.

"Well…" Hilda stroked her beard. "Behemoths are almost unkillable. They have armored hides that are magically resistant, and aside from the blood mages of the Northern Guard, I don't know anything that can truly hurt them. Dragons are tough, but they do have weak points and have been slain on occasion. Raglan the Magnificent turned back a red dragon single handedly. In a fair fight, I'd put my money on the behemoth."

"No way." Frida looked at her grandmother like she had two heads. "Dragons breathe fire. And they can fly. It could pick up the behemoth and drop it in the sea."

Hilda laughed at the absurdity of the statement. "If we're playing that way, then the behemoth could rip the dragon's leg off while it was flying. Its hide is so tough that it might even survive the fall. And if its scales can withstand a fire mage attack, I think it can outlast a dragon flame."

"You make a good point." Frida tapped her chin.

Before she could continue, Hilda took the opportunity to turn the tables on her granddaughter. "Now, you tell me. Who would win between a dragon and a kraken?"

"That depends. Are they fighting in the water or on land?"

"I think it's only fair to give them a chance to prove their worth on both."

And so, Frida debated the merits of each while Hilda navigated them toward the northern gate.

The girl was in the middle of describing the effects of a dragon's teeth against a kraken's tentacles when Hilda heard a gurgling sound from nearby. She paused, pressing a finger to her lips for Frida to be quiet. There was a loud splash, followed by another. She closed her eyes, listening for the source of the noise.

Hilda ordered Morsel to wait and quietly approached the next street, Frida following closely.

In the courtyard of what might have been a bank at one point, a water fountain burbled. The circular fountain had a statue of two goats facing one another, and water dribbled from their mouths.

Hilda and Frida exchanged a glance. It was odd that the fountain still worked, even this poorly, after so long.

The water sputtered, and then a jet shot from one of the goat's mouths as a stream of crystal blue arced into the mouth of the second statue.

"What the hells…" Frida's voice trailed off.

A moment later, another spurt shot from the second statue, as if propelled of its own accord. Water splashed on the face of the goat, and then congealed, falling into the basin and forming an amorphous blob that rippled as it moved, dancing and splashing in the fountain.

"It's a water elemental," Hilda whispered. They were the most tranquil of the elemental spirits, often playful and curious.

They watched in awe as water swirled around the fountain's base, creating a miniature whirlpool before disappearing into a drain, only to erupt from one of the goats a moment later. The elemental continued its performance, oblivious to their presence until the clack of hooves announced that Morsel had joined them.

The blob rose from the water. It was nearly as tall as Frida, swaying like a reed in the breeze as it appeared to watch them.

"Morsel, go back," Frida hissed. "You're going to scare it away."

The war goat bleated loudly, her cry bouncing off the stone walls. The elemental froze. There was a tense moment, and then it squelched, showering them all with water before collapsing into a puddle and vanishing through the drainage pipe at the bottom of the fountain.

Frida growled as she pressed her head to the goat's. "You can be so rude sometimes."

Morsel bleated right in the girl's face.

Hilda breathed a sigh of relief when they finally arrived at the northern gate. It wasn't barred and had likely been left open to allow those living in the mountains to escape through the city.

They passed through without issue, and by late afternoon, Hilda, Frida, and Morsel were climbing the ridge that separated Deepwarden from the dragonlands.

Stone paths stretched before them, overgrown from millennia of disuse but still traversable. They'd been designed for carts hauling lumber or stone and occasionally branched off toward a mine or terraced housing.

"A dragon and a water elemental." Frida clapped her hands together. "What do you think we'll see next?"

"This far out, there's no telling." Hilda surveyed the land where pines, firs, and spruces covered the mountain in a thick layer of dark green. There could be any number of creatures lurking in its depths.

Aside from a glimmer around a tree hole that may have been evidence of fae, the day passed without much excitement. When Frida spotted a stream that passed underneath the road, she took off running.

"Finally!" The girl raised her hands to the heavens. "Maybe we can eat something other than stonebread tonight."

Hilda scanned the horizon. "We might as well make camp here. We can enjoy a couple of hours of fishing before nightfall."

"Now we're talking." Frida went to grab the fishing pole from Morsel's pack when Hilda swatted her hand away.

"We make camp first."

Frida huffed. "It's always work with you."

"You chose this life, remember?" Hilda gave her a knowing look.

The girl's frown twisted into a smile. "How could I forget?"

Once they set up camp, Hilda and Frida gathered around the stream. Frida let the fishing line dangle in the water while Hilda rested against a tree. A cool breeze swept through the mountain, sending ripples across the gurgling brook.

"Come on." Frida tugged at the line. "I can see you in there. Take a bite of the tasty worm. There it is. Just a nibble." She jerked, and the hook flew from the water, worm still wriggling on the end. "Dammit!"

"Patience, youngblood." Hilda grinned. "Fishing is a sport of patience."

Frida groaned. "But I want to eat now."

Hilda pulled a piece of stonebread from the pack and waved it in the air. "Be my guest."

"I think I'd rather eat this worm." The girl tossed the line back into the water.

"I'll hold you to that." Hilda put the bread away. "Keep an eye on things for me. Your gram is going to rest her eyes for a bit."

A couple of hours later, Frida had managed to catch two fish. Hilda had them sizzling in a pan, the savory scent of whitefish blending with wild onion and garlic that she'd foraged nearby.

Frida rubbed her stomach. "All this time we could have been eating like queens, and you forced us to eat stonebread."

Hilda snorted. "Apologies. If I'd known I'd be traveling with royalty, then I would have packed the kitchen." She slid a piece of fish onto a plate for Frida. "I'm but a simple servant, my liege. I hope you can find it in your magnanimous heart to forgive such a lowly serf as myself."

Frida rolled her eyes. "I'm just saying. You're a great cook. I'd happily hunt and fish if it meant we could eat like this every night."

"Sometimes, it's not practical to hunt. And it's nice not to have to worry about tracking your next meal after you've been traveling all day."

They ate dinner in a ravenous silence. Afterward, Frida rinsed the plates and pans in the stream. With full bellies, they settled in for the night. The whisper of trees sang a gentle lullaby.

***

Hilda woke to the sound of soft, guttural growls as something rummaged about their camp. One of the packs lay on its side, potions and other supplies scattered around. Her fingers curled around the handaxe at her side, sleep retreating as decades of instinct took over.

She glanced at Frida. The girl was still fast asleep.

Across from Hilda, several pairs of large reptilian eyes glinted in the moonlight. Scaly, humanoid creatures stood on their hind legs, huddling together and grunting.

Kobolds.

She counted three of the creatures, each one less than three feet tall, with long ears that jutted upward and a ridge of short horns that ran from head to neck. Kobolds tended to avoid combat, preferring to lay traps and use cunning tactics to catch their enemies unaware, but their hands and feet were tipped with dangerous claws that could be deadly in a fight.

Those claws scratched against stone, and a pit formed in Hilda's stomach as she realized what they were holding. Frey's urn. The creatures fiddled with the golden latches, but couldn't seem to unlock the dwarven mechanism.

No, no, no, no. She couldn't lose Frey. Not like this. *Don't you dare open that urn.*

Hilda's heart raced as one of the kobolds hissed and snatched the urn from the other. A scuffle broke out, and the urn toppled to the ground with a thunk as they rolled in the grass.

She reached for her bow and nocked an arrow. Her shoulder groaned as she pulled the bowstring.

"Wait!" Frida whispered.

Hilda paused. When had the girl woken?

The kobolds turned around in unison, hissing and growling as they moved to guard the urn protectively as if it was some great treasure.

Hilda could have easily taken out one of them at this range, and probably stopped a second from escaping, but there was a good chance at least one of the creatures might vanish into the darkness with the urn before she could nock the third arrow. She'd never forgive herself if she lost Frey's ashes.

"What are you doing, child?" Hilda whispered between her teeth.

Frida's eyes were wide as she looked from the kobolds to her grandmother. "I think they are looking for food."

Hilda fought the urge to snap at her granddaughter. Of course they were looking for food; the little bastards were scavengers. But they were also fascinated with foreign objects, and on more than one occasion, she'd found kobold lairs that were filled with the most random assortment of trash and trinkets imaginable.

"Move quietly. Grab your bow," Hilda ordered under her breath, trying to remain calm. With Frida's help, they could likely eliminate all three of the vultures.

One of the kobolds reached for the urn, and Hilda drew her bowstring tighter.

Her eyes narrowed. "Don't even think about it."

The kobold growled, and Hilda heard the wrinkle of waxed paper to her side. She glanced over to see Frida holding a piece of stonebread, offering it to the kobold. All three of the creatures perked up, snouts sniffing at the air.

"I thought you might like this." The girl grinned, waving the stonebread.

"What the hells are you doing?" Hilda hissed.

One of the kobolds approached cautiously, stopping a few feet in front of Frida. The girl tossed the bread, and it landed at the kobold's feet.

It snatched up the biscuit and scurried back to its clan members. They sniffed at the stonebread and broke out in a flurry of grunts. One took a bite and then shared it with the others.

They chittered excitedly, slitted eyes greedy for more.

Frida held up another, and their tongues licked at the air. "Tasty, right?" She waggled her brow. "There's plenty more where that came from."

Hilda swallowed hard as she realized what was happening. This was a gamble, but it just might work. This wasn't how she'd choose to get the urn back, but she had to applaud the girl's ingenuity.

Frida gave each of the kobolds a piece of stonebread, which they devoured greedily. At this point, they only had eyes for Frida. She pulled out the remaining stonebread, dangling the bag in the air.

The kobolds chittered, prancing on clawed toes like a dog waiting for a treat.

"Not so fast." Frida pulled the bag to her chest. "I want that." She pointed at the urn.

The kobolds looked from the urn to the bag of stone-bread and back again. Frida pointed from the urn to the bag several times, and Hilda wondered just how much of the girl's message was getting across. They might not understand her words, but they seemed to comprehend the gesture.

One of the kobolds picked up the urn and set it midway between them. It kept one hand on the urn, the other outstretched.

"Good, good." Frida approached, placing the bag next to the urn.

The kobold's lips curled into a sneer, and Hilda pulled on her bowstring, but then the creature licked its snout and grabbed the bag, scurrying back into the woods with its compatriots.

Frida let out a shaky breath. "Gram, did you see that?" The girl's hands were shaking from the excitement. "I just bartered with a kobold."

Relief flooded through Hilda as she retrieved the urn. She turned to her granddaughter, shaking her head. "You're going to be the death of me, child."

18. THE CIRCLE OF LIFE

Hilda's heart pounded, not from the encounter with the kobolds but from almost failing her dearest friend's quest. She examined the urn, the polished stone cool against her skin. Aside from a little dirt caked around one of the latches, it was in pristine shape.

She placed it on top of the bedroll. *I'm sorry, old friend.*

"Gather your things." Hilda began retrieving the contents of the overturned satchel that were spilled about the campsite. "We need to be moving before they decide to come back."

"You think they'll be back?" Frida's brow knit as she looked in the direction the kobolds had fled.

"I don't want to be here to find out."

Once they were packed, she doused the remaining embers from the fire. It hissed, smoke swirling in wispy tendrils. At the edge of the ash, she saw something slender and white—the bones from the fish they'd eaten the night before.

"I thought I told you to dispose of this?" Hilda snapped, holding the bones by the tail.

Frida's cheeks flushed. "I did."

"Dispose means bury or toss in the stream." Hilda threw the remains into the ash. "It doesn't mean toss them in the fire as a beacon for anything with a nose. If you're going to burn them, you have to burn them completely. Look at this."

She held up the bones, which still had pieces of flesh caked on.

"I'm sorry. I just thought—"

"No, you didn't think. That's the problem, Frida. You do whatever you feel is best for you, without a thought for how it might affect anyone else. If I hadn't woken when I did, the urn might be halfway down the mountain by now." Hilda picked up the pack and searched for Morsel, but the goat was nowhere to be seen. Emotion roiled inside of her, threatening to erupt. She tossed the bag to the ground in frustration. "Where is that damned goat?"

"Gram," Frida said softly.

"What?" Hilda barked, but when she noticed the hurt expression on her granddaughter's face, the fire inside her extinguished. "I'm sorry I yelled. I thought for a moment that I..." She sighed, pressing her knuckles against her eyes. "I don't know what I would have done if something had happened to him."

"I'm sorry about the bones." Frida sniffled. "It won't happen again."

"I know, child." Hilda wrapped an arm around her granddaughter. "It was a mistake. I understand that. Gods know I made plenty in my youth. What matters is that you got the urn back." She brushed a strand of hair behind Frida's ear. "Which was pretty clever, by the way."

"That was the last of the stonebread, though." Frida grimaced.

"I don't suppose you'll be too sorry about that." Hilda smiled, trying to let go of her nerves. "We can finally put that bow of yours to use."

Something stirred in the bushes, and Hilda drew her hand axe. A massive head poked through the underbrush, Morsel's mouth full of leaves.

"Where did you run off to?" Hilda admonished the goat, grabbing her by the reins.

Morsel bleated and licked Hilda on the cheek.

"Yeah, yeah. You're just full of excuses." She scratched the goat behind the ears.

Frida helped load the gear, and soon they set off up the mountain. They traveled in silence for miles, aside from Morsel's occasional commentary, a thread of tension still hanging in the air.

Hilda had always done a decent job of keeping her cool under pressure, but the thought of losing Frey had touched something inside that she hadn't expected. Although she'd paid her respects at the funeral, she'd yet to truly say good-bye.

She tugged on the reins, and Morsel came to a stop.

"Everything okay?" Frida watched her hesitantly.

"No." Hilda shook her head and climbed down from the goat. "I owe you an apology."

"An apology?" Frida frowned. "For what? I'm the one who left the bones out."

"You made a mistake. One that could have been dangerous, but luckily, it wasn't. It was a learning experience and could have been a teachable moment, but instead, I let my fear cloud my judgment. I lashed out at you, not because I was angry but because I was afraid. I was afraid of losing my chance to say good-bye to Frey. For that, I am sorry." Hilda spread her arms. "Do you think you could forgive me?"

Frida embraced her grandmother. "I didn't think you were afraid of anything."

"Everyone is afraid of something, child." Hilda squeezed. "That's part of living."

Without the stonebread to give them sustenance, they quickly went through the remaining rations of cheese and jerky. They'd yet to pass another stream since the kobold incident, and although Frida set traps each night, they came up empty each morning.

They made the best of what they had, foraging for carrots, wild onions, and mushrooms as they trekked through the mountains.

Early one morning, Hilda was stoking the fire when she heard Frida scream. Grabbing her bow, she set off in the direction of the sound.

She found Frida beneath a shaggy pine, crying over a pile of carrots.

"Are you hurt?" Hilda asked as she surveyed the area for signs of a threat.

Frida turned around. She was holding her thumb, but she wasn't crying. Hilda thought she might be imagining it for a moment, but she could clearly hear the sound of someone whining. Then the pile of carrots shook, and one of them stood up. It was nearly a foot tall, its roots a golden brown that split halfway up to form legs. It had two shorter root-like appendages for arms just above its paunchy midsection, and a crown of dark green foliage adorned its head. Tiny knobs formed a distressed face as the creature opened its mouth and shrieked.

Hilda burst out laughing as the creature scurried away down the mountain. Frida scowled as it ran away but said nothing.

"Was that your first mandrake?" Hilda asked, examining the girl's hand. There was a red mark around her thumb, deep enough to pinch but not enough to draw blood.

Frida sucked on her thumb. "No one told me they bite."

"They're nasty little buggers. Don't take too kindly to being disturbed. One time, Brok pulled one while foraging and it kicked him in the eye. It got him so bad that he needed a potion to heal the damage." Hilda swallowed another bout of laughter at the mental image. "Let's get you back to camp and you can put my coldstone on that for a bit."

Upon returning, Frida iced her thumb while Hilda boiled a pot of wild carrots and mushrooms. The smell was inviting and cozy, but it was far from filling. They could survive on such things, but if they wanted the energy to trek such mountainous terrain, Hilda was going to have to hunt.

Hilda knelt atop a ridge, overlooking a ravine where a herd of deer wandered below. A buck, three does, and a fawn grazed on foliage.

Frida watched them hungrily, bow at her side. "They're practically begging us to eat them." She licked her lips. "I can already taste the venison with carrots and onions, the hint of smokiness from the open fire..." She gazed at the deer wistfully as one nibbled on a leaf.

"We're not so desperate that we need to hunt more than we can eat. There's plenty of game in these woods that won't go to waste if we kill it." Hilda's eyes scanned their surroundings as she spoke, searching for movement in the underbrush. "Nature provides, but we don't take that for granted. Take what you need, nothing more."

Frida nodded. "I understand."

One of the deer raised its head and the rest of the herd froze. Hilda signaled for Frida to stay quiet as she searched the area for signs of predators. The birds had quit chirping, and all that could be heard was the whisper of leaves.

There was a crunch, and the herd bolted. Branches snapped as a shadowy outline of a cat darted in pursuit, its paws padding against the earth, springing the beast forward with rippling power.

"What in Pidros's shiny anvil was that?" Frida stared blankly as the hunt disappeared around the bend. "Was that a demon?"

"Shadowcat." Hilda stood and nodded in the opposite direction. "They're mostly solitary creatures. Adept at camouflage, especially among the shadows. They're not much of a threat to dwarves, as they tend to go for smaller game. That one is probably after the fawn since I doubt it could take down the others."

"Aww." Frida's lips pressed together in a thin line.

Hilda raised a brow. "Two seconds ago, you were ready to eat them, and now you feel sad?"

"I wasn't going to eat the baby." She huffed. "I hope it gets away."

"The adults will fight to protect it, but nature doesn't play favorites. Out here, the strong survive and the weak get eaten." Hilda nudged the girl with her elbow. "Now, come on. Let's try to feed ourselves while you ponder the circle of life."

Frida grabbed her grandmother's arm. "Do you think we should check on Morsel?" she asked, urgency in her voice.

Hilda laughed. "The only creature Morsel need fear in these woods is a dragon."

"Really?" The girl's brow arched.

"She has thick fur, legs that could kick through a stone wall, and horns that could hammer an anvil." Hilda gave her a knowing look. "There's a reason our people chose them as mounts. Don't worry about—"

Frida stuck out her arm, stopping her grandmother. Her other hand pointed in the distance where two large birds were pecking at the ground. Hilda recognized them as mountain pheasants. They were ground birds, and the mountain variety tended to be larger and darker than their grassland counterparts.

Hilda raised her bow and nocked it, nodding for Frida to do the same. "I'll take the one on the left. You take the one on the right."

"It's kind of far." Frida frowned. "Should we move closer?"

Hilda shook her head. It was a long shot, but moving any closer risked frightening the birds. "You can do this." She drew the bowstring. "We loose on three." Frida nocked an arrow, and Hilda counted. "One. Two. Three."

There was a twang as they released. The bird on the left dropped, and the second pheasant crowed, its wings flapping loudly as it flew away. Hilda had hit her mark, but Frida's arrow stuck in the dirt a foot from her target. While Hilda's eyesight might not be what it once was, her aim was as good as ever.

"Dammit!" Frida kicked the ground. "I told you it was too far."

"Don't worry about it. It takes time to master the bow. You have the fundamentals; all you need is practice." Hilda patted her on the back as they walked to retrieve the pheasant. "And since you bartered away our stonebread, there will be plenty of opportunities for you to perfect your aim between now and home." Hilda picked up the pheasant by the tail. "In the meantime, cheer up. Meat's back on the menu."

19. FUN AND GAMES

The pace slowed in the days that followed, but with the added hunting practice, Frida's skills continued to improve. Each night, they went to bed with full bellies, and Hilda shared stories of the travels of her youth before going to sleep.

She found herself experiencing a strange sensation, like two parts of her life had blended into one. The young girl who'd once sat upon her grandmother's lap listening to tales of exploration and daring feats was now part of her very own adventure, spending her mornings training and evenings hunting.

As hesitant as Hilda had been to let her granddaughter join her, she had to admit that Frida was up to the task. While the girl still held onto the stubbornness of youth, she learned from her mistakes and was better for them. Frida had a thirst not only to be good, but to be great. That was something Hilda resonated with.

They were hiking up a narrow path when Frida

stopped and sniffed at the air. "You smell that?" She sniffed again. "I think it's going to rain."

Hilda's shoulder tended to agree with the assessment. She massaged the growing ache, then smiled. "I think you're right."

Frida grinned. "I'll keep an eye out for somewhere to camp."

Hours passed as the sky continued to darken. Thunder purred overhead, yet they still hadn't found a cave or cliff to camp beneath when the first raindrops began to fall.

Hilda was about to suggest they make do with a canvas tarpaulin between two trees when Frida started jumping excitedly.

"Gram, there's an old watchtower." She pointed beyond the dense trees, where moss-covered stone blended into the surroundings.

The ancient-looking tower had seen better days. Pieces of broken stone jutted from the earth where parts of the spire had collapsed. The tower had the appearance of a broken spear that had been snapped off at the head, and there was no mistaking the claw marks etched atop the jagged stone from where something had perched.

Luckily, the watchtower remained intact enough to serve as shelter from the storm. The wooden entry had long since deteriorated, leaving rusted hinges attached to the stone doorway. Inside, there was brush and debris scattered about, along with broken glassware and clay cups from when it had served as a watchful protector.

The stairwell and floors on the lower levels had survived, offering protection from the rain that pattered above.

"This will do just fine," Hilda said as she unloaded Morsel.

Once they were unpacked, she and Frida explored the upper levels. The walls were ringed with arrow slits, and abandoned bird nests and spiderwebs now filled the openings. There was a small armory of rusted weapons piled in a corner on the second level.

On the third floor, there was a bedframe, the mattress long gone, and a bookshelf, the contents of which had been gnawed to nothingness by mice and other creatures. A stairwell led to a higher level, but the entry was blockaded with stone from the collapsed spire.

"I don't think anyone has been here in a while," Frida said as she looked around the room.

Hilda ran her finger along the bookshelf, collecting a thick layer of dust on her fingertip. She blew it, sending plumes of fuzz into the air. "What gave it away?"

Frida waggled her brows. "Like you said, I'm perceptive."

Hilda scoffed. "You're something, child."

By the time they returned to the ground level, Morsel had wandered off, but Hilda could see the goat through one of the arrow slits, fur soaked as she munched on leaves from a thorny bush.

Frida started a fire using some of the timber she found within the tower. Once it crackled merrily, she grabbed her cloak. "I'll go gather us some firewood for tonight. And I'll set some traps while I'm at it."

"Hold on," Hilda called as Frida was stepping through the doorway. She removed her own cloak and offered it to the girl. "This will keep you dryer."

Frida held it reverently and slipped it over her shoulders. There was a noticeable aura about the girl as she donned the fabled dreamweave cloak. Hilda smiled as she watched her leave.

Later that night, thunder rumbled, shaking the walls of the watchtower. Hilda rested against her pack, Frey's urn tucked close beside her as she basked in the calming sounds of rain battering the landscape. Morsel slept at her feet, legs tucked underneath so that the goat again resembled a giant loaf of bread.

Frida sat by the fire, using the light as she wrote in her journal. She bit her lip, pencil moving swiftly across the page.

"What are you writing?" Hilda asked.

The girl finished the sentence she was working on and looked up. "Just keeping notes. I want to make sure I remember everything when I recount my first adventure."

Hilda laughed. "It makes for a better story if you leave out the boring bits."

"I don't know." Frida tapped the pencil against her chin. "There might be someone who wants to know what happens in between the action. I know I would."

"In that case, don't let me hold you back." Lightning flashed, igniting the night, followed by a thunderous crash that reverberated in Hilda's chest. "We're in the thick of it now. Hopefully, it passes by morning."

Frida closed her journal and moved to sit beside her grandmother. She cuddled up close, resting her head on Hilda's shoulder. "Will you tell me a story?"

She kissed Frida on the top of the head. "What kind of story?"

"I don't know. Something calm and relaxing."

Hilda pondered for a moment. While there had been plenty of downtime during her adventuring days, things were rarely calm or relaxing with Frey and Brok in her party. There had been evenings in taverns, which usually ended with a brawl or a hangover. There was the occasional stately dinner for royal quest completions, which sometimes ended in a similar manner to the taverns. Even the nights spent camping under the stars often culminated with Brok and Frey trading blows.

Calm and relaxing. She stroked her beard. "Well, there was that one time in Fernhill…"

Many years ago…

Hilda sat in the back of the wagon, watching the rolling hills of Tyne as the wagon bumped along the dirt road. The halfling lands were beautiful in their autumn glory, trees brandishing leaves of gold and crimson. A cool breeze swept across the land, sending untamed tendrils of red hair across Hilda's vision.

Across from her, Brok leaned against the wagon frame, head bobbing as he slept. Hilda chuckled to herself. The old dwarf could sleep through a dragon attack.

In the front of the wagon, Snorri drove while Frey kept her company. After the past few days spent tracking down a nest of hill wyrms that had invaded several vineyards south of Honeydale, Hilda was grateful for a little solitude, even if it was fleeting.

Frey turned around, rapping his knuckles against the wagon's wooden frame. "There's a town up ahead. Fernhill, I believe. We'll stop there for the night and make for Hillside in the morning."

Hilda nodded her acknowledgement, and a mischievous grin split Frey's face as he set his gaze on the slumbering Brok. Frey took a grape from the basket they'd been given as a token of thanks and tossed it, hitting the sleeping dwarf in the neck.

Brok stirred and grunted, but he didn't wake.

"Will you stop?" Snorri elbowed Frey in the side.

"What?" He feigned innocence.

"Do you always have to goad him?" Snorri asked.

Frey tossed another grape, this one disappearing into the neck hole of Brok's armor. "Does he have to make it so easy?"

Snorri grabbed the basket and passed it to Hilda. "Sometimes, I wonder why we put up with him."

Frey had the gall to look taken aback. "I'm right here, you know."

Snorri's gaze bored into her friend. "Oh, I know."

Hilda plucked a few grapes and returned her attention to the scenic view while Snorri and Frey bickered. The fruit was a beautiful greenish-gold, a far cry from the rich reds and purples that grew in Mount Tor. She took a bite, and sweetness exploded in her mouth, soft and refreshing with a hint of honey that lingered.

A couple of hours later, the wagon rolled into Fernhill. For a small town, it was full of life. They'd arrived during the harvest festival and a gathering of halflings, along with a couple dozen humans and dwarves, drank wine, laughed, and bustled about the crowded square. Everyone seemed to be enjoying one another's company as music carried across the town.

The festival was in full swing with events and festivities for the townsfolk. Local vendors sold their wares, and the scent of cinnamon bread and caramel corn hung in the air. Homes and businesses were adorned with autumnal wreaths, and pumpkins carved with monstrous faces lined the streets.

"Look at that!" Frey managed to convey a sense of childlike wonder upon his grizzled features as they passed an area where people were playing games and bobbing for apples from wine barrels. "You know I can't turn down a challenge."

After they'd checked into the inn, where they were forced to share a room, he was adamant they return to the festival.

"Who wants to take on the Rogue Ember of Ashborn?" Frey asked, eyes settling on each of them in turn.

"You have fun." Snorri patted him on the back. "It's been too long since I've partaken in halfling pipeleaf, and I see a cloud of smoke that's calling my name."

Brok shook his head. "I think I'll have a gander at the scented candles. We'll need something to cover up Frey's natural odor in such close quarters."

"You little…" Frey took a step toward Brok, but Hilda grabbed him by the arm.

"Come on," she said, pulling him toward the festivities while trying to hide her grin. "Let's see what you've got."

They stood in line behind a group of halflings, each about half a foot shorter than the dwarves. They all wore colorful jewel-toned tunics with matching vests, and they took turns at the various games. Some played a game where the goal was to knock down wooden pins with a dried-out corn cob. Cheers erupted as one of the group managed to knock over a pin on her third attempt.

Next to them, others were playing ring toss. The goal was to throw colored rings around matching colored stakes in the ground. They were allowed five misses before elimination, but the rings got progressively smaller as the player moved down the line from blue to green, yellow, orange, and then red. The final red ring was barely bigger than Hilda's palm.

Two halflings were playing against one another. One managed to make the blue ring but was unable to secure the green stake. The other, poor soul, had missed the blue stake five times in a row. On the fifth try, he threw his hands in the air and stormed off.

"That looks like fun." Hilda nudged Frey in the arm. "Want to give it a go?"

"You think your skills with a bow extend to wooden rings?"

Hilda grinned. "Only one way to find out."

They waited their turn, watching as every challenger failed to complete the circuit. One halfling managed to get the orange ring on his fourth try, but no one had claimed the red stake.

When it was time, Hilda stepped aside and gestured for Frey to go first. "After you."

"I see how it is." He tossed the blue ring, and it landed around the blue stake. "Trying to steal my technique."

Hilda went next, claiming the blue ring with ease.

Frey winked, then tossed the green ring, once again circling the matching stake on his first attempt. Hilda rolled her eyes and then mirrored his shot. At that, several of the halflings abandoned their game of cob throw to watch Frey and Hilda's competition.

"Let's see what you've got now." She waggled her brows.

He set his eyes on the yellow stake and tossed. It barely caught the wood, rattling as it spun around the tip before finally dropping to the ground. "Nervous?" He smirked.

"I could make this with my eyes closed."

"Pssh." Frey dismissed her with a wave of his hand. "I'll believe it when I see it."

Hilda closed her eyes and tossed the ring.

The resounding gasps told Hilda that she'd succeeded, and when she opened her eyes, the crowd was twice the size it was before.

"Showoff," Frey muttered under his breath as he picked up the orange ring. His gaze fixed on the stake as he practiced his throwing motion. He released, and the ring clattered as it bounced off the wooden stake. Frey cursed as he retrieved the ring. With a look of fierce determination, he tried again. This time, the ring landed on the stake. "Your turn."

"Are you worried, Frey?" A smile tugged at the edge of her lip. "You look worried."

He narrowed his gaze. "Enough stalling. Shit or get off the pot."

Frey loved to heckle his opponents. He'd been that way for as long as she'd known him. Whether it was a friendly game of dice or a confrontation at the tavern, he thrived on getting into someone's head. But when it came to games of skill, Hilda had the slow-beating heart of a behemoth. There was nothing more dangerous than cold, collected confidence.

She tossed the ring without acknowledgment, and it encircled the orange stake.

The crowd had multiplied tenfold at this point, and there were halflings standing on tables and fence posts to get a better view.

Hilda caught a familiar minty-pine scent and turned to see Frey dabbing his lucky frostbloom oil into his mustache. "You think that's going to help you?"

"No." His ears flushed. "My mustache was feeling a bit dry."

Hilda grinned. "Of course it was."

Hushed whispers snaked through the crowd as Frey gathered the red ring.

He took a deep breath, practicing his movement. Hilda said nothing, letting the silence build like a mounting wave. He tossed the ring and it hit the top of the stake, circling twice before dislodging and landing several feet away on the grass.

He retrieved the ring and tried again. This time, the wooden ring clacked as it hit the stake two inches below the top. Three strikes, two to go. On his next attempt, the back of the ring clipped the stake, flipping end over end onto the ground.

"Godsdammit," Frey barked as he picked up the ring for his final attempt.

The crowd waited in silence. Frey's arm swung forward, and that's when Hilda let the wave crash down as she whispered, "Don't choke."

The ring slipped from Frey's fingers, shooting from his grip like a wet tadpole. It sailed over the stake, missing by a fraction and landing in the grass. He shook his head, too furious for words.

Hilda watched with amusement until he regained his composure.

"Real funny," he croaked. "Not that you'll be able to do any better. The ring is barely wider than the stake."

"Oh, hon." Hilda placed the ring on her thumb and launched it like a coin. It flipped through the air, end over end, and she turned to Frey while it was still airborne. "You've got skill. I'll give you that. But you're no ranger."

The crowd erupted into cheers as the ring fell over the stake like it had been dropped from the heavens.

Frey scowled. And then his frown shifted into a smile as he howled with laughter. He grabbed Hilda's hand, raising it overhead. "Hilda Flintbreaker, ladies and gentlemen. The best damn ranger in all of Aedrea."

***

Present Day.

Outside the watchtower, the rain had stopped. A dense fog had gathered in its wake, making it look as if they were camping among the clouds. Water dripped from tree branches, singing a soothing lullaby, and Frida's snores purred softly as she slept against Hilda's shoulder.

Hilda was surprised at the mist gathering in her eyes as she finished the story. It was moments like that which showcased the breadth of Frey's character. He could be an ass at times, but even in defeat, he'd acknowledged Hilda's skills.

After a showing like that, neither she nor Frey had paid for a drink the rest of the evening. Some twenty years later, they'd passed through Fernhill again, and there were still locals who spoke of that day fondly.

Those were the days, huh? She placed her hand on Frey's urn.

Hilda cradled Frida behind the neck, gently lowering her granddaughter to the ground. She covered the girl with the thin blanket from her bedroll, and for a moment, she admired the young woman. This was likely Hilda's last real adventure, but for Frida, it was only the beginning.

A howl shattered the silence, near enough to set Hilda's hair on end. Morsel stirred, head rising as she sniffed at the air.

Hilda grabbed her bow, peeking through the arrow slit for signs of wolves, but with this much fog, it was impossible to see anything more than a few feet.

Something sparkled in the distance, and she thought her eyes were playing tricks on her as a deep orange glow moved through the fog. She watched, mesmerized by the floating light.

And then it turned, revealing a second source of condensed light. Molten eyes that burned like embers stared at her. Hilda stared back, unable to look away even if she wanted to. There was something wise and ancient in the way they watched her.

Then the eyes closed, and another howl cried into the night.

20. EYES OF THE MOUNTAIN

"What am I supposed to do?" Frida stood in the doorframe before a wall of fog that obscured the landscape. "There's no way I'll be able to find the traps in this. I can barely see five feet in front of me."

Hilda joined her granddaughter to look upon the gloomy setting. She hadn't slept particularly well that night after her encounter with the glowing-eyed…

She frowned, not quite sure what it had been. The realm was full of mysterious happenings. When one lived as long as she had, especially as a ranger, they learned that some things defied explanation. Mysterious lights, strange noises, and the inexplicable came with the territory. Whatever she'd seen the night before had been unsettling, but it hadn't seemed dangerous. It had left them in peace once it disappeared.

"Looks like a tidal fog." Hilda stepped outside, and the cool, damp air settled on her skin. All around, a heavy fog rose high into the tree line. It was dark gray at the bottom and shifted to a bright white among the tree branches, where presumably the sun was shining above. "It's a rare phenomenon named after how unusually high it rises. We'll have to be careful."

"How long does it last?" Frida asked, eyes looking skyward.

"Hard to say. I've only witnessed it twice in my life, but if we keep climbing, eventually we'll crest it."

"You think it's safe to travel?" Frida's expression was uncertain.

"I've been through worse."

Behind them, Morsel grunted as she leaned forward, stretching her powerful back legs. Then, she forced her massive frame between the two dwarves to lick Frida on the nose.

"Gross." Frida wiped away a string of slobber.

Morsel bleated her disagreement, licking the girl again. While Frida fought off the war goat, Hilda grabbed a length of rope from her pack.

"Check your traps." She handed the rope to Frida.

Frida blinked several times before holding up the rope. "What am I supposed to do with this?"

"Oh, sweet child." Hilda chuckled. "Anchor it nearby so that you don't get lost."

"Brilliant." Frida grinned as she tied the rope to a loose stone. "You think of everything, don't you?"

"New recruits always complain about packing rope, but let this be a lesson to you. Gold may fill your pockets, but rope will save your bones." She smiled at another one of the sayings she'd inherited from Snorri.

Frida nodded before disappearing into the fog.

While the girl checked the traps, Hilda set Frey's urn by the fire, talking to it as she started packing. "I remember the first time we encountered a tidal fog. Brok nearly fell off the mountain, and you dove after him, catching the neck hole of his armor with your fingertips. He kept sliding, and you were going with him, so Snorri had her arms wrapped around your midsection, pulling with all her might, boots scraping against the earth until she caught her foot on a rock." Hilda laughed as she rolled her bedding. "It was like watching a boulder on a precipice where the slightest breeze might send all of you tumbling below."

It had been Hilda's quick thinking that saved them that day. She'd attached a length of rope to the saddle of their war goat and wrapped the other end around Snorri so that the goat could pull them back up. Just another reason to never leave home without it.

By the time Hilda had finished, Frida returned with a squirrel, holding it up like a prize. "Might not be much, but it's still better than stonebread."

Hilda mixed the squirrel into the leftover stew from the night before, and after eating, they set out across the shrouded mountain. While war goats were sure-footed, a great deal of their steadiness came from a cautious anticipation of where to place their hooves. By midday, the fog still hadn't receded, keeping the pace slow going, with Morsel huffing and snorting her irritation at the lack of visibility.

"It's okay, girl," Hilda said as she scratched the goat on the shoulder. "We'll be through it before you know it."

A loud rumble sounded in the fog ahead of them, and Hilda pulled Morsel to a stop.

"Is that thunder?" Frida asked, her gaze toward the light-colored fog above them.

"I don't think so. It's not coming from the sky." Hilda tilted her head, listening. Minutes passed before there was another rumble. She could almost trace the sound as it moved down the mountain. "Sounds like falling rock. All that rain must have saturated the soil."

Frida's eyes widened. "And you want us to walk through it?"

Hilda stroked her beard. They could always return to the watchtower, but that was no guarantee of safety either. If there was loose stone from the rain, they needed to steer away from it. "We could try to climb higher to see if there is visibility, but our best bet might be to find cover, wait, and hope that the fog clears."

Frida tilted her head back and groaned. "It's always something."

She climbed down from Morsel and placed a hand on her granddaughter's shoulder. "Welcome to the life of an adventurer."

"Still beats going to school." Frida grinned mischievously as she set her pack down and pulled out her journal.

Hilda tied Morsel behind two trees growing close enough together to block any falling rock that might come. The goat bleated her discontent at the lack of freedom.

"I know, I know," Hilda said as she removed Frey's urn from the pack and settled in behind a tree.

The falling rock was sporadic in its appearance. Sometimes, the noise was lighter and distant. At other times, it was almost thunderous as something crashed down the mountainside, followed by the squawk of birds and the shudder of leaves. Once, she swore she heard a deep cachinnation, as if the mountain was laughing at the destruction.

In all her years, Hilda had never heard such continuous rockfall. In her experience, rockslides were sudden and rapid. She was beginning to think they might have to find another route when a sonorous howl erupted from the direction of the falling rock. The howl was singular, deep and resonant, as if it had come from the mountain itself. The same as the previous night.

"Gram?" Frida closed her journal and turned toward the noise, concern coating her voice. "What was that?"

Hilda stood, clutching Frey's urn to her chest as she followed her granddaughter's gaze. The air shifted around them, fog swirling and roiling as it moved across the mountainside. Falling rock ceased as the fog continued to recede, like it was being pulled away by godly bellows.

Frida gasped, and when Hilda saw the reason, chills erupted along her body.

Up the mountain stood a wolf, bigger than the largest warhorse she'd ever seen, easily twice as tall as a dwarf. Its body was composed of fog, soft, yet somehow powerful at the same time. Wispy gray tendrils flared like flames as the fog continued to condense into the wolf. Deep orange embers burned in its eyes, blazing as it stalked toward them, paws hovering inches above the ground as it walked.

Hilda felt herself drawn to the magnificent creature. Though it carried a power that radiated, she felt no fear.

The wolf stopped a few dozen yards away from them as the last of the surrounding fog vanished within its body.

"Gram?" Frida asked again, her voice uncertain.

"I think it's a mountain spirit," Hilda whispered.

Frida swallowed hard. "Is it dangerous?"

"I don't believe so." She'd heard legends of nature spirits that guarded mountains, forests, and lakes across the realm, but she'd never encountered one until now. They were said to be watchful guardians, protectors of the natural world. "I saw it near the watchtower last night, just the eyes among the fog. Whatever it is, I don't get the feeling it wants to harm us."

"That's a relief." Frida raised a hand and waved at the wolf spirit. "Hello there!"

Hilda stared, awestruck, as the spirit's eyes flared, and fog swirled within its body like a raging storm. It turned, taking a few steps away before stopping to look over its shoulder.

"I think it wants us to follow," Frida said.

The spirit took another step before looking over its shoulder again.

"I'll be damned," Hilda whispered. "I think you're right."

"No one is going to believe this." The girl wore a look of astonishment, as if she couldn't believe it herself.

Hilda was equally mystified as she packed away the urn and untied Morsel, leading the goat on foot as she followed the wolf spirit. Morsel didn't seem the least bit hesitant or concerned that they were following a wolf larger than she was, which solidified Hilda's opinion of the spirit. The goat might be annoying at times, but she was a great judge of character.

The spirit led them across the mountainous terrain, following paths tread by deer and other large beasts. Everywhere they trekked, the fog receded, pulled into the wolf's massive frame. Occasionally, the spirit would turn to make sure they were following before continuing onward.

They followed until they came upon a ravine, where an old, decrepit-looking bridge stretched across a narrow gorge. The bridge was wooden, anchored with large metal spikes and stabilized by copious amounts of rope and nails. Hilda had no idea how it was still standing after all these years. Perhaps there was some sort of enchantment holding it all together.

The spirit stepped onto the bridge, paws hovering inches above the wooden planks. It turned, once again beckoning them to follow.

"You think this is safe for Morsel?" Frida petted the goat.

Normally, there was no way Hilda would risk traversing something so ancient, but even though she couldn't explain why, she trusted the mountain spirit. If it needed their help, then that meant the bridge had to be safe to cross.

Hilda let go of Morsel's reins and tested her weight on the bridge. The wooden planks swayed slightly, but it felt secure. Once she was confident in its integrity, she beckoned Frida to join her.

The girl took two steps and then looked into the ravine below. "Ahh," Frida shouted, and her hands clenched desperately around the handrail.

"Eyes in front of you," Hilda ordered. "Take it one step at a time."

Frida nodded, and with the effort it might take to move a mountain, she turned her gaze forward.

"That's it. Keep your eyes focused on the other side. It's just like walking down the street."

"Uh-huh." Frida's voice shook as she passed her grandmother.

"Keep on going. Morsel and I will meet you on the other side."

Hilda watched as Frida slowly crossed the bridge, where the mountain spirit waited. Once her granddaughter was safely across, she took Morsel's reins. "Come on, old girl."

The bridge swayed with each step of Morsel's powerful legs, forcing Hilda to keep her knees bent for added balance, but the goat was steady, and she voiced her opinions of the situation every step of the way. Hilda's knees popped and creaked, adding their own remarks.

They made it across without issue, and Frida wrapped her arms around her grandmother.

"That was a rush." She let go and showed her shaking hands.

Hilda grinned. The girl was going to go far with an attitude like that.

Ahead of them, the wolf spirit stood in the center of an old trail that wound its way around the mountain. There was a steep drop to one side with a churning river far below.

They followed the spirit until Morsel suddenly stopped. She bleated, her massive frame tensing as her hooves pawed at the ground in agitation.

"What is it, girl?" asked Hilda, but the goat continued to thrash and step backward.

She was focused on Morsel when she heard a loud rattle emanating from beyond Frida and the wolf spirit. Her granddaughter had one hand over her mouth as she pranced with glee, and the other hand pointed at a recess in the cliffside that Hilda couldn't see. The rattling intensified, and a cold sweat erupted along Hilda's spine as she realized what she was hearing. She let go of Morsel's reins and sprinted toward her granddaughter.

"Frida!" Hilda shouted. "Get away. That's a—"

The words choked in her mouth when her gaze fell upon the source of Morsel's distress. The mountain spirit hovered over a purple dragon coiled into a defensive posture, its side pressed against the mountain. The dragon's scales shimmered like amethysts in a myriad of purple hues. Golden eyes narrowed upon them, and its lips curled back, revealing a set of dangerous white teeth. It was still a juvenile, only slightly bigger than Morsel, with claws as large as the goat's hooves and a lithe, muscular body. Jewel-like spikes ran down the ridge of its back and along its tail, ending in the large, black rattle that defined the venomous rattledrake. It vibrated ominously as the dragon released a low, threatening growl.

"It's hurt," Frida whispered, pointing at the dragon's wing.

Hilda noticed, too. The bony part of the appendage was bent at an odd angle and crusted with indigo-colored blood. The wing hung lopsided, unable to fully retract. One of the dragon's front claws was also injured, and it kept its paw clutched against its chest. Perhaps it was the unfortunate victim of a falling rock, but that didn't change the fact that rattledrakes were deadly. Hilda had never seen one in person, but she'd read about them. They weren't known to be aggressive, as evidenced by the rattle on their tail. Rattles were a defensive mechanism, a warning, but she'd heard the horror stories of those unlucky enough to cross their paths. Rattledrakes might be one of the smaller dragon species, but a fully-grown one was still capable of carrying off a horse between its talons, and their venom made them a threat to creatures much larger.

Morsel must have sensed the gravity of their situation, because for once, the mouthy goat was silently watching the scene unfold from a safe distance. There were very few creatures that could intimidate a war goat, but a dragon was high on the list.

"I'm sorry, but there's nothing we can do." Hilda squeezed Frida's shoulder. "It's too dangerous. Healing potions don't work on rattledrake venom."

"We can't just leave it here." Frida's face twisted in anguish. "Look at it."

The wolf spirit turned to Hilda, orange eyes blazing, as if agreeing with Frida's point. After a tense moment, it lowered its head and nuzzled the dragon. The injured creature's growl shifted to a whimper.

"Please," Frida pleaded. "We have to do something."

Hilda stepped closer, and the dragon's tail shook the black rattle furiously. Its lips curled back into a snarl, and its golden eyes narrowed menacingly. A low catlike growl emanated from the dragon's chest.

Hilda sighed. She hated to see any creature suffer but keeping Frida safe was her priority. "There's not much we can do if it won't let me approach."

"It's just scared." Frida knelt, her eyes locked on the dragon. "You're just scared, aren't you?" She spoke with a soft, kind voice, similar to the one Hilda had used to comfort her own children and grandchildren over the years. "We aren't going to hurt you." She scooted closer, and the dragon's tail swished. "It's okay. It's okay." Frida held up her hands. They shook slightly, though whether from excitement or nervousness, Hilda couldn't tell. "You're hurt, and I know that's scary, but she—" Frida nodded to the wolf spirit. "—or he… I don't really know how foggy spirit beasts prefer to be addressed. The point is, the spirit led us here so that we could help you."

The wolf spirit nuzzled the dragon again, and the

rattling slowed. Every rational part of Hilda said that this was a terrible idea, but looking into the burning eyes of the spirit, her instincts said to trust it. But if she was wrong, they were weeks from civilization. How could she ever explain to Flint and Maela that she'd willingly let their daughter approach a dragon?

"Be careful," Hilda whispered. She watched in awe as her granddaughter continued to soothe the dragon.

"That's it." Frida smiled. "We want to help you, but we can't do that if you attack us." The dragon's snarl faded, and it sniffed at the air. "There we go. That's a good dragon." Frida inched forward, and there was a slow rattle. She waited until it stilled and then moved again. "We just want to help you and then we'll be on our way."

Hilda watched cautiously, one hand on her bow out of instinct, as the girl moved closer.

Frida stopped when she was about six feet away. "This is the part where we trust each other." She held out her hand. "I trust that you won't bite me, and you trust that we mean you no harm."

"Trust." The words hissed from within Hilda's mind, raspy but with a youthful and feminine quality to them. Based on Frida's stiffened posture, the girl heard it too. *"Why would a dragon trust a two-legged?"*

"The spirit led us here." Frida's voice quivered. "I can see you're in pain, and my gram will help you if you let her, but we have to trust one another."

"Gram..." The dragon's eyes narrowed as she projected the words. *"What is 'gram'?"*

"Grandmother," Hilda was so enraptured by the fact that a dragon was speaking to her telepathically that she found herself answering the question without realizing. "I am her father's mother. You can call me Hilda, if you wish."

"I see." The dragon's forked tongue licked at the air. *"My gram is called Corcyra, known throughout the lands as the Shattered Gem."*

"And what should we call you?" Frida's hand was still extended.

"My name is Amethyra, but the elders call me Tinktink." Her tail swished slightly, and the sound was like the plink of beans in a metal bowl. The dragon's eyes focused on Hilda. *"The young one says you can help me."*

"I will try. But first, can you tell me what happened?"

Tinktink shifted uncomfortably. *"I was feeding when the mountain fell upon me. I cannot bend my wing nor bear weight upon my forepaw. I have been here for three days waiting for my kin to pass over."*

"You poor thing." Frida let her hand fall to her side.

Tinktink huffed. *"I do not need your sympathy."*

Frida crossed her arms. "You don't need to be such a—"

"Easy now," Hilda cautioned. "The spirit brought us here to help. None of us expected to be in this situation, so let's just stay calm."

Hilda had read a great deal about dragons in her youth, but there was very little information on their ability to communicate. Dragons kept to themselves, only occasionally appearing within range of dwarven settlements. According to the legends of old, the first dragon riders were said to form bonds with their drag-ons, but there was no mention of how the process worked. If Tinktink had been here for three days, unable to contact other dragons, then that meant there was a range on how far their communication could travel.

"May I examine your injuries?" Hilda asked.

Tinktink lowered her head. *"You may."* The dragon whimpered as she moved from the mountainside, shambling from the shadows upon three paws to the path. Tinktink's scales glittered in the sunlight, and the spikes that ran down the ridge of her back sparkled like polished jewels. The wolf spirit followed, hovering over the dragon like a protective parent.

"Beautiful," Hilda said softly. In her many years of adventuring, she'd seen countless treasures, but none of them compared to the beauty before her now. Tinktink was like gemstones brought to life, and even in her wounded state, she radiated grace and power.

The dragon stopped a few feet from Frida and rested on her haunches. Hilda approached. There was a moment when Tinktink's tail vibrated slightly, but then she calmed and allowed Hilda to continue.

"I'm going to touch you, just to check the damage." Hilda swallowed hard as she tried to hold back her nerves at being this close to something so dangerous. "It may hurt a bit."

"I understand."

Hilda's heart thundered as she placed her hand on Tinktink's wing. The dragon flinched and unleashed a tight hiss. For a moment, Hilda froze. Tinktink calmed, and Hilda continued. The dragon's scales were smooth to the touch. Heat radiated from the wounded areas, and there was a clear deformation underneath the scales where the bony structure had snapped.

She knelt, taking Tinktink's paw in her hand. The

dragon bared her teeth as Hilda extended her paw, and there was another rattle.

"It's okay." Frida stepped closer. "It will all be over soon." She stroked Tinktink behind the ear before Hilda could warn her to stay back. "Wow. Your scales are so smooth," the girl said with reverence.

Surprisingly, the dragon leaned into Frida's touch while Hilda examined her paw. The paw dwarfed Hilda's hand, and it was caked in congealed, crusted blue blood. Several of the claws were bent at odd angles.

"I've never used a healing potion on a dragon before, but I know they can work on some animals. We once had a pony step in a hole and break his leg. A potion had him good as new within a couple of hours." Hilda gently returned the paw to Tinktink's chest and stood. "But if the potion doesn't work, I can make a splint and try to reset the bones. It will take longer to heal, but it will allow you to travel back home."

"Do what you must."

"Gram will fix you right up." Frida continued to pet Tinktink like she was a common housecat and not a creature capable of unleashing destruction on a whim.

"Let me grab my supplies," Hilda said as she turned to leave.

Morsel had watched the entire exchange, her head peeking around the mountainside. When Hilda returned, the goat pressed her massive head to Hilda's chest and released a bleat layered with desperation.

"I understand that feeling," she said as she patted the goat on the shoulder. Her spine was still doused with nervous sweat. She pulled several healing potions from the pack and then cradled Morsel's jaw. "Stay here while I go attempt to heal a dragon."

The ridiculousness of those words was not lost on her as she made her way back.

She found Frida sitting on the ground with her legs crossed in front of Tinktink.

Frida looked at Hilda, eyes wide with excitement. "Did you know that Tink is seventy-two years old and still considered a child by her tempest?" She turned back to Tinktink. "That's what it's called, right, a tempest of dragons?"

"You are correct, young one."

"I can't imagine having to listen to Ma and Pa tell me to clean my room at seventy-two. Do your parents make you do chores, Tink?"

Tink. Hilda held back a snort at the familiarity. All of this, from the mountain spirit to the dragon, was absurd. Had Frida become friends with a dragon in the few minutes it took her to gather the potions? The girl was just full of surprises.

"Once a hatchling is able to fly on their own, they are considered a broodling and have the same freedoms of the tempest. Though I will not be permitted to attend council meetings until I reach a hundred winters."

"All of the freedom and none of the responsibility." Frida nodded approvingly. "Sounds like you are living the dream."

"It is a great honor to sit upon the council." Tinktink adjusted herself, and a prism of light reflected off her spikes and onto the wolf spirit, igniting a section of its foggy appearance with violet. *"I look forward to the day I am able."*

Hilda placed two of the three health potions she'd brought on the ground. "If you were a dwarf, a single potion would be enough to heal you, but I brought extras just in case. Are you ready?"

Tinktink inhaled deeply before her words spoke in Hilda's mind. *"You may proceed."*

Hilda uncorked the bottle and moved beside the dragon. "Open your mouth."

Tinktink did as instructed, revealing the full breadth of her teeth. She had four long, sharp canines at the front of her jaw, perfect for latching onto and incapacitating prey. There was a small gap to the inside of the upper canines where two hinged fangs rested against the roof of the dragon's mouth, allowing her to choose when to activate her venom. A line of equally sharp chisel-like incisors about a third of the size ran between the canines for biting and gripping. Along the sides, premolars and molars with serrated edges were capable of grinding and shearing through flesh and bone.

Under any other circumstance, to look upon the mouth of a dragon was to look upon death. Hilda tilted the bottle, pouring the cherry-red liquid into Tinktink's mouth.

The dragon grimaced as the liquid touched her tongue. She huffed and puffed, shaking her head in disgust.

When she finally stilled, her words resonated in Hilda's mind. *"That was unpleasant."*

"I doubt we have the same affinity for tastes." Hilda corked the empty bottle and set it on the ground. "We'll wait a few minutes before I give you another."

While they waited, Frida talked with Tinktink like they were new friends.

"Do you have any siblings? I have three brothers and a sister. I'm the oldest."

The dragon kept licking at the inside of her mouth and smacking her lips at the unpleasant taste. *"I do not. It is not often that my kind bears more than one offspring."*

"That's sad. My siblings can be annoying at times, but it's nice to have them to play with."

"When we are young, the hatchlings are raised together by the den mothers. It is not that different from your siblings in that regard. I was raised among three other hatchlings."

"Ooh! That sounds fun." Frida clapped her hands. "Were they all rattledrakes as well?"

"No. It is uncommon for there to be hatchlings of the same species. Our den consisted of a golden, an ironside, and a mirrorwing hatchling."

Frida was about to launch into another round of questions, which Hilda had to admit was fascinating, but it was time for the second bottle. The heat around the wounds had lessened, but they had yet to heal.

Hilda uncorked the second bottle, and an involuntary snarl passed across Tinktink's features.

The second potion was no more palatable than the first, and Hilda found herself concealing a smile as the dragon stated her revulsion. The wounds began to stitch themselves together, but it took another half-hour and a fourth bottle before the wing reset itself.

With her body mended, Tinktink extended her forepaws, stretching like a cat after a long nap. She extended her wings, nearly knocking Hilda over in the process. Each wing spread at least fifteen feet across, with beautiful golden coloring on the underside.

The mountain spirit, who had been watching silently, approached, weaving between the three of them. It nuzzled against Tinktink and then turned its burning eyes upon Hilda.

She froze as the spirit gazed into her soul. Then, as suddenly as it had appeared, the spirit dispersed. Its foggy body dissipated into the ether.

Tinktink preened as she tested her repaired wing and paw. Once she was satisfied, the dragon bowed in front of Hilda. *"You have aided me in a time of need. I owe you a debt of service."*

"That's not really necess—" Hilda stopped herself. "Actually, there is something you could help us with."

"Name it, and if it is within my power, it shall be done."

Hilda told Tinktink about their quest to scatter Frey's ashes and the journey ahead.

"Perhaps it is fate that we met, for my kin do not take kindly to interlopers upon our lands. I will guide you to your destination, but first, I require sustenance. It has been days since I last fed." She sniffed at the air. *"I smell prey."*

Tinktink took off in the direction of Morsel. The goat bleated, and started backpedaling toward the bridge.

"Wait!" Hilda shouted. "Wait, wait! You can't eat Morsel."

Tinktink skidded to a halt and looked at Hilda with suspicion. *"It is not wise to name your food."*

Hilda moved in front of the dragon, her hands held up defensively. "She's not food. She's our mount."

"Very well," Tinktink grunted. *"But I still require sustenance."*

Frida grinned as she held up her bow. "Then I guess it's time to hunt."

Hilda bit into a steaming piece of duck. The meat had a rich, savory flavor, almost like a blend of chicken and steak. Ducks were fattier than most birds due to their aquatic nature, and they had a distinct earthiness that came from wild game.

Frida had shot the bird from an impressive distance when they came upon a small pond earlier in the day. Now, she sat next to Hilda, lips smacking as she devoured the fruits of her labor. A fire crackled before them, offering a gentle warmth against the evening chill.

Tinktink lay on the ground, ripping into the carcass of a deer she'd caught, while Morsel stood a great distance away, watching the dragon warily. Hilda didn't blame the goat. Watching Tinktink tear through meat with ease was a not-so-subtle reminder of just what she was capable of.

"I thought dragons cooked their food," Frida said, wiping grease from her chin.

Tinktink looked up from her quarry as she chewed.

"Not all dragons breathe fire." She tore away another strip of meat. *"And charred meat is an acquired taste."*

"You don't breathe fire?" Frida's mouth hung agape as she turned to her grandmother. "Did you know this?"

Hilda shrugged. "As much as we might like to pretend we know the ways of dragons, we have barely scratched the surface of their culture. They are still mysterious creatures." She took a sip of water from her flask and looked upon Tinktink. "Can I ask you something?"

"You may."

"The mountain spirit, were you able to communicate with it?"

The dragon's golden eyes twinkled in the moonlight before she spoke. *"Not in the same way I am able to speak with you, but I could understand its intentions. It sensed my distress, and I knew the spirit was there to aid me."* There was a crunch as Tinktink snapped a bone in half. *"Spirits of the earth do not exist on a single plane like you and I. They are ever-present, a part of the mountain itself. When the need arises, they can take a physical form."*

"It's a good thing we were in the area," Frida said with a full mouth.

"It is fortunate," Tinktink echoed.

After she finished eating, Frida offered the dragon her leftover bones. Tinktink crunched upon them as the two dwarves settled in for the night.

Hilda placed Frey's urn by her bedroll. The two of them had witnessed some incredible moments during their travels, but nothing like this. Not only had she helped heal a dragon, but they'd gained a rattledrake as a traveling companion. In the words of her granddaughter, "No one was going to believe this." But Hilda didn't care.

There was a special comfort in the fact that on her last journey with Frey, there were still memories to be made.

"Good night, old friend." Hilda pressed her fingertips to the cool stone and waited for sleep to claim her.

Loud thunder startled Hilda awake. She hadn't sensed a storm coming, and her shoulder was only mildly uncomfortable, but she reached for the tarpaulin to cover their campsite, nonetheless. She looked up, puzzled. There was nothing but clear sky overhead. The thunderous noise rumbled again, and trees shook and rustled in the distance, followed by the angry squawk of birds as they flocked the air.

Another rockslide? Hilda wondered, though she'd never known this region to experience them so frequently. She tilted her head as the rumbling faded and something else took its place. This time, there was no denying the deep laughter that rolled down the mountainside.

Tinktink growled as she took to the air, her violet scales gleaming in the morning sun.

"Where are you going?" Hilda called after the dragon, but all she saw was a streak of purple moving above the trees.

Frida sat up at the disturbance, wiping sleep from her eyes. "Whasgoinon?" she mumbled, then frowned at the resounding cachinnations above them. "Is that laughter?"

"Certainly seems that way. Whatever it is has Tinktink in a mood," Hilda said as she searched for Morsel. She found the goat hiding behind a tree, her gaze fixed in the direction of Tinktink as she flew toward the mountaintop. Hilda whistled the goat over, then turned to Frida. "Stay here. I'm going to investigate."

She didn't wait for Frida's protests that were certainly coming as she climbed into the saddle. Morsel bleated her disapproval as they set off in pursuit of the dragon.

Unlike Tinktink, who could soar above the treetops on powerful wings, Morsel and Hilda were forced to traverse the steep mountainside. There were deep grooves in the earth with freshly upturned soil. Hilda had written the rockslides off as the aftermath of the storm before, but now, she believed there was something deeper at play.

Morsel ascended the unstable terrain with natural instincts that had been honed over thousands of years. Hilda jostled back and forth, holding on to the saddle horn for dear life as the rumble of deep laughter grew louder.

After a few intense moments, they reached a well-trodden path that led to the mountaintop. Through a break in the tree line, Hilda could see Tinktink hovering. She roared, and the sound set Hilda's hair on end.

"Come on, girl." She flicked the reins and Morsel sped up the path.

At the top, she found Tinktink baring her teeth as a giant heaved a boulder off the mountain. The dragon's scales sparkled in the sunlight, and the spikes along her back gleamed like polished jewels. There was a crash as the rock hit the ground, crushing trees and foliage as it rolled away.

Two other giants stood behind the first. All three howled with laughter, deep and boisterous like the thrum of a drum. The creatures were massive, ranging in height from eight to ten feet tall. Their bodies were powerfully built, all knotted muscle and calloused skin the russet brown of dried earth. Gray hair grew in patches about their bodies, and they wore rudimentary clothing made of fur and leather.

Tinktink dove at the first giant, and before it could react, she pinned it to the ground with the force of a creature twice her size. She bared her teeth, venomous fangs descending to hover inches from the giant's neck. The giant made a sound somewhere between a whimper and a groan, and all laughter died as the other two cowered behind a pile of boulders as tall as Morsel.

"What's going on here?" Hilda asked, though she'd already begun to fit the pieces together.

"Imbeciles." Irritation was evident in Tinktink's tone. She met Hilda's gaze but kept her fangs an inch from the giant's neck. Her golden eyes burned with intensity. *"I've seen hatchlings with more sense than the lot of them combined."*

Hilda held up a hand in a peaceful gesture. "Maybe we should calm down for a moment."

A deep growl emanated from Tinktink's chest. *"I should drain the life from every last one of them for what they did to me."*

"I'm sure they didn't intend to hurt you." Giants were simple creatures, after all. Powerful, but simple in their nature. They could be dangerous when provoked, based on their size and strength, but she'd never known them to be aggressive. She'd heard stories of giants amusing themselves by uprooting trees or throwing large objects from cliffs, but she'd never witnessed it herself until now. "They were just having fun."

"Fun." Tink let her fangs retract into her upper jaw, choosing to inject the venom into her words. *"This is not*

fun. This is idiocy. It would be a mercy to prune their bloodline."

She removed her paw from the giant's chest, and it backpedaled to join the others, speaking in a tongue Hilda could not understand.

Tinktink prowled back and forth, her tail swishing ominously with each step. Its rattle was a stark reminder of how close the giant had come to death. All three hid behind the pile of boulders like it might protect them, and every time Tinktink took a step closer, they would cower like frightened children. It was all Hilda could do not to laugh at the absurdity of the scene.

One of the giants, a female judging by her ample bosom, finally noticed Hilda and Morsel. She mumbled something unintelligible.

"What is she saying?" asked Hilda.

"To summarize such doltish ramblings: she asks for your help. She says that they were only making mischief and did not realize that such a magnificent creature as myself was in their midst." Some of the bite had left Tinktink's words as she held her head proudly. *"I suppose they cannot be blamed for their nature. They are dense creatures, after all. And their taste leaves much to be desired."*

Tinktink flicked her paw, and the giants bounded down the path without sparing a second glance in the dragon's direction.

"Ahh!" Frida dove to the side of the path as the giants passed by. When she stood, the girl was gasping for breath. "What..." She sucked in air. "...did...I miss?"

Without the threat of falling rock and the low visibility of fog, they made decent progress over the remainder of the day. Tinktink assured them that they would cross into dragon lands within a day or two.

"I bet it was fun," Frida said as she tossed a small rock and watched it bounce down the mountain. "I know it was dangerous, and they could have seriously hurt Tink, but I bet it was fun watching the boulders tear through the forest."

"*Two-leggeds.*" Tinktink huffed. "*Why are they always so infatuated with destruction?*"

"Excuse me?" Frida arched an eyebrow. "Was it your kin or mine who destroyed an entire city?"

Tinktink narrowed her gaze upon the young dwarf. "*Pyrrax had his reasons, but tell me, young one, how many cities have your people plundered? How many kingdoms have risen and fallen so that one may claim that which belongs to another?*"

"Fair point. I guess we've both been pretty destructive." Frida shrugged. "But that was in ages past. Since the Age of Unification, we've had peace and prosperity for nearly two thousand years now."

Tinktink snorted.

Hilda had no intention of antagonizing the dragon, so she changed the subject. "Pyrrax. Was that the name of the red dragon that destroyed Hells' Crag?"

"*Perhaps, though I am not familiar with the modern names for your cities. The elders still refer to it as Verrundral, the Dragon's Spear, from when dragons still conversed with the two-legged. It is said that Pyrrax unleashed his wrath upon the city and then battled a storm mage of great power. The elders*" *say Pyrrax flew north after the battle and has not been seen since."*

"That was over five hundred years ago." Frida's mouth dropped open. "Do you think he's still out there? How old can dragons live?"

"I do not know if he lives, but there are still ancients who flew the skies before the first two-legged had learned to conquer stone."

"Wow, I can't imagine living that long. That's even longer than the elves." Frida shook her head in disbelief. "So, hatchlings are the youngest, and then broodlings like you are old enough to wander on their own, but not old enough to be on the council. And then you have the elders who are at least a hundred years old. How long does one have to live to be an ancient?"

Tinktink turned to face Hilda. *"Do all of your young ones ask this many questions?"*

Hilda laughed. "In my experience, if they're not eating or causing trouble, then they're probably asking questions."

"Not that different from a hatchling." Tinktink unfurled her wings. *"You know what we do when hatchlings ask too many questions?"*

"What do you do?" asked Frida.

Tinktink launched herself into the air.

Frida chased after the dragon as she disappeared above the trees. "Tink! What do you do?"

The dragon kept flying away.

The morning chill kissed Hilda's cheeks, tousling the wispy ends of her silver beard. In the distance, she could see the white caps of the Forgotten Peaks, and nearer, the last ridge before they crossed into the dragon lands.

Ahead of her, Frida walked beside Tinktink. The girl had been especially inquisitive this morning, peppering the dragon with questions.

"If I ate something that you killed with your venom, would I get sick?" Frida asked.

"Unlikely." Tinktink's tail rattled softly as it swished through the air. *"Venom is not poisonous."*

Frida stopped. "What the hells does that mean?" A deep crease formed in her brow as she looked to her grandmother for insight.

Tinktink huffed, and Hilda did her best not to laugh.

"I thought you paid attention during class?" Hilda smirked.

Frida rolled her eyes. "I'm supposed to remember every little thing that's said to me?"

"It would save us from repeating ourselves." She enjoyed teasing her granddaughter, but truthfully, she liked sharing her knowledge. "Snorri had a saying that helps me remember the difference between the two. 'Venom is injected. Poison is ingested.'"

"That's good to know." Frida pulled her journal from her pocket and scribbled some notes. "But what does it mean?"

Hilda chuckled. "It means that venom is toxic when injected into the bloodstream, like a snake bite or a scorpion sting. Poison is toxic when ingested, either through the lungs, skin, or mouth. This could be from a mushroom, a plant, or a secretion like some frogs or slimes produce. Poison is usually a defense mechanism, while venom is for attacking."

Frida frowned. "So why wouldn't I get sick if I ate the venomous meat?"

"Because venom needs to enter the bloodstream to have an effect." Hilda rolled up her sleeve, pointing to a vein. "I guess, technically, it could be harmful if you had an open wound in your mouth or stomach."

"Which is unlikely," Tinktink reiterated before taking to the sky. A telltale sign that she'd had enough questions for the time being.

Hilda watched as the dragon soared overhead, her body radiant in the morning sun. She wondered if the dragon riders of old ever got used to seeing such beauty.

Due to Frida's curious nature, they'd learned more about dragonkind in the past two days than most scholars learned in their entire lives. Hilda knew a few academics who would happily part with their right arm for the opportunity to speak candidly with a dragon.

Tinktink had no reservations sharing her knowledge, and whenever she'd had enough questions, the dragon would fly away for a moment of respite, much to Morsel's appreciation.

The goat seemed to be warming to the dragon, at least as much as prey could toward a predator. She still watched Tinktink with a wary eye, but she no longer hid out of sight while in the dragon's presence.

Hilda scratched the goat behind the ear. "You're a big, tough girl, aren't you?"

Morsel bleated her agreement.

"Are we there yet?" asked Frida.

Hilda sighed. "How many times do I have to tell you—"

"I'm just messing with you." The girl waggled her brows.

Hilda chuckled at the amused expression on her granddaughter's face. "Very funny, Frida."

By midafternoon, they'd reached the final stretch leading to the ridge between the dwarven mountains and the dragon lands. The dense trees grew sparser, and the landscape transitioned to lush grass, strewn with giant boulders and patches of wildflowers still in bloom. Morsel frolicked among the daisies, eating them in droves.

Tinktink had flown ahead and was waiting for them at the top of the ridge. The white-capped mountains of the Forgotten Peaks loomed beyond.

Frida stopped, pausing to look at the far-off mountains. "What do you think it'll be like on the other side?"

Hilda pondered. She didn't really know what to

expect. Dragonkind were known for their destruction, but did that mean they'd be walking into scorched and ruined lands or were dragons more mindful of the areas they called home?

"I don't know." Hilda stroked her beard. "You'd think at my age, there would be very little that surprises me, but this journey has been proof of just how wrong that sentiment can be. The world is full of wonder, and I'm grateful for a chance to experience it, whatever lies in store."

"Adults." Frida let out an exasperated sigh. "Always dodging the difficult questions. I bet we're going to see a giant graveyard where all of the dragons leave the bones of their prey. It's going to be epic!" She rubbed her hands together mischievously. "Race you to the top!"

Frida took off running, her pack jostling with each step.

"You don't seriously think I'm going to—" Hilda abandoned the words as her competitive nature took over, and the urge to run consumed her. "You're on!"

Frida looked over her shoulder to see if her grandmother was actually following and stumbled, dropping to one knee.

Hilda nudged her granddaughter in the shoulder as she passed. "Not bad for an old lady, eh?" She barked with laughter.

The girl tossed her pack to the ground for added speed. Hilda had no such worry with her pack strapped to Morsel, who was enjoying a mouthful of wildflowers. When the goat noticed the excitement, she tossed her head and kicked at the earth before bounding up the mountain after them.

Frida was closing the distance, now only a few paces behind.

Halfway up the ridge, Hilda's muscles began to cramp and her lungs were burning, but she refused to quit. It had been at least fifty years since she'd run like this, back when her children were young. Old age might have softened her a bit, but she still had the heart of an adventurer. She still had the fervor that had taken over in countless taverns and guild halls across the realm when she'd been challenged at anything from darts to drinking.

Frida pulled even with Hilda, but this time, she kept a safe distance between them. "See you at the top, old lady." She grinned as she gathered her second wind and increased her pace.

Hilda growled. Frida had made the mistake of challenging the great Hilda Rockfall, and now her granddaughter was about to learn just how unwise a decision that was.

She removed the handaxe attached to her belt and tossed it. The head of the axe buried in the ground just as Frida's foot touched the earth, tripping the girl and sending her sprawling.

"Gram, what the hells!" She grimaced as her grandmother passed her by.

Hilda looked over her shoulder and winked. "Sorry, kid."

At the top of the ridge, Hilda doubled over, trying to catch her breath. A painful stitch throbbed in her side, and the muscles in her legs trembled, but it was worth it to see the look on Frida's face. She chuckled between heaving breaths. "I've still got it."

"It is the job of elders to show the young ones their place."

There was a humorous tone to Tinktink's voice. *"Many times have I had my scales counted by those greater than myself."*

"Gram, you nearly chopped off my—" There was a long pause. "Oh, my." The words were barely a whisper.

Hilda followed her granddaughter's gaze, taking in their surroundings for the first time. Sprawling hills and gorgeous meadows stretched across the valley, where low-lying clouds hung in the air like soft pillows. Further out, more mountains than she could count extended beyond the Forgotten Peaks and into the Frozen North.

The scene reminded her of a painting, serene and beautiful. She gasped when she saw the first dragon pass through a cloud on the far side of the valley. It soared across the sky, golden scales shimmering brighter than a hoard of treasure. There were at least two dozen dragons in various shapes and sizes. Some she could identify, but many more she'd never seen or heard of. A pair of iron-hide dragons perched on a mountain, their dark metallic scales giving the appearance of iron sculptures. In the distance, the silver wings of the mirrorwing dragon produced a blinding reflection as they caught the light. Below, a dragon with a large, hooked snout burrowed in the earth while a statuesque stone dragon nearly three times as large as Tinktink bathed in the sun. The two heads of a twin-headed dragon nipped at one another before taking flight on their powerful wings.

"I didn't expect there to be so many," Frida whispered. "And so close to one another."

"This is but a fraction of our numbers." Tinktink gestured with her front paw at the distant mountains. *"Hundreds of my kin reside among the mountains beyond."*

"That's a lot of dragons." Frida spared Morsel a look of concern. "Do you think it's safe to bring Morsel with us?"

"Do not worry about the hairy four-legged. She will be safe under my protection."

"No offense, Tink, but those dragons are a lot bigger than you."

Morsel bleated her own concerns.

The dragon huffed. *"It is not the breadth of wings but the fire in the heart."*

Frida leaned in close to her grandmother and whispered, "But Tink said she doesn't breathe fire."

"I heard that." Tinktink's gaze narrowed on the young dwarf.

"It's not that I doubt you." Frida gestured at the sprawling lands. "I'm just saying that is *a lot* of dragons."

The girl truly was fearless. Three days with a dragon and Frida was already teasing it.

Hilda shook her head as she pulled the map from her pocket and opened it. Based on the route they'd taken through Deepwarden and the position of the lake and valley, she was able to approximate their location. She turned the parchment until the mountain ranges lined up before them. Among a section of six mountains, one rose above the others, its top curved like the tooth of a dragon.

She swallowed at the prospect of crossing such dangerous terrain. The location Frey had chosen wasn't taking them to the edge of dragon country; it was taking them through it. *Gods, he was such a bastard.*

Hilda drew an X in the air where the mountain loomed. "That's where we're going."

24. DRAGONLANDS

Hilda wasn't sure how much time passed as she and Frida stood atop the ridge simply watching the dragons exist in their natural habitat. There was something mesmerizing about the creatures. As nervous as she was, Hilda could have spent the entire day content just to be in their presence.

Tinktink had no such notions, reminding them that they still had a ways to travel, so they set off deeper into the land of dragons.

Walking through an open meadow surrounded by dozens of the realm's most dangerous creatures went against Hilda's every instinct, no matter how beautiful they were, but Tinktink insisted everything would be fine. So far, the other dragons seemed oblivious to their presence, but that did little to put Hilda's racing heart at ease. Morsel was visibly uncomfortable, clinging especially close to her owner.

Hilda scratched the goat behind the ear, offering comfort even though it felt like she was bringing a glazed ham into a den of wolves.

"I am with you. Do not worry." Tink held her head high, her amethyst scales gleaming as she led their party across the valley.

"You keep saying that." Frida walked beside the dragon with the confidence only youth could provide. "But it's kind of like if I took Gram down to Basilisk Bay and said everything would be fine just because I used to play pirates with my brothers."

"I do not know this Basilisk Bay."

"It's a pirate stronghold in the far south," Hilda answered, holding tightly onto Morsel's reins. "It's known for attracting the more unsavory sort."

"Like giants." Tinktink's lips curled back in a display of revulsion. *"They are truly vile-tasting creatures."*

"Not quite what I meant." Hilda chuckled.

There was a loud screech as a brownish-green dragon appeared in the sky.

"Look. Gram!" Frida pointed. "It's a clubtail."

The dragon had a ball-shaped knob on the end of its tail, similar to Tinktink's rattle. Behind it, a larger clubtail followed, its scales much darker. It roared as it pursued the smaller dragon, which darted back and forth through the air as if they were playing a game of cat and mouse. The smaller dragon landed on the mountainside, hiding behind a rockface, and the larger dragon dove, using its hardened tail like a mace to smash the stone to rubble.

The smaller dragon screeched and darted in the direction of two massive ironhide dragons perched nearby. It nestled between their wings for safety while the larger clubtail hovered in the air, roaring its challenge.

One of the ironhides stirred, extending its wings and stretching its forepaws.

"Are they fighting?" asked Frida.

"Worse." Tinktink's tail rattled slightly. *"They are siblings."*

Frida frowned. "How is that worse?"

Hilda cackled, remembering how many vases and stoneware her own children had broken while frolicking through the house. "Some things transcend species."

She watched as the largest ironhide leapt from the cliff and soared to a more peaceful location. The smaller clubtail peeked around the wing of the remaining ironhide. Its tongue licked at the air, and its tail twitched back and forth as if taunting its sibling.

The larger clubtail dove, but it quickly retreated at the threatening growl of the remaining ironhide.

"Come." Tinktink looked back from several paces ahead. *"There is still far to go before we reach Raeth's Tooth."*

"Raeth's Tooth?" Hilda scrunched her brow. "I've never heard that name before."

"Raeth was an obsidian. Wise beyond measure. The elders say she led the council for two thousand years, and that she used to sit upon the highest peak to watch over all of dragonkind."

"What happened to her?" Frida asked.

"There was an attack." Tinktink paused a moment before continuing. *"Long before my time. Before the Cursed Ones protected the north, and before your people had settled the mountains. A behemoth came into our lands and located our hatching grounds. Raeth attempted to defend the eggs from the interloper. She was a mighty dragon, one of the few obsidians to rival a red in size. It is said that she lost a leg when attempting*

to carry the creature away. With no other options, she consumed the behemoth and flew north."

Frida gasped. "It killed her?"

"From the inside."

Hilda didn't need further details. She'd heard the horror stories of behemoths that had made it past the Northern Guard and into Mount Tor. There were some tales that were embellished as fables to warn children of what might happen if they didn't eat their vegetables or go to sleep at a proper hour. When it came to behemoths, the tales of their destruction failed to do them justice. Hilda had scoured the archives as a young adventurer, and some of the accounts still sent chills down her spine.

Behemoths were unlike anything else in the animal kingdom. They were like gargantuan bears, but with armored scales, steel-like claws, and magically resistant hides, unkillable by the most powerful elemental mages and immune to dragon fire. Only blood mages were capable of bringing one down, and there were precious few of those poor souls throughout the realm. Only at great personal cost could a blood mage stop the beating heart of a behemoth.

"I'm sorry," Hilda said. "That's a terrible way for anything to go."

Tinktink didn't answer as she turned to lead them on. Hilda was grateful that in all her years of adventuring, she'd never had to travel into the Frozen North. The wilds were plenty dangerous, as were many of the southern outposts, but if one went too far north, they didn't return.

By late afternoon, they'd left the valley behind and were once again traveling among mountainous terrain. Dragon sightings became more infrequent, but Hilda would occasionally hear a nearby roar or the flap of wings.

As she settled down for the night, Hilda lay against the coldstone, relishing the icy touch against her aching shoulder. The weeks on the road were beginning to catch up to her, though she'd never admit it in front of Frida. She closed her eyes, listening to the distant rumblings of nocturnal dragons. There was such variety in their calls. Some were deep and cavernous, others more grating or screech-like, but they were all fascinating.

Morsel chose to sleep close this evening; her massive frame pressed to Hilda as if the goat didn't weigh more than a boulder. Frey's urn rested on Hilda's chest as she listened, and it wasn't long before Frida's snores joined the draconic lullaby.

Hilda gazed into the flecked stone of the urn. "Our journey is nearing its end, old friend." She held her hand to its cool surface. "You're a real ass for sending me here, but truthfully, this has been a gift I didn't know I needed. It's been amazing to watch Frida come into her own, and though my body may not be what it once was, I feel a fire burning inside me again. The call of adventure never really goes away, does it?"

"It is strange that you talk to the vessel as if it can hear you."

Hilda jumped at Tinktink's words, and Frey's urn fell onto its side. "Gods. Tink! You startled me." She picked up the urn, ensuring the latches were still fastened. "I thought you were asleep."

Frida mumbled something under her breath before turning over.

"I was resting."

Hilda sat up, cradling the urn in her lap. "Do your kind not talk to those who have passed on?"

Tinktink stretched, and there was a soft rattle as she moved to face Hilda. *"We carry their memories with us, but we do not commune with them."*

"We do. Some cultures bury the dead so that their loved ones may return to them." She held up the urn. "Others burn the bodies and keep the ashes to honor their memory. Frey was like a brother to me, and I like to think there is still part of him that's holding on until this quest is over."

"Perhaps it is you who is holding on."

"On that, we can both agree." Hilda returned the coldstone to its traveling box and settled in once again.

Tinktink lowered her head to the ground, saying no more on the subject.

The dragon was right; Hilda wasn't ready to let go. As wonderful as this quest had been, she was dreading the end of it. Sure, she missed her husband, children, and grandchildren, and the beautiful chaos of a home filled with family, but she'd missed this, too. She'd forgotten just how much.

Hilda wondered what Boric was up to right now. She imagined her husband in the kitchen, tired but unable to sleep, with a flour-stained apron around his neck as he made his best attempt at her honey crumble.

The dwarf loved her with the fiery passion of Pidros's hammer. She could only imagine how empty the bed must feel to him without her presence. Hilda wasn't sure what she'd done to deserve the love of such an understanding dwarf, but she was grateful all the same.

And poor Flint and Maela. Those two must be worried sick about Frida.

Not for much longer, though.

For the first time since Hilda had left Stonefist Hold, her shoulder hurt more upon waking than the night before. She grimaced as she packed away her bedroll.

"Everything okay, Gram?" Frida asked as she helped load the gear onto Morsel.

"Just the aches and pains that come with age." Hilda winked. "Nothing your gram can't handle."

"We can slow down if you need to. I know we're close, but we still have a long way back home."

Hilda wrapped an arm around her granddaughter. "I appreciate the concern, but I'm fine. I promise."

"There is a watering hole up ahead." Tink spread her wings, revealing a myriad of purple-hued scales. *"The four-legged can drink, and you may replenish your stores. Then, we will be on our way. Follow me."* Tinktink didn't wait for acknowledgment before taking to the air.

Frida pumped her fist. "Off we go!"

A half-hour later, they found Tinktink beside a pool of water, the sun warming her jewel-colored body. A waterfall poured from the mountain with a dull roar, leaving a prismatic mist that sparkled in the morning light. The water was crystal clear. Silver fish darted beneath, and a family of turtles sunbathed on a log. Beyond the rushing water, a cave system disappeared into the mountain.

Hilda filled her canteen and sat upon the bank,

soaking her tired feet in the frigid water. "Ah, that feels good."

Gooseflesh sprouted along her legs. Even this late in the year, the mountain peaks were snowcapped, and their run-off provided plenty of water for its springs and waterways.

Morsel stepped into the pool, splashing water and drinking as if she might not have another opportunity.

A moment later, Frida removed her boots and joined them, putting her stubby toes in the water. "Oh, wow, that's cold."

Hilda grinned. "Cold, but great for tired feet. If you ever have the chance, you should try the hot springs near Crowhold. One bath and you'll feel like a new person."

"Crowhold?" Frida raised her brows. "That's on the other side of the realm."

"If you become an adventurer, you never know where the quests will take you."

"When." Frida splashed Hilda with water. "It's not *if* I become an adventurer. It's when." She leaned back on her hands, letting the sun kiss her cheeks. "And technically, I already am."

Hilda scooped a handful of water and flung it at her granddaughter. "When you join the guild, then, how about that?"

Frida stuck out her tongue. "That sounds better. I can't wait to—"

There was a loud thud behind them, followed by a rush of air. Morsel whimpered, and the large goat tried to hide behind the two diminutive dwarves.

Hilda turned to see a blue dragon towering ominously, a low growl rumbling in its chest. The dragon was massive, dwarfing Tinktink like a rabbit next to a dire-wolf. Most of its scales were a deep, sapphire blue, except for a streak of white that ran down its chest and along the interior of its wings. It had a single white horn just above its brow and several smaller ones along its lower jaw. Thick, black talons dug several inches into the ground as it sniffed the air.

There was another gust as a slightly smaller golden landed, though it was still easily three to four times bigger than Tinktink. A moment later, a twin-headed dragon joined, this one rivaling the blue in size.

Frida gasped, and her hand clenched Hilda's arm.

Whether because of fear, admiration, or a combination of both, Hilda found it difficult to take her eyes off the golden. Its scales shimmered with every movement, so intense that its entire body could have been sculpted from the metal. She forced herself to look upon the twin-headed dragon, and when she did, it was equally as mesmerizing. One half of its body was solid black, the other a vibrant white, as if two separate dragons had been stitched together at the middle. A singular tail forked halfway down, each end twitching like a cat about to pounce. The black head had ram's horns that curled around its angular face, while the white had two short nubs and a wider jaw. Both had their eyes locked on Morsel.

Tinktink's tail rattled threateningly as the smaller dragon stepped protectively in front of the dwarves and the frightened goat.

25. A TASTE

Hilda's heart thundered in the presence of the three giant dragons. There was no escape from their fearsome gaze. Even if her legs weren't as gelatinous as an ooze, it was unlikely they could make it to the caves behind the waterfall without being burned alive.

She placed her hand on top of Frida's and forced herself to take a deep breath. In situations like this, it was crucial to remain calm. For now, their fates were tied to the young rattledrake standing protectively in front of them.

To Tinktink's credit, she showed no fear, even as her tail rattled like a swarm of bees.

The blue dragon's lips curled back in a snarl. *"What cause do you have to bring outsiders into our lands?"*

His voice rumbled in Hilda's mind, harsh like the grind of metal on rock. Beside her, Frida's face twisted as she rubbed at her temple. Hilda applied pressure to her granddaughter's hand, offering the only comfort she could in this situation.

Tinktink stood between them and evisceration, but what could she do against three adults?

"My business is my own," the juvenile rattledrake said defiantly.

The blue dragon lowered his head, and Hilda could smell the stench of sulfur on his breath. *"What business does a broodling have with a two-legged?"* his voice boomed.

Tinktink's tail rattled in warning. *"It is none of your concern, Sapphyrax."*

The golden dragon stepped forward, every movement of its body like molten gold. *"Your business concerns us all, Amethyra. Especially when you bring it into our lands."* Her tone was less aggressive than the blue's, alluring in a way that could spell the doom of many.

The white head of the twin-headed dragon sniffed at the air. *"We smells something tasty. Don't we, sister?"*

"Not now, Sollak." The black head nipped at the jaw of the white.

"Just a taste." Sollak licked his lips as he eyed Morsel greedily.

Tinktink hissed, and her fangs descended from her jaw. *"Try and it will be the last thing you taste."*

"Little Tinktink," Sapphyrax spoke with a mocking tone. *"Do you really wish to challenge an elder?"*

Tinktink's wings flexed. *"I will challenge any who threaten those under my protection."*

"As is your right." The golden dragon was the only one who seemed to have a level head at the moment. *"But are you prepared for the consequences?"*

Tinktink took a step forward, and to Hilda's surprise, the twin-headed dragon stepped back. *"Are you?"*

"So small, yet so violent." Sapphyrax laughed. It was a

disturbing, savage sound. His neck twisted to face the twin-headed dragon. *"Lunnak, I suggest you control your lesser half, lest little Tink give you both a taste of her rancor."*

Lunnak, the black head, snorted. *"It is a cruel joke that the young have the most potent venom while their minds are still so feeble."*

This time, it was Tinktink's turn to laugh. *"How insightful, considering half of you has an empty flame and the other has hollow scales and ashes for brains. Tell me, which one are you again?"*

Frida leaned in close to her grandmother and whispered, "Why is she insulting them? That seems like a bad idea."

Hilda pressed a finger to her lips. The last thing they needed was attention on them. She agreed with her granddaughter, but then again, she knew very little of the ways of dragons.

"You insolent little wretch, I'll show you an empty flame." Lunnak's voice held a furious edge as both heads reared back like they were about to attack.

"ENOUGH!" The golden dragon's voice cut like sharpened steel. *"Sollak, Lunnak, if your scales are this thin, then take them elsewhere. We did not come here to fight. We came for answers."*

The two dragon heads continued to fume. Lunnak huffed, and then they flew away to the mutterings of her twin.

Hilda took another steadying breath and squeezed Frida's hand. Perhaps there was hope, after all.

Sapphyrax picked at his teeth with a massive claw, dislodging a piece of red meat that could feed an entire dwarven family. *"Aurelia never lets them have any fun."*

The golden, Aurelia, glared at Sapphyrax. *"They should learn to better control their impulses. We are dragons, not felines in heat."*

"And yet..." The blue dragon's gaze lingered on Tinktink. *"This one flies beyond our borders whenever she wishes, even though she is not of age to do so, and now, she brings interlopers into our lands. How much insolence must we endure?"*

"You know she wishes to become a warden."

"Then she must wait like I did. Like everyone else. There is no special treatment, even for the progeny of the great Shattered Gem."

Aurelia turned to Tinktink, but she lacked the disdain Sapphyrax seemed to carry. *"Amethyra, I trust that you have your reasons for bringing the two-leggeds into our lands. It is not forbidden, but it is unwise. If you would help us understand, we can inform the council and be done with this."*

Tinktink put her fangs away, and the rattle in her tail faded to a soft rustle. *"They are under my protection for providing aid when I was injured. I was feeding beyond the borders when a rock fell upon me, crushing my wing and paw. Stupid giants and their games. I was unable to fly, and so the spirit of the mountain found me, bringing aid so that the elder two-legged could heal my wounds. On my honor, I agreed to guide them to Raeth's Tooth."*

"Why does a two-legged need to go to Raeth's Tooth?" The words rumbled in Hilda's mind as Sapphyrax's eyes narrowed.

Tinktink looked over her shoulder.

"It's a long story. I—" Hilda gulped, immediately wishing she hadn't spoken as the dragons' gaze fell upon her.

"She wants to scatter the ashes of her oldest friend

upon the mountain," added Frida, who didn't have the same concern. "It was his dying wish. If you allow us to pass, we'll leave as soon as we are done."

The two elder dragons watched the girl, almost puzzled that she could speak.

"*Very well.*" Aurelia turned her attention back to Tinktink. "*I do not approve, but it is not within my power to deny you.*" She turned to leave, pausing for the blue dragon to do the same.

Sapphyrax lowered his head until he was only a few feet away from Tinktink. "*Your mother will hear of this.*"

Tinktink huffed, but she said nothing. The blue dragon kept his gaze upon her, and after a long, tense moment, he took to the skies.

The golden remained, her watchful eyes taking in everything until finally, she spoke. "*I was once like you, young Amethyra. I pushed boundaries and took risks, earning the ire of many elders. For all of his bluster, Sapphyrax is a rule-follower. Both the council and the wardens thrive off order, but there is a place for those like us. You must choose when to push boundaries and when to fall in line. There is a time for controlled burns, but a wildfire consumes everything in its path.*" She turned without waiting for a response.

Tinktink watched silently as Aurelia took to the air.

Frida collapsed on the ground, her breaths heavy for a moment until she sat up like a corpse raised from the dead. "That. Was. Awesome!" she shouted, her braid whipping behind her with the sudden movement.

Hilda watched the girl with amazement. She'd known grown men who would have soiled their pants under the circumstances. Her granddaughter had not only remained calm, but she was itching for more.

The girl held up her hands, which were still shaking, and showed them to her grandmother, smiling the whole time. "I was so scared but, wow, that was a rush. Is this what it's always like when you're in a dangerous situation?"

"Sometimes." Hilda paused to calm her own racing heart. "But I only ever knew one person who became calmer the more intense a situation was."

"Who?"

Hilda turned toward Morsel, who was still cowering in the water. She pointed at the satchel containing the urn. "Frey." She chuckled. "Somehow, the more chaotic the circumstances, the better of a leader he became. It was like a lever flipped. One minute, he'd be a complete menace, teasing Brok and looking for danger, but once the danger came, he never faltered, almost like he could see two steps ahead. He still took his lumps from time to time, but that comes with the territory."

"I wish I could have known him."

"He would have loved you." Hilda grinned.

Frida turned to Tinktink. "Thank you for protecting us, Tink. That was the bravest thing I've ever seen."

Tinktink snorted. *"Sapphyrax looks a terror, but he is all smoke, no flame."*

Frida shrugged. "He's still pretty scary-looking, though."

"Size does not make one great." Tinktink's tail flicked back and forth, and Hilda had the impression the young dragon was still agitated. *"I thought you would understand that."*

"Oh, I do." Frida grinned. "I just meant that you looked

fearsome standing your ground against three bigger dragons."

"The odds are irrelevant. I promised to escort you safely through these lands, and that is what I intend to do."

There was a splash as Morsel climbed out of the pool. Water dripped from her shaggy coat as she approached Tinktink, and to Hilda's surprise, the goat nuzzled against the dragon, a slight whine escaping as she did so.

Tinktink appeared so shocked by the display that she just blinked at Morsel. *"What is the meaning of this?"*

Frida's mouth twisted into a smirk. "I think she likes you."

As if in agreement, Morsel pressed her wet tongue to Tinktink's neck and licked. Frida burst out laughing.

Tinktink let out a low growl and unfurled her wings. *"It is time to go."*

The dragon took off, and Morsel followed.

26. OUT ON A LIMB

By evening, thick clouds had formed above the mountains, obscuring the sun and casting the land in a dreary gray. Without the forest for cover, the wind had a biting chill that nipped at Hilda's cheeks. She pulled up her hood and leaned forward, stroking Morsel's fur. This high above the tree line, the air was thinner than she was used to, and she was thankful for the goat's steadfast constitution.

Frida seemed unfazed by the change in elevation as she trudged up the ridge alongside Tinktink. "What did Sapphyrax mean when he said, 'Your mother will hear of this'?"

The dragon huffed. She'd been quiet for the majority of the day after their encounter with the three wardens, choosing to walk or fly ahead of their party, but she'd finally slowed enough for the young dwarf to catch up.

"My mother is the archwarden. It is her duty to maintain the integrity of our borders, and Sapphyrax will take great

delight in informing her of my deeds. The two are alike in many ways, and she is not always as understanding as my gram. Some call her the Thorn Warden, though they would never say it in her presence."

Hilda smiled at the dragon's use of their vernacular.

"Why do you do it if you know you'll get in trouble?" asked Frida.

The elder dwarf barked with laughter at the sincerity of the question.

"What?" Frida looked over her shoulder, brow scrunched.

"Oh, nothing." Hilda grinned. She leaned forward and scratched Morsel behind the ears to keep from laughing again. "Carry on."

"Dragons were not meant to be caged. There is a wide world beyond our borders, and I wish to see its beauty."

"I'd hardly call this a cage. There's nothing but open wilderness for as far as we can see. And beauty…" Frida gestured at the mountains stretching in perpetuity all around them. "This is beauty."

"But how am I to know unless I see for myself?"

"That makes sense." Frida nodded. "I guess it's not that different from me following Gram on her adventure." She turned, narrowing her eyes at her grandmother. "Hey! Is that why you were laughing?"

Hilda held up a hand. "Guilty, but I'm glad you came to the conclusion on your own."

The girl crossed her arms. "I told you I was perceptive."

Tinktink stopped and sniffed the air.

"Is everything okay?" asked Frida.

The dragon closed her eyes, and there was a long pause before she answered. *"It would be wise to rest for the night."*

Morsel nuzzled against Tinktink's side. Her fear of the predator had seemingly evaporated after their earlier exchange.

Tink's lip curled in a snarl, and she pushed Morsel away with a paw. *"This is most unwelcome."*

The goat bleated and then pressed her horns to the dragon's chest. Tinktink sighed in resignation.

A shiver passed through Hilda as she woke the next morning. She snuggled deeper into her bedroll for a few more minutes of rest, closing her eyes tighter to fight against the orange glow of daylight creeping at the corners of her eyelids. As she settled in, she had a sinking suspicion that something was off. Everything was unnaturally quiet.

In the wilderness, that was never a good sign.

Something crunched softly behind her, and Hilda peeked above the bedroll, wincing at the unnatural brightness. Several moments passed before her eyes adjusted to the blinding white snow blanketing the landscape.

"Seven hells," she muttered.

There was another odd, muffled crunch before Morsel's giant head hovered above Hilda. The goat had a mouthful of snow, and her fur was dusted with frost.

Frida was still asleep nearby, a thin layer of snowflakes

dusting the girl's red hair. She looked peaceful as her slow breaths steamed against the cool air.

Tinktink was nowhere to be seen, but there was a grassy, dragon-shaped indentation on the other side of the fire's smoldering embers. The snow must have stopped falling before she left.

Hilda sat up, her bones creaking from the movement. She patted Morsel on the jaw as slobber fell, melting a crater in the snow. "Any idea where Tinktink is? Off hunting is my guess."

Morsel bleated her agreement, and Frida stirred at the noise, pulling her blanket up to her chin.

Hilda scooped a handful of snow and let it fall through her fingers. She sighed. "This is unfortunate, old girl."

Every so often, an early snow would cover the top of Stonefist Hold, but never this early in the year. The leaves had barely even begun to change, but perhaps the weather was more erratic this far north.

Hilda raised a hand over her eyes, squinting as she surveyed their surroundings. The clouds had disappeared during the night and now, the sun beamed in all its glory. There was a chance the snow might melt if the temperature rose, but it was impossible to predict what the higher elevations had in store. Mud and runoff would be difficult to navigate, but ice was the real danger.

Tinktink could fly, and Morsel was skilled enough to cross dangerous terrain, but Frida might be forced to join Hilda on a saddle meant for one going forward.

She shook the snow from her cloak and wrapped it around her shoulders. She picked up Frey's urn and wiped the frost off the dark stone. "I'm sure you're getting a real laugh out of this, aren't you?"

She called Morsel closer and unfastened the satchel for storing the urn. As she raised it, the slick stone slipped from her cold fingers. She tried to gain control, but it was like trying to squeeze an ooze. Her left leg slid in the snow, and her footing gave way. The urn shot from her grasp like wet soap, landing on the ground and sliding down the sloping terrain. Frey's remains carved a trench through the untouched snow, its smooth surface gliding like a sled.

"No!" Hilda shouted as she chased after the runaway urn. She stumbled in her panicked state, falling face-first before pursuing in a mad dash. "No, no, no, no, no."

The urn's momentum slowed as it neared the edge of the cliff and drifted to a stop, teetering on the precipice.

"Easy," Hilda said as she cautiously approached. "Pidros, Elohr, Ahteus, if any of you are listening, I could use some help right now," she prayed to the Gods of Mining, Fire, and Fortune. "Please, please, please, don't let me lose this urn."

"Gram," Frida called groggily from up the mountain. "What's going on?"

Hilda ignored her granddaughter. Right now, every bit of her attention was focused on the urn. She stepped forward, and the snow around the urn shifted. There was a soft crunch as snow dislodged, and the urn tumbled over the cliff.

She rushed forward, crawling on her stomach to peer over the edge. Her heart sank as she saw the drop into rocky terrain below. Tears brimmed at the edge of her vision. They'd gotten so close.

She searched for pieces of broken stone among the rocks. There was nothing. Then she noticed the urn.

By the grace of the gods, it had lodged in the skeletal branches of a tree sprouting from the cliffside. The tree was dead, its bark dried and brittle, and the specks of snow upon the dark wood nearly camouflaged the vessel.

Snow crunched as Frida joined her grandmother, crawling beside her to look over the edge. "Uh-oh."

"Yeah," Hilda concurred. This was a big uh-oh. The branch was about ten feet down, impossible to reach from their current position and too high to grab from below. If Tinktink were here, she could grasp it with her claws, but the dragon was nowhere to be seen. The thin branches didn't look very strong, and there was no telling how long they could hold the weight before snapping. If Hilda was going to save her friend, she needed to act fast.

She stood, mapping out the best way to reach the bottom of the cliff. There were a few places where they could descend onto outcroppings, but nothing that led to the bottom unless they traveled back down the ridge.

"What are you going to do? And where is Tink?" Frida looked over her shoulder toward camp. "And why is it so cold all of a sudden? It didn't look like it was going to snow."

"I don't know," Hilda answered, her response covering all three questions.

She walked along the ridge until she found a rocky decline to an outcropping halfway down the cliff. It didn't reach the urn, but it allowed for a better view of the situation.

The urn was balanced precariously on the old branches. It had landed on its side with one of the handles facing skyward. Cracks had formed along the bark from the impact, revealing lighter-colored wood. It was a miracle it hadn't fallen already.

Hilda had an inkling of an idea.

She called up to Frida, "Run back to camp. Grab my bow, arrows, and the spool of fishing line."

Frida gave her grandmother a questioning look before the crunch of snow announced that she was following the request.

While she retrieved the gear, Hilda surveyed the cliffside, searching for somewhere she might be able to anchor the waxed string on the other side of the urn. From her current angle, there was nothing but solid rock along the cliff. She climbed back up, her shoulder aching from the effort, and set off further down the ridge. She found a small ledge, about fifty yards away, and waited for her granddaughter to return.

Frida ran through the snow, nearly slipping several times in her haste. Morsel followed. The girl's breath came in heaving clouds as she handed the gear to Hilda.

"Thank you," Hilda said as she tossed the quiver over her shoulder. "I'm going to need your help in case this doesn't work."

Frida's eyes sparkled with anticipation. "Tell me what to do."

"If you go down the ridge a little further, there's an embankment that will take you to the path beneath the cliff. Go down there, and if the urn falls, I need you to catch it."

"You can count on me." Frida set off down the mountain.

"Be careful!" Hilda called after her.

While Frida got into position, Hilda climbed down

onto the ledge. It didn't descend as far as the previous one, but with the drop in elevation from the ridge, it was nearly level with the urn. She found what she was looking for—a tree growing in the distance directly beyond the urn. It was far, but it was better than nothing.

Hilda nocked an arrow and aimed. The handle on the urn had a narrow opening, wide enough to fit a few fingers through but not much else. If she squinted, she could see the tree through the hole. She frowned. If her aim was even a little off, the best-case scenario was knocking the urn from the branches. Worst case, she risked shattering the stone and sending Frey's ashes into the snow below.

She let the tension fade from the bow. Using the fishing line, she tied it around the area between the fletching and the nock. It would throw off the balance somewhat, but with enough power, the arrow should fly straight.

Once her granddaughter had positioned herself below the urn, Hilda called out, "Ready?"

"Ready!" Frida confirmed.

Hilda swallowed hard. She likely had one shot at this. Closing her eyes, she breathed deeply. This wasn't that different from many of her adventures. She'd made tougher shots, stopping a charging direhog from a great distance with a well-placed arrow to its eye. When they'd been pursued by pirates off the coast of Basilisk Bay, she'd shot the halyard of the main sail from two hundred yards on rough waters. She'd even managed to down a thieving fairy through limbs and foliage using only the light of the moon for guidance.

She could do this. Her bow was as much a part of her as the hair on her chin.

Hilda unwound the spool of waxed string and placed it on the ground before her. Then she drew the bowstring until her knuckle kissed her cheek. She breathed in, tightened her body, and released.

27. FROST WARDEN

Amethyra sent out a telepathic echo as she soared above the clouds, warning any dragons in the vicinity that they were not to harm the two-leggeds or their annoying companion.

Frost gathered on her scales, the tiny crystals twinkling in the moonlight. Far below, snow blanketed the landscape.

There was only one reason such an unseasonable chill would descend upon the mountains. Crythra had returned from the north, and everywhere the Frost Warden flew, ice and snow followed. The ancient warden could not have picked a worse time to return.

Amethyra did not relish the prospect of encountering an elemental ancient, even if Crythra was one of her gram's allies. She rolled her eyes at the word choice. Not gram, no, the Shattered Gem was her high-mother. A week with the two-leggeds and she'd already adopted some of their jargon.

She pushed the thoughts away and focused on the task

at hand. The rattledrake had held her ground against Sapphyrax and his boorish need to put his snout where it didn't belong. If it came to it, she would stand before Crythra as well. She had made a promise to protect the two-leggeds and guide them to Raeth's Tooth. She would do what she must to ensure her debt was repaid.

The two-leggeds were small and weak, yet they had saved her, proving the wisdom of her high-mother's words: *even the smallest ember can start a wildfire*. The elder two-legged had the wisdom that came with age, but the young one held a spark similar to Amethyra's own. The dragon had grown fond of her time in their company. Even the annoying mount was endearing in its own way when it wasn't clinging to her scales.

Amethyra flapped her wings, and the frost shattered, shards falling in her wake like a comet trail as she tucked her wings and dove through the clouds.

Warden's Cavern was located near the top of one of the tallest peaks across the dragon lands. The cavern had been hollowed out ages ago by a band of hooksnouts and was spacious enough for even the largest wardens to gather. The entrance appeared as a gaping maw with icicles descending above the opening like giant teeth. Drifts of snow had gathered along the landing, a sign that Crythra was inside.

Amethyra landed on the ledge and shook the frost from her wings. Beyond the cavern's mouth, pyres burned within the sprawling cave system, casting shadows of wardens upon the walls.

The young rattledrake clung to the darkness as she crept inside, thankful for the snow to muffle the clack of talons against stone. It was rare for Crythra to fly this far south before winter. Frost dragons preferred the far north, where they had no need of their glacial aura. If she was here, something must be amiss.

Amethyra snuck down the cavern, and the voices of the wardens became clearer.

"I agree it is odd." She recognized the crisp, authoritative voice of her mother, the archwarden. *"Behemoths are solitary creatures. Why would so many of them congregate?"*

"I do not know." Crythra's voice sounded like cracking ice. *"But we must be prepared. I request two additional wardens to the north."*

"You were wise to return," the archwarden said. *"Take Sapphyrax and the twins with you."*

Crythra let out a contemptuous growl. *"The twins are fools. I would prefer Aurelia."*

"All the more reason for someone as renowned as yourself to take them under your wing. For the good of the tempest."

The temperature dropped suddenly at Crythra's displeasure, a thick layer of frost forming along the cavern walls. Amethyra repressed the urge to howl with laughter.

"You know you are not permitted here, little Tink," Sapphyrax's voice rumbled in Amethyra's mind at the same time as the dragon appeared.

The rattledrake jumped at the blue dragon's unexpected presence, her fangs descending and tail rattling involuntarily. *"I am here to see the grandwarden."* Amethyra did her best to sound calm.

Sapphyrax lowered his head until he was a few feet from her. *"What makes you think she is here?"*

"The Frost Warden has returned. That means there will be a warden council."

"And you are not a warden."

Not yet, Amethyra wanted to say, but she held her tongue.

"I know what this is about." Sapphyrax's mouth curled into a mocking grin. *"Are your playthings cold?"* Smoke poured from the dragon's nostrils. *"Shall I warm them for you?"*

"Sapphyrax." The archwarden's voice held an edge of irritation. *"Why have you left the council?"*

Amethyra froze at the sound of clawsteps approaching.

The blue dragon flashed a mouthful of teeth. *"I found an intruder."*

Amethyra turned to see her mother—Virrelia, Archwarden of the Border Guard—approaching. She was twice the size of her daughter, with scales the deep purple of elderberries and spikes running along her spine so dark that they'd earned her the name Violet Abyss. Her tail rattled as it flitted back and forth, and her yellow eyes narrowed upon Amethyra.

Behind her, the massive form of Crythra dwarfed the archwarden. Her scales were the silvery blue of a frozen lake. Tiny barbs covered her body like jagged ice, and four solid white horns protruded from the top of her head. One of the frost dragon's giant paws was nearly half the size of Amethyra.

"Amethyra," her mother sighed. *"You know you are not permitted here."*

Amethyra lowered her head in deference. *"I know."*

"Then why have you come?"

"I felt Crythra's presence when the snowstorm passed over us." Amethyra sheepishly met her mother's gaze. While she might stand her ground against Sapphyrax and the other junior wardens, she knew better than to test her mother. *"I'm sure Sapphyrax has taken great joy in informing you of the situation. The two-leggeds aided me, and I am honor-bound to guide them to Raeth's Tooth. I fear the journey will be perilous under the current conditions, so I have come to ask for aid."*

Sapphyrax snorted.

Virrelia's icy glare was so frigid that the blue dragon stepped back several paces. *"You chose to bring these inter-lopers into our lands."* Her gaze returned to her daughter. *"While I respect your oath, it is your burden to bear. If you wish to become a warden someday, then you must learn to overcome such obstacles."*

"But—"

"This is not a discussion, Amethyra."

The young dragon clenched her jaw. Arguing with her mother would get her nowhere.

"Now, now, Virrelia," came the voice of the grandwarden, lifting Amethyra's spirits. Unlike her mother's sharp intonation, the Shattered Gem's was like a tooth that had been dulled over time. It might not be piercing, but it could still bite. *"Why turn away young Tinktink when she calls for aid?"*

"We have bigger issues than the honor of a broodling who makes her own trouble," Virrelia said flatly.

Crythra stepped aside so that the elder rattledrake could pass. Corcyra, the Shattered Gem, was only slightly bigger than her daughter, but her mere presence commanded the respect of every dragon in the cavern. Her scales had lightened with age, resembling the lavender that grew upon the southern meadows, and scars mapped her body, each one earned over thousands of years of service. The ancient spikes along her spine were a reminder of her namesake, each one like a cracked gemstone.

"It is good to see you, Tinktink." She lowered her neck and pressed her head against Amethyra's. When she rose back to her full height, her faded gray rattle flicked, garnering the other dragons' attention. *"Honor is not a chain that weighs us down. Whether broodling or ancient, honor is the wind that lifts our wings, propelling us to greater heights. Without it, we are little more than monsters."*

Crythra nodded along to the grandwarden's words. *"Well spoken, Corcyra."*

The Shattered Gem shook her rattle in front of Amethyra like she had done when the young rattledrake was only a hatchling. *"Now, do as your mother says and return to your duty."*

"But what about the snow?" Amethyra's defiance threatened to unravel.

Crythra stepped forward. *"I will take Sapphyrax and the twins into the north. Your lands will thaw soon enough. May the scales of fortune gleam upon you, young Tinktink."* Her glacial eyes moved from Amethyra to Sapphyrax. *"Find the twin-headed simpletons. I do not like to be kept waiting."*

Amethyra straightened as the ancient ice dragon passed by. Sapphyrax hurried deeper in the cavern, his gaze straight ahead.

Corcyra wrapped a wing around Amethyra. *"Let your honor guide you, Tinktink. Leave your mother to me."*

28. FAMILY FLIES TOGETHER

Hilda held her form as the arrow zipped toward its target. The waxed fishing line trailed along behind it, uncoiling from the spool with a soft purr. Below, Frida watched with anticipation, covering her mouth with both hands.

The arrow passed through the urn's handle with a *thwip*, the fletchings grazing the stone before the arrow thunked into the tree on the far side. Relief surged through Hilda, and her knees wobbled, forcing her to lean on the cliff for support.

Frida shielded her eyes from the sun as she squinted at the urn. "Did you get it?" From her vantage point, it was impossible to tell if the arrow had pierced the handle or merely shot over it.

"I got it." Hilda slung her bow over her shoulder and tied the end of the fishing line to her belt. "Wait for me to climb up."

She scaled the steep rockface, her shoulder burning with the effort. Once she was atop the cliff, she began coiling the fishing line as she went to ensure that the arrow was securely lodged in the tree. Confident that the arrow would hold, she returned to the area just above the urn.

Standing at the edge of the cliff, Hilda pulled the line until it was taut. "I'm going to use the tension on the fishing line to lift the urn, and then I'll lower it down to you. Ready?"

Frida nodded. "Ready."

Hilda tugged on the string, and there was a soft groan as stone rubbed against aged bark. She pulled harder until the urn rose from its nest. Hilda swallowed hard as the fishing line took the full weight. The arrow held, and she stepped to the side, guiding the vessel along the waxed line. Once it was clear of the branches, she carefully released the slack little by little, lowering the vessel until it reached Frida.

The girl cut the line and held the urn up for her grandmother to see. "Got it!"

"Good. Now, be careful on your way back." Hilda sat down in the snow and collapsed onto her back. Gods, that had been close. She couldn't remember the last time she'd felt so stressed. "So much for a relaxing journey through the countryside." She dug her fingers into the snow. "No, that'd be too easy. How about we add in dragons, giants, mountain spirits, and snowstorms that come out of nowhere. That would be much more fun."

There was a muffled crunch before Morsel's head appeared in Hilda's vision.

"Hey, old girl." She reached up to pet the goat on the cheek.

Morsel bypassed her hand, planting a wet kiss across her forehead.

Hilda waited by the fire for the stew to boil. Frey's urn rested in her lap, a rope tied securely to each handle so that she could wear it slung across her body like a satchel.

Nearby, Frida frolicked in the snow with Morsel, making snowballs and tossing them at the goat. Morsel tried to eat the snowballs from the air, and more often than not, they splattered against her massive head. This produced a bout of laughter from Frida, which made the goat even more excited.

Pieces of wild carrot and venison bobbed as Hilda stirred the pot. Her gaze drifted across the sky in search of Tink. It was midday, and the dragon still hadn't returned. She wasn't sure how long they should wait before moving on.

All around them, the snowfall had started to melt, making it all the more blinding as sunlight reflected off the slick surface. If the runoff froze overnight, they would be in dire trouble. Without Tink to guide them, the journey would slow to a crawl.

Hilda had never imagined she'd have a dragon guiding them through these lands, but it had been nice. Not only had Tink shared meat from her hunts, she'd also defended Hilda and Frida from the three larger dragons. That made her disappearance seem particularly odd. Hilda wasn't sure if dragons felt compassion on the same scale as dwarves, but it had seemed like Tink and Frida had formed a bond during their brief time together. She hadn't expected the dragon to abandon them without a word.

Hilda was still ruminating when a shadow appeared

across the snow. She looked up just in time to see a deer falling from the sky. It thudded against the snow, and Frida nearly jumped from her skin.

"What the hells!" the girl shouted.

Morsel bleated loudly and bolted away, nearly trampling Hilda, who clutched Frey's urn to her chest and fell backward into the snow. Lying on her back, her heart raced as she looked skyward. Tinktink hovered above them, her outline a silhouette against the blue sky.

"What the hells, Tink?" Frida stared at the dragon with an open mouth before rushing to help Hilda.

Tinktink landed near the deer carcass, her scales shining brilliantly against the frosted landscape. *I thought you might require sustenance.*

"Where have you been all day?" Frida crossed her arms. "Gram nearly lost the urn, and we could have really used your help."

"There was a matter I needed to see about." Tink did not elaborate further as Morsel returned, nuzzling against her. The dragon huffed.

Hilda shook the snow from her cloak. "Does it normally snow this early in the year?"

"Occasionally, but this is not natural. It was an elemental snow." Tinktink looked over her shoulder at the far-off mountains. *"There was a disturbance in the far north, and so Crythra returned to request that more wardens join her. She is an ice dragon, and whenever she flies to warmer climates, a snowstorm follows in her wake."*

"Really?" Frida's eyes lit with excitement. "So, she's like a dragon mage? That's so cool!"

"I suppose she is similar to a mage in a way. She has the

ability to control the aura around her, but she does not conjure spells in the same way your mages are able."

Frida shook her head in disbelief. "That's amazing."

"You said there was a disturbance." Hilda adjusted the urn's strap around her shoulder. "Should we be concerned?"

"Crythra patrols the far north." Tinktink growled at Morsel as the goat continued to show affection, but it wasn't very effective. *"There is no reason to be concerned, but as wardens, the situation is worth monitoring."* Tinktink picked up the deer carcass with her teeth and moved it closer to the fire. *"Now that you have sustenance, I suggest you eat so that we may continue our journey."*

While Frida prepared the deer, Hilda approached Tinktink. The dragon was cleaning herself of Morsel's slobber. "Should we be worried about the runoff freezing?"

"With Crythra gone, the temperature will return to normal. Nothing should freeze, and most of the snow at the lower elevations will be gone by morning."

That was good news. She'd take mud over ice any day of the week.

Frida butchered enough venison to feed them for a little while, and soon had it roasting in a pan with some wild onion she'd foraged the previous day. The aroma was heavenly—rich and earthy with a mild sweetness that had Hilda's mouth watering.

Morsel sniffed at the pan before stealing a raw onion Frida had left in the open. The goat sat in the snow across from Tinktink, eating her onion while the dragon devoured the remaining deer.

Hilda tried not to think about what might be

happening in the far north that would require more than one dragon to monitor. For an elemental dragon to request backup, it had to be concerning.

Tinktink's head cocked as she looked up from her meal, and Morsel's ears twitched before she let out a worried bleat.

A moment passed before Hilda heard the flap of wings, and two rattledrakes more than twice the size of Tinktink descended on their camp. One had dark purple scales, and its yellow eyes darted around their campsite as if assessing every minuscule detail.

The second dragon was bigger, though not by much, with light purple scales that were almost gray in places. White scars lined much of this dragon's body. It looked over Hilda and Frida once before turning its gaze to Tinktink. Hilda had the impression that the dragon had gathered everything it needed to know in that brief moment. Unlike the three dragons they'd met earlier, these two did not present as aggressive.

Nevertheless, Morsel hid behind Tinktink, a whine escaping the frightened goat.

Tinktink stood. *"Mother, high-mother."* She dipped her head in deference. *"What are you doing here?"*

The elder—high-mother, who Hilda assumed was the Shattered Gem—nuzzled her head against Tinktink's. *"We have come to aid you."* Her voice was graveled with age.

Tinktink's tail flicked with a low rattle as she turned to her mother. *"I thought you said this was my burden to bear?"*

"It is." Tinktink's mother's voice had the coldness of authority. *"But your high-mother was right. Just because it is your burden to bear, it doesn't mean you must bear it alone."* Her gaze turned to Frida and then to Hilda. *"And once the*

two-leggeds are back beyond our borders, we can all rest easier."

Frida opened her mouth to speak, but upon the dragon's icy glare, thought better of it.

"While I do not welcome you into these lands, you aided Amethyra when she was in need. For your compassion, we will fly you to Raeth's Tooth so that you may complete your task."

Hilda gulped. "I'm sorry, did you say fly?"

A grin spread across Frida's face. "Oh, hells yeah!"

29. RAETH'S TOOTH

The three dragons sat across the fire from Hilda and Frida as the dwarves ate. Tinktink chewed on the bones of the deer she'd hunted. A few paces away, Corcyra, the Shattered Gem, seemed enthralled with Morsel.

After discovering the dragons weren't going to eat her, Morsel showcased the same fondness toward the elders that she had displayed toward Tinktink. Virrelia was not amused by the goat, growling every time Morsel came near, but Corcyra toyed with Morsel the way a cat might entertain itself with a mouse.

Hilda prayed the elder had the same restraint as her grandchild.

Tinktink's mother watched the two dwarves as they ate. The claws of her front paws rapped against the scales of her thigh like an impatient teacher.

Hilda found it hard to eat under the archwarden's penetrating gaze, but Frida had no such trepidation. If anything, the girl was eating with more gusto.

"Is it true, then?" Frida mumbled between bites. "Did there really used to be dragon riders?"

Virrelia's rhythmic tapping paused. *"Long ago."*

"I always knew it was true." Frida gestured with her spoon. "So, that must mean we'll be the first dragon riders in over three thousand years."

Tinktink raised her head in what Hilda could only describe as a look of warning.

"We will carry you to Raeth's Tooth." Virrelia's tone sharpened. *"That does not make you a dragon rider."*

Frida shrugged. "If you say so."

"I do say so." The dragon huffed. It was a huff that Hilda knew all too well from raising six children. *"A draconic bond is not something to be taken lightly. It is a relic from ages past, when dragons chose to involve themselves in the affairs of men."*

Hilda let her spoon rest on the edge of the bowl. "Why did you stop?

There was a long silence punctuated by the crunch of bones before Virrelia finally answered. *"Many ages past, the first civilizations of the two-legged began to arise across the continent. There were the elves who claimed the forests, and dwarves who delved within the mountains. Many tribes of men unified along the open plains, but the mountain tribes continued to war against one another, none wishing to cede their authority to the others. There was one among them who feared rowhat would happen if they could not unite, so in his desperation, he approached our ancestors in the hopes of using the dragon's might to unify the tribes. Most of my kin desired to remain neutral, but there was a subset who wished to honor the two-legged's bravery. Those few formed a bond with men, and for an age, there was peace in the shadow of dragons and their riders. Eventually, war spread across the realm. Kingdoms fractured and expanded. My ancestors did not wish to be used as weapons of war, so they left, promising to abstain from interfering in the squabbles of the two-legged evermore."*

Hilda let the words sink in. Much of what Virrelia said lined up with what she'd read of the Age of Empires. It was a time of conquest, when hillside and mountain dwarves had been united under a single banner, and the elves had yet to splinter. What was now known as Nelderland and Gannett had been a single human empire that stretched across half of Aedrea. It was during this time that the warring tribes of Warminster finally united.

What followed was known as the Age of Strife, an era defined by the Elvish Separation and nearly a thousand years of war as empires broke into what resembled the nine kingdoms of today.

Very few historical texts survived from that time. Most accounts of those periods were dated after the formation of the Order of Clerics thousands of years later. Hilda wondered how much their histories differed from what the dragons experienced.

She thought of the fall of Deepwarden. An entire city forced to flee the shadow of dragons. For her people, it was marked by sadness and fear, but what had been the dragon's reasoning for showing their teeth?

Although she was curious, Hilda was hesitant to broach the subject.

"You seem troubled." Virrelia's gaze bored into her.

"Just thinking." Hilda set her bowl aside. "We know so little about dragonkind, let alone your history."

"We would prefer to keep it that way. The two-leggeds have a way of forgetting the past, or viewing it differently from what

it was. Dragonkind live too long to be afforded such luxury."
Virrelia leaned forward to stretch her forepaws. Her deep
violet scales were like an abyss against the melting snow.
"We will fly when you are ready."

Hilda shivered as cool air whipped against her face. She
clutched Frey's urn to her chest, glancing down at the line
of white that trailed across the landscape from where
Crythra had flown. Her stomach lurched. It looked as if
the gods had taken a white paintbrush across the region.
If she hadn't been so terrified, she might have thought it
beautiful.

Virrelia cradled the dwarf in her arms, and her wings
flapped like sails upon the high sea. When she'd said the
dragons would carry them to Raeth's Tooth, she'd meant
it literally.

"This…is…so…awesome!" Frida screamed over the
wind as Tinktink held her, the young dwarf's arms flailing
with delight.

Once again, Hilda found herself in awe of her granddaughter's fearlessness.

"She reminds me of Amethyra," Virrelia spoke in Hilda's
mind, and by the lack of acknowledgment from anyone
else, the dwarf had the impression it was a closed conversation. *"Too often, the young believe that sternness is a sign
that we don't respect them. They fail to see that our guidance
comes from hard-earned experience, that our rules exist for a
reason. I admire Amethyra's adventurous nature a great deal,
but it would be a failure on my part to let her follow every
whim."*

Hilda understood that feeling all too well. "It's easier when you're not the parent. I had to be tough with my children, but now that they have children of their own, I can spoil the little ones."

Virrelia cast a sideways glance at her mother, the great Shattered Gem. *"You are not wrong."*

Somewhere behind them, Morsel bleated, which sounded an awful lot like a scream. The war goat was too big for any of the rattledrakes to carry without hurting her, so they'd enlisted the help of Tarrun, a massive obsidian. The dragon was so large it could have grasped the goat in one claw, but after some convincing, Tarrun agreed to cradle Morsel like a cat in his forepaws.

Corcyra passed overhead to take the lead, and her scarred body shimmered in the light of the cloudless sky as she began her dive. Hilda could see Raeth's Tooth as they approached. It was hardly imposing from such great heights but grew quickly. She clenched the urn tighter, closing her eyes and praying to the gods that Virrelia didn't let go.

There was a soft crash as the four dragons landed atop the mountain.

Virrelia gently lowered Hilda to the ground. *"We will be waiting beyond the trees when you are ready to return."*

"Thank you." Hilda nodded solemnly.

Frida hollered with excitement, and Morsel bleated her indignation at being carried. Hilda found herself at a loss for words. Her throat tightened as a wave of emotion washed over her.

This was it.

They'd traveled for weeks, and now the journey was at its end. Frey's urn felt unnaturally heavy, the cool stone like an anchor in her arms. She blinked back her tears and released a shaky breath.

"You knew this was coming," she whispered to herself.

Frida's arm rested gently on her grandmother's shoulder. "Do you mind if I say a few words before you go?"

The question took Hilda by surprise. She cleared her throat. "That would be nice." She offered the urn to Frida.

Frida sat on the ground, legs crossed, with the urn between them. "I never had the chance to meet you, but Gram says we would have gotten along well. If her stories are anything to go by, I think so, too." She smiled, hand resting on the cool stone. "I've learned a lot about you during our travels. Gram says you were a pain in the ass at times. I think she probably feels the same way about me sometimes, too. I know you loved adventure, that you were a good leader, and you were an even better friend. I hope that one day, I have a friend as fearless as you were, and that when I'm in trouble, I never have to second-guess if they have my back. Gram says that life is fleeting, but our stories have a chance to live forever. I hope that's true, because this is an adventure I will never forget. None of this would have been possible without you, Frey. I hope you find peace and know that my gram loved you enough to see this through."

The world was a blur beyond Hilda's tears-filled eyes. She took the urn and draped the makeshift strap over her shoulder, sniffling as she embraced her granddaughter. "That was beautiful."

Frida squeezed hard. "Thanks for letting me come along."

"It wouldn't have been the same without you." Hilda meant it. At the start, she'd been worried if the girl could keep up or could deal with the rigors of open travel, but at every hardship, her granddaughter had risen to the challenge.

Frida met her grandmother's gaze with an understanding the elder dwarf didn't think was possible. "I'm going to go explore while you say good-bye."

Good-bye. Those words were like a punch to the gut.

Hilda took a deep breath to gather her courage. She turned toward the overhanging rockface that made up Raeth's Tooth, and for the first time since they'd landed, she took in the view.

The vista was awe-inspiring. Nothing but endless mountains in all directions. They stretched so far that they disappeared into a blue haze along the horizon. In front of her, a verdant green path led from the grove of trees down to the rocky overhang.

Hilda sat a few feet from the edge, Frey's urn resting on her lap. Her mind wandered back to that unexpected knock on her door. That felt like so long ago. So much had happened since then. What had begun as a straightforward journey had taken twists and turns she never would have imagined.

She unfastened the clasps securing the lid and placed it beside her. Light gray ash filled the stone vessel. All that was left of one of her dearest friends.

"I wish we had more time." Hilda sighed, feeling the tears well up at the edge of her vision. She blinked several times and then shut her eyes, but the tears flowed down her cheeks anyway. "We both know that all good things come to an end. All we can do is look back on the good times with fondness. You and I, we had so many good times. Part of me is sad that I didn't spend more time talking to you on this journey. But the other part, the part that knows this was more for me than for you, that part knows that our story ended long ago. This was a chance for something new." She sniffled. "I suppose I owe you my thanks." Hilda smiled sadly. "Without your ludicrous request, Frida never would have followed me on this journey. Truth be told, having her by my side has made this one of my life's greatest adventures. We flew with dragons, for gods' sakes!" She shook her head, chuckling as her gaze drifted across the landscape. A mirrorwing flew in front of a distant peak, its silver wings glinting in the afternoon sun. "I don't know if you truly believed I would take your wish seriously, but I did. And I can't think of anywhere better to put you to rest. You were a wild spirit, beautiful and untamed to the very end."

Hilda stood and removed the strap from around her neck. She tilted the urn upside-down, and gray ash scattered on the wind.

As Frey's ashes dispersed across the mountains, Hilda caught the faintest smell of mint and pine, just like the frostbloom oil he used to wear. She turned, her breath hitching at the sight of a frost laurel bush growing on the mountaintop, its pale blue flowers in full bloom.

She smiled. "Rest easy, old friend."

30. DARK PATHS

The sun peeked from behind the mountains, casting long shadows and painting the sky with streaks of tangerine and pink. Hilda jostled in Virrelia's arms as the dragon landed on the high ridge just beyond the border of the dragonlands. A moment later, Tinktink landed, followed by Tarrun and Corcyra.

Hilda's muscles complained, and her back cracked as she stretched her arms overhead. Morsel bleated loudly once the giant obsidian dragon released his hold on the goat.

Hilda scratched Morsel on the chin. "You might be the only goat in history to fly in the arms of a dragon and live to tell the tale."

Morsel bleated her opinion on the matter as Tarrun took to the sky.

Virrelia tucked her wings by her side. *I trust you can find your way home.*

"I think we can manage." Hilda smiled as she adjusted Morsel's saddle to make sure it was secure. When she noticed the empty satchel where Frey's urn used to rest, a mixture of sadness and relief swelled inside her. After scattering his ashes, she'd left the urn beside the frost laurel bush atop Raeth's Tooth as a monument to her friend. The quest was complete. Now, it was time to go home. "Thank you for your help. All of you."

"*I accept your gratitude.*" Virrelia watched Hilda with an unblinking gaze. "*I have no ill will toward you, but now that Amethyra's debt has been balanced, I hope that our paths do not cross again.*"

"*Mother!*" Tinktink's tail twitched with a sharp rattle as her mother flew away.

Hilda laughed at Virrelia's directness.

Corcyra nuzzled her head against Tinktink's. "*You should know by now that your mother does not mince her words for the benefit of anyone.*"

The younger dragon huffed. "*I am well aware.*"

The Shattered Gem turned her gaze on the two dwarves. "*My daughter's tongue may be barbed, but she speaks the truth. There is enough space in the world for dragonkind to be left in peace. I wish you safe travels upon your journey home.*"

Corcyra took flight, leaving Tinktink alone with her traveling companions.

"Good-bye!" Frida shouted as the elder dragon flew away.

They all stood in silence, watching the Shattered Gem disappear into the distance. Hilda knew this next part was going to be difficult for her granddaughter. She and Tinktink had been practically inseparable since they'd met.

She wrapped an arm around Frida and pulled the girl

close. "We'll need to find somewhere to make camp for the night. Take a moment to say good-bye."

Her granddaughter bit her lip and nodded, the emotion already evident on her face.

Hilda turned to Tinktink. "I'm glad to have made your acquaintance. You've given this old dwarf an experience she'll never forget, and that's saying a lot. Take care of yourself, and try not to give your mother too much trouble."

"I can't make any promises." Tinktink's tail swished. *"I will remember you fondly."*

Hilda nudged Morsel in the side with her elbow. "Say good-bye to Tink." The goat bleated loudly and leaned her full weight into the dragon. Surprisingly, Tinktink didn't push her away. "Alright, alright. That's enough. Let's give Frida a moment, shall we?" Hilda grabbed the reins and led Morsel away.

Frida stared at the ground, kicking rocks and refusing to meet Tinktink's gaze.

"Why are you upset, young one?" The dragon lowered her head until she was on Frida's level.

"I'm going to miss you." The girl sniffled. "And I don't want to leave you."

"It is not every day that a dragon befriends a two-legged. Know that I will carry your memory with me."

Frida rushed forward, wrapping her arms around Tinktink's midsection. To Hilda's surprise, the dragon hugged her back.

"Will I ever see you again?" Frida asked.

"All paths are dark until the sun finds them." Tinktink released her hold. *"But there is always hope."*

Frida nodded as tears streamed down her cheeks. "Good-bye, Tink."

"Good-bye, little one."

In the days that followed, they kept a leisurely pace, enjoying the countryside and taking time to hunt and fish. Frida's bow skills continued to improve and by the time they passed through Deepwarden, she was able to clean a rabbit in half the time she had initially.

As they slept within the walls of the abandoned city, Hilda had a new understanding of the great migration. The dragons could have easily destroyed the city, razing it to the ground like Hells' Crag, but they'd allowed the citizens to leave peacefully, if albeit fearfully. The two-legged of Aedrea had claimed most of the continent, and it only seemed fair that dragons have a home to call their own if they wished.

The journey back proved less exciting than the way there. There were no run-ins with giants, though they did have a close encounter with a direbear. After flying with dragons, Morsel was fearless in the face of the giant bear, ramming it so hard that the beast scurried into the woods with a yelp. Hilda made sure to forage for extra carrots that day.

They saw a troll bathing in a stream from a distance, and one night, will-o'-wisps set the valley alight with their golden glow. Hilda would often catch Frida scribbling in her journal during their downtime, and she made sure to never interrupt.

Eventually, they came upon the ruins of civilization,

and later, the sparsely traveled path where they found the Inn'd of the Road hidden behind a dense thicket. The old, dilapidated stone building wasn't much, but after so long in the wilderness, the prospect of a warm meal under an actual roof was exhilarating.

Several cats lay upon the old wooden porch, scattering when they saw Morsel approaching.

Hilda grinned at her granddaughter. "Would you like to stay in the barn again, or will you be sleeping inside this time?"

Frida rolled her eyes. "You'd have made a good jester."

Hilda tied Morsel to a post and knocked on the door. A moment later, the hinges groaned as the door swung inward. Gwynera wore the same tattered clothing Hilda remembered, and the elderly dwarf's beard was once again remarkably braided.

Gwynera frowned behind her bushy eyebrows. "You again." She peeked beyond Hilda. "Ya find this one on the road?"

"More like she found me." Hilda winked.

Gwynera puffed on her pipe, blowing smoke from her nostrils like a dragon before stepping aside. "Ya comin' in or just taking the view?"

Hilda laughed. "We'd love to stay the night if you'll have us."

They stepped inside, where a herd of cats basked in the warmth of the hearth.

"You have lovely braids," said Frida. "Did you do them yourself?"

"It sure weren't the cats." Gwynera laughed, though it sounded more like a cough.

"You're so talented." Frida held up the end of a braid

that was tangled with twigs and other debris. "I wish I could braid my hair like that."

Gwynera ignored the compliment as she gestured toward the kitchen, where an assortment of carrots, potatoes, and turnips sat on a cutting board. "I'm making root stew tonight. Dinner will be ready in a couple hours. Make yerself at home. Mind, the beds haven't grown any softer since you left."

Frida held up her bow. "If you'd like, I can try and find some meat for your stew."

Gwynera took another long drag of her pipe. "If ya manage that, dearie, I'll braid yer hair."

The girl grinned. "Deal."

A few hours later, the hearty aroma of roasted vegetables and wild rabbit wafted across the old inn. A half-dozen cats gathered around the hearth, lured by the smell. Beyond the grime-covered windows, night had settled on the land.

"You sure do have a lot of cats." Frida said as she played with a small orange one, bobbing a piece of string over its head.

"They keep me company. Not too many folk pass through these parts anymore." Gwynera stirred the stew, and scooped a small amount. She waited for the steam to fade before tasting it. "That'll do."

The trio sat at the table, surrounded by a clowder of hungry-eyed cats. While the two younger dwarves ate, Gwynera smoked her pipe, the vanilla and caramel aroma of the sweet tobacco blending with the earthiness of the stew.

"Were ya able to keep yer promise?" she asked as a calico cat climbed into her lap for a better view of the food.

Hilda nodded. "I was." She still had an ache in her heart for her old friend, but it had softened over the return journey. Grief wasn't something that was severed with the axe-stroke of a single action. It would take time, fading a bit with each passing day.

Gwynera tilted her head in acknowledgement but left the conversation at that.

After dinner, they gathered around the fire. Gwynera motioned for Frida to sit between the old dwarf's legs. She loosened Frida's braid and brushed through the dirt and tangles with an intricately designed silver comb. Compared to how battered and dingy the rest of the inn was, the comb's elegance seemed out of place.

Gwynera caught Hilda admiring it. "Family heirloom. One of the few luxuries my ancestors brought with them."

Hilda smiled. "It's lovely." She suddenly understood why the woman kept her hair in such meticulous order despite the disarray around her. This comb, such a simple thing, was a tether to her past. A reminder of her family's history.

She supposed, in a way, this journey hadn't been all that different. Carrying Frey's urn for all those miles had reminded Hilda of who she once was. As much as she loved being a grandmother, she'd missed the call of adventure. She was grateful to have experienced that thrill one last time.

Gwynera combed and braided Frida's hair while

listening to the young dwarf recount her adventures through the wilderness. Occasionally she would pause, eyebrow raised as she looked to Hilda for confirmation of events that seemed too farfetched to be true.

When she finally finished, Frida's fiery mane was braided into two intricate fishtails, the end of each tied with a piece of string.

The girl strutted around the inn, holding her braids by their tips and admiring the exquisite work. "How do I look?" she asked her grandmother.

"Gorgeous as ever," said Hilda.

Frida tossed the braids over her shoulder and mimed drawing her bow. "Just because you're an adventurer, it doesn't mean you can't look good."

Hilda chuckled. "You're going to go far, kid."

31. HOME SWEET HOME

The next morning, Hilda and Frida bid farewell to Gwynera with a promise to visit again in the future. The location was close enough to civilization that they weren't truly isolated, but far enough away that Frida could train her skills in true wilderness without forcing Hilda to camp on the ground every night. Even though the Inn'd of the Road was a trek from Stonefist Hold, there were enough towns and villages in between to make the journey not burdensome if they took their time.

"She's a nice lady," Frida said, walking alongside Morsel. "I don't know why she'd want to live out here all by herself, though. Seems like it would be quite lonely."

"I'm sure it is." Hilda glanced over her shoulder, where the inn had disappeared behind the tree line. "But I don't think she's ready to let go. This inn was her family's legacy. After uprooting everything they'd known, they formed a new life here, only to watch it slowly wither away. There was a time when this route went all the way from Stonefist Hold to Deepwarden, but after the city was abandoned, the towns and villages in between slowly shriveled and eventually faded away. Dragonkind didn't just force the citizens to leave the city; they removed the beating heart of the region. In many ways, Gwynera is the last thread connecting the old world with the new."

"I never thought of it like that. It must have been hard watching everyone move closer and closer to Stonefist Hold and one day realize she really was the end of the road."

Hilda thought about her own life and how the years kept ticking by. One day she'd had the smooth skin of youth and hair so red it could have been crafted by the gods, and before she knew it, her hair had grayed and wrinkles told the stories of a thousand laughs and smiles.

Life came fast, whether you were ready for it or not.

In the days that followed, Hilda and Frida enjoyed the comforts that came with the return to civilization. A hot bath at the Griffin's Nest Inn wasn't enough to calm the pain in Hilda's shoulder, but it soothed achy muscles and washed away the grime of travel. Morsel was rewarded for her efforts with a brushing and pampering at the Stone Shadow Stables. They stopped for a meal at the One-Eyed Raven and had bread fresh from the oven for the first time in over a month. They indulged in custard tarts and stewed fruits, and the night before they were set to arrive in Stonefist Hold, Hilda splurged on a bowl of sugared almonds. She and Frida ate them by the fire while listening to a bard regale them with songs of adventure and heartache.

That night, as Hilda lay in bed with the coldstone pressed to her aching shoulder, she thought of her husband. She longed to be in Boric's sturdy arms once again and feel the scruff of his beard upon her cheeks.

They woke early the next morning and shared a breakfast of herbed potatoes, sausage, and stewed oats. Once they were back on the road, the white fist of Stonefist Hold beckoned them upon the final stretch home.

By the time they arrived at the city, twilight had descended on the land, and the sounds and smells of the mountain welcomed them home as they scaled the wide streets. The tang of metal and dust seeped from the open tunnels, comforting in its own way. Pickaxes clinked within the mines, and dwarves barked orders as cargo moved up and down the massive shafts to the city above.

At the summit, they passed through the gates, where lamps cast the streets in a dull glow. Frida stopped and let out a long sigh. The time for her reckoning was near.

"Don't slow down now." Hilda gave her a knowing look. "You swung your axe, and now it's time to meet the mountain's judgment."

Frida looked up with the innocent eyes of a newborn foal. "You think they're going to be mad?"

"I think they'll be happy to see you're safe and sound," said Hilda. At that, Frida perked up. "And then they'll be mad."

Frida tilted back her head and groaned. "Fine. Let's get it over with."

Morsel licked the girl's face.

Flint and Maela's home was similar to most of the others on Rockdale Lane. The stone building was two stories tall, square, with scale-shaped shingles and a small chimney that streamed smoke against the starry sky. The Rockfall crest was carved into the stone above the door. Frida stared into the glow of the smoked-glass windows.

"Wait a moment, youngblood." Hilda climbed down from Morsel and pulled Frida aside. "I don't relish being in your situation, but it's time to see where the stone falls." She kissed the girl on the top of the head.

Frida smiled at her grandmother. "Whatever happens, it was worth it." She hugged her grandmother and then opened the door.

Hilda followed her inside. There was chatter from the rear of the house before Frida's youngest brother, Elrik, peeked around the corner. The boy's mouth hung open as he stared up at his sister. A second later, Killy, Zarra, and Brom joined him.

Killy grinned at the sight of her sister. "Ma! Pa!" she shouted. "Frida's home."

"You're in trouble," Elrik said the last word in a sing-song voice before sticking out his tongue.

Feet shuffled as Flint and Maela hurried over. Maela rushed past, wrapping Frida in her arms. "Oh, Frida. Are you okay? We were so worried about you."

"I left a note," Frida said as Flint joined her side, enveloping his daughter and wife in his powerful arms.

"Well, I guess that makes everything fine, then." Flint frowned as he met Hilda's gaze. "We were worried sick, but then the guild brought us a letter from two elven fellows who said you crossed paths on the road. After hearing the way they talked of you at Frey's funeral, I figured if there was anyone who could make sure she got home safe, it was you."

"She kept me safe more often than not." Hilda winked at Frida. "Come by for dinner tomorrow and I'll tell you all about it."

Flint and Maela released their hold on their daughter and each hugged Hilda in turn.

"Thank you, Mum." Flint kissed her on the cheek.

"I don't know how you still do it." Maela gestured to her children. "Sometimes, it's a chore for me just getting them out the door."

Hilda squeezed her daughter-in-law's arm. "It wasn't easy, but some things are worth the effort."

Hilda tugged on the reins, guiding Morsel to a stop outside her home. She smiled at the sign above the door that read "Home is where the hearth is." For a moment, she just sat there, grateful to have finally made it back.

A soft glow came from the living room, but there were no signs of activity. That was good. She'd see her children tomorrow, but for tonight, she only wanted the company of one person.

She tied Morsel to the post out front. "I'll take you to the stables soon. Just give me a moment."

Morsel bleated, and Hilda saw a shadow move past the window toward the door.

The door slowly opened, and Boric stepped outside. He had his beard oiled and braided with small clasps that jingled when he walked. His gray mustache twitched as he set his eyes on her. "I thought I recognized that voice."

Morsel bleated. Boric gave her a scratch behind the ear, but his attention was on his wife. "Hey, Mama."

Hilda let herself melt into his arms. "Hey, Papa."

"I've missed you." Boric pressed his lips to Hilda's, and the prickly hairs of his mustache tickled her nose.

"I'm glad to be back." She rested her head against his broad chest. "I still need to take Morsel to the stables, but I wanted to see you first."

"Nonsense." Boric rubbed her back. "I'll take Morsel and then I'll draw you a hot bath when I return. Go inside and take a load off."

Hilda kissed him again. "I knew there was a reason I liked you."

"This is divine." Hilda leaned against the tub as steam rose from the bath. The scent of lavender and rose petals filled the room.

"Not as divine as you." Boric sat in a chair nearby, sipping a glass of red wine. "Only you would travel to dragon lands to keep a promise to an old friend. Was it everything you'd hoped for?"

"Everything and more." Hilda took a sip of wine, consequences be damned, and passed it back to her husband. "Frida was a natural. I don't want to rob her of the chance to tell you what happened, but I think Frey would have been proud. If she chooses the life of an adventurer, she has a chance to do special things."

"That's not surprising with a grandmother like you."

Word spread quickly of Hilda and Frida's return, and so, the next evening, the house was full of children and grandchildren. After the solitude of the wilderness, Hilda welcomed the chaos of family with open arms. She made sure to hug everyone, telling them just how much she'd missed their company.

They all gathered in the living room as Frida recounted their journey.

"I don't believe it." Darrin furrowed his brow when Frida got to the part where the mountain spirit led them to Tinktink.

"Gram, tell him." Frida scowled at her uncle.

Hilda chuckled. "Darrin has always been a skeptic." She winked at her granddaughter. "Don't worry about him. You and I both know the truth of what happened."

"I believe you," Tilda said adamantly, the young girl casting a menacing glance at her father.

"I know you do." Frida stuck her tongue out at Darrin. "You're proof that skepticism is a character defect and not a family trait."

"Why, you little... I ought to—" Darrin burst out laughing before he could finish his threat. "You're just like your father."

Hilda sat back in her chair, listening to her granddaughter recount their adventure while their family laughed and bickered. The girl had a natural talent for storytelling, knowing exactly when to pause for dramatic effect. As the tale unfolded, young and old alike were on the edge of their seats, gasping when Sapphyrax appeared and cheering as Tinktink defended the two dwarves from certain doom.

When she told them about waking up to a snow-covered landscape, a buttery sweet aroma wafted into the living room. Hilda savored the smell of the honey crumble baking in the oven and intertwined her fingers with her husband's. She gave a gentle squeeze, grateful for the life she had.

She'd come to understand that she didn't have to split her life into sections. Grandmother, adventurer, baker, storyteller, and everything else. It had taken her far too long to learn things didn't have to be either-or. The truth was that she could have it all if she wanted, and she couldn't wait to see what adventures lay in store.

EPILOGUE

30 years later.

"Gods, it's hotter than Pidros's forge." Sweat beaded down Frida's back. She leaned forward in the saddle, scratching Grimble behind the ears. The shaggy black war goat huffed his displeasure as he leaned into her touch. "What do you say we take a load off for a little bit?"

He bleated his approval.

Frida wiped away strands of red hair that clung to her damp forehead and climbed down from the saddle. It had been an exceptionally warm summer, even at the higher elevations. Only the most distant mountains were still snowcapped, and streams and rivers overflowed with run-off from the nearer peaks.

Her adventuring party, Braids & Quivers, hadn't been too pleased to learn Frida was abandoning them during pruning season to take a solo trek into the far north, but she'd put this venture off for the past two years while they traveled the realm, adventuring from Barrowsturm to Whispering Vale and everywhere in between. Her mouth twisted into a smile as she recalled the week they'd spent in Harpy's Roost.

They could manage one tour without the Ember Ranger. Frida would reconvene with them in a few months once they returned from the wilds. Besides, Tilda had become a cunning ranger in her own right. It was time to let her cousin showcase her worth.

Frida set her pack down beneath the shade of an old oak and pulled out a piece of stonebread. It had taken her a while to appreciate the bland bread, but she finally understood why her grandmother swore by the stuff. It might be hard as a rock, but it was packed with energy providing nutrients, was lightweight, and required a lot less effort than hunting every single day.

In her youth, Frida would have rather spent hours hunting or setting traps, but with age came wisdom. The bread crunched as she bit into it.

Grimble was lying on the ground, panting like a dog, when a throaty roar sounded in the distance. The goat's ears twitched, but he didn't seem alarmed. Frida smiled. He'd protected her from goblins, ogres, wargs, and countless other creatures. Once, the war goat had squared off with a direhog and sent it whimpering into the forest. Frida had never met such a fearless goat, but she wondered what even he would do in the presence of a dragon.

She'd find out soon enough.

Last night, Frida had heard the leathery flap of wings as several dragons passed overhead. The sound of their call had sparked gooseflesh across her body. In the thirty years since she'd left the dragonlands behind, not a day had passed that she didn't think about Tinktink.

She often wondered if the young rattledrake remembered her fondly. Their time together had been brief, but it had left a lasting impression.

Frida let Grimble rest during the hottest part of the day, and once the sun touched the highest peaks, they set off under its golden glow.

"We should cross into dragon territory tomorrow if we're lucky. Are you excited?"

Grimble bleated.

"Me, too, Grim." Frida ruffled the long hair between his ears. "Me, too."

They made camp within earshot of a gurgling stream. While Frida cast her line, Grimble roamed the hillside eating foliage. Soon, she had a fish roasting in a pan over a low fire. She removed a packet of spice from her dreamcloak—the same one that the great Hilda Rockfall had worn as she traveled the realm—and sprinkled it on the fish.

She wondered if she'd ever live up to the reputation her grandmother had earned. In truth, it didn't matter. This was her life, full of its own triumphs and challenges. She took gratitude in having someone who understood the life she'd chosen. Every time she visited Stonefist Hold, she and her grandmother would spend an afternoon together recounting their adventures.

After eating, she spent a few minutes writing in her journal before dousing the fire and settling down upon her bedroll. Frida closed her eyes and fell asleep as crickets and owls sang a wild lullaby.

A panicked bleat tore Frida from her slumber. Hooves trampled by as she rolled to her side, grasping for her dagger in the dark. Her fingers wrapped around the grip, and she scrambled to her feet.

Golden eyes twinkled in the moonlight where a dragon loomed several paces away. Grimble stood between the dragon and Frida, a wall of muscle and violence. The war goat lowered his head, heaving and pawing at the earth.

"A worthy companion." The familiar voice held a trace of amusement, though it had lost some of the youthful edge that Frida remembered. *"Be at ease. I have no intent to harm you."*

As Frida's eyes slowly adjusted to the night, she began to make out more of the dragon's appearance. Not much had changed over the past thirty years. Tinktink's scales were still a vibrant amethyst, and the spikes along her spine were like dazzling jewels. She had been the size of Morsel during their last encounter, but now she was bigger than a male war goat. In a few hundred years, she might be the same size as her mother and grandmother.

Frida stepped forward and patted Grimble on the shoulder. The goat's muscles were as tense as wrought iron.

"It's okay, Grim." She stroked his fur. "She's an old friend."

He let out an uncertain bleat. His hooves settled in the earth, but the goat didn't retreat.

Tinktink's tail rattled softly as she sat on her haunches. *"It is good to see you again, young one."*

"I'm not so young anymore." Frida chuckled to herself. By dragon standards, forty-six was still a child. "How did you find us?"

"It is a warden's duty to patrol our borders."

"You're a warden?" Frida beamed. "Congratulations, Tink! That's wonderful."

The rattledrake straightened her neck and preened. *"It is a great honor."*

"That's amazing. I'm so proud of you." She moved toward Tinktink, and Grimble stepped protectively in front of her. Frida smiled at the goat, cupping his massive head in her palms. "It's okay. I promise."

Grimble huffed, but he let her pass.

Tinktink lowered her head, pressing the cool scales of her forehead to Frida's. *"You have grown."*

"I was a child the last time I was here."

"How have the years treated you?"

"They've been good. Better than I could have hoped for." Frida sat in front of Tinktink, legs crossed, which Grimble took as an opportunity to hover over his rider. "Enough of that." She tried to push the massive beast away, but he didn't budge. "I told you, Grim, everything is fine."

Grimble bleated in her ear and then tucked his legs underneath his body as he sat like a giant loaf.

Frida rolled her eyes. "For such a massive creature, he's awfully clingy."

Tinktink extended her neck until she was inches from the war goat and sniffed. *"He is protective. It is an admirable quality."*

"That he is." Frida rested her head against his fur. "I'm

lucky to have him. He and I have traveled across the realm together."

The dragon's eyes sparkled with curiosity. *"Tell me about it."*

For the next several hours, until the sun rose, Frida shared stories of her apprenticeship. As the day unfolded, breakfast passed as she reminisced about adventures with her first party, the Dawnseekers. She ate lunch while describing how she left them to follow through on her childhood dream of forming the all-female party Braids & Quivers with her cousin Tilda. The afternoon was filled with more of their adventures.

Although Tinktink had only been a warden for two years, she had plenty of tales to recount herself. *"I've flown beyond our borders many times in the past two years. On occasion, I've even passed over settlements of the two-leggeds under the cover of night. I often wondered if you might be somewhere below."*

Frida smiled. "That's sweet of you, Tink."

Tinktink stood, stretching out her forepaws in the grass. *"I must patrol soon."*

The dwarf opened her mouth to ask if she would see Tinktink again when the dragon continued.

"Would you care to join me?"

Frida grinned. "Are you going to carry me again?"

Tinktink lowered herself to the ground. *"I had other intentions."*

HILDA'S HONEY
CRUMBLE RECIPE

To view Hilda's Honey Crumble Cake Recipe, head over
to **slrowland.com/honeycrumble**

ACKNOWLEDGMENTS

Thank you for reading *There Be Dragons Here*! If you enjoyed your time with Hilda and Frida, please consider rating, reviewing, and sharing your thoughts on social media using the hashtags #ThereBeDragonsHere or #TalesofAedrea. **Word of mouth is one of the best ways to support indie authors like myself. It helps to ensure my books find their way into libraries, bookstores, and the hands of readers like you.**

When I think about the people who have supported and believed in me over the years, my grandmother, **Peggy**, is at the top of the list. She's a strong, kind woman, and an amazing cook. I live across the country nowadays, but every time I visit, she asks me when my books are going to be turned into movies. I give a little laugh, and without hesitation, she always says, "Just you wait."

While I'm on the topic of support, **Caroline,** you have been the bedrock of my support system through all the ups and downs that come with being an independent author. I'm grateful to have you by my side through all life's chaotic adventures.

Thank you to my alpha reader, **Cindy Koepp**. Your feedback is invaluable as I take the raw stone of an idea and slowly (so slowly) chisel it into something resembling a story.

If you picked up this book without having read any of the others in the *Tales of Aedrea* series, I have to thank **Brent Minehan** for the gorgeous cover art that lured you here. He captured the cozy adventure aesthetic perfectly.

To my amazing **beta readers**—your feedback was invaluable, and I can't thank you enough for catching all my blunders. **Aaron Eichler, Cheryl Deal, Emma Ewert, Erica Nadvornik, Gregg Trotti, Janet Beane, Loren Foster, Nancy Ann Gazo, Sean Flint, Chiara Masnovo, Ava Van den Bergh,** and **Cindy Koepp**

A special thanks to my **Patreon supporters**—your comments and encouragement between releases mean the world to me.

Diamond Tier: Lance Krautlarger

Platinum Tier: Joel Southard, Willa Elliot, Jon Hopkins Jr., Jae and Courtney Lane, Nichole Hall

Gold Tier: Robert Schaefer, Michael Percell, Laura Lea Davidson, Amanda Blackburn, Angie F, Jess Worgo, Preston Leigh, Kevin Wagner, Michelle Benavides, Elise Raposa

Silver Tier: Rickie Brookes, Nick Kelly, Jon Kilcrease, Cristopher Walters, Emmi Junkkari, Amanda Parcheta, Zachary Stout, Lara Reichart, Nichole Hall, Kyle Wilkinson, Crystal Mayberry, Kumiko Sakata-Williams, Bill Holmes, Missy Jovic

ALSO BY S.L. ROWLAND

Tales of Aedrea

Cursed Cocktails

Sword & Thistle

The Halfling's Harvest

There Be Dragons Here

Pangea Online

Pangea Online: Death and Axes

Pangea Online 2: Magic and Mayhem

Pangea Online 3: Vials and Tribulations

Sentenced to Troll 1-6

Path to Villainy: An NPC Kobold's Tale

Collected Editions

Pangea Online: The Complete Trilogy

Sentenced to Troll Compendium: Books 1-3

Sentenced to Troll Compendium 2: Books 4-6

ABOUT THE AUTHOR

S.L. Rowland is a cozy fantasy and LitRPG author known for crafting immersive worlds filled with adventure, heart, and a touch of humor. A lifelong gamer and fantasy enthusiast, he draws inspiration from tabletop RPGs, video games, and the fantastical. When he's not writing, he enjoys weightlifting, hiking with his Shiba Inu, and enduring the heartbreak of being an Atlanta sports fan.

SLRowland.com

Patreon-For signed paperbacks, advanced chapters, exclusive short stories, art, merch, and more.

Newsletter: For updates on new releases, sales, and behind the scenes content!

Email: slrowlandauthor@gmail.com

Find out more at https://linktr.ee/SLRowland

9 781964 567280